# MAXWELL'S WAR

*By the same author*

Fiction

*Maxwell's House* (1994)
*Maxwell's Flame* (1995)
*Maxwell's Movie* (1998)

*The adventures of Inspector Lestrade* (1985)
*Brigade: further adventures of Inspector Lestrade* (1986)
*Lestrade and the hallowed house* (1987)
*Lestrade and the Leviathan* (1987)
*Lestrade and the brother of death* (1988)
*Lestrade and the Ripper* (1988)
*Lestrade and the guardian angel* (1990)
*Lestrade and the deadly game* (1990)
*Lestrade and the gift of the prince* (1991)
*Lestrade and the magpie* (1991)
*Lestrade and the dead man's hand* (1992)
*Lestrade and the sign of nine* (1992)
*Lestrade and the sawdust ring* (1993)
*Lestrade and the mirror of murder* (1993)
*Lestrade and the Kiss of Horus* (1995)
*Lestrade and the Devil's Own* (1996)

Non-fiction

*Let him have it, Chris: the murder of Derek Bentley* (1990)
*The wigwam murder* (1994)
*Open Skies, Closed Minds* (with Nick Pope) (1996)
*The Many Faces of Jack the Ripper* (1997)

# MAXWELL'S WAR

M. J. Trow



Hodder & Stoughton

First published in Great Britain in 1999 by
Hodder and Stoughton
A division of Hodder Headline PLC



10 9 8 7 6 5 4 3 2 1



British Library Cataloguing in Publication Data
Trow, J. J.
Maxwell's war
1. Maxwell, Peter (Fictitious character) – Fiction
2. Detective and mystery stories
I. Title
823.9'14 [F]

ISBN 0 340 70756 9

Typeset by Palimpsest Book Production Limited
Polmont, Stirlingshire
Printed and bound in Great Britain by
Mackays of Chatham PLC, Chatham, Kent

Hodder and Stoughton
A division of Hodder Headline PLC
338 Euston Road
London NW1 3BH

For Carriston

# Chapter One

Time and tide, they say, wait for no man. They certainly didn't wait for Tom Sparrow, but used him for their sport, rolling him 'twixt tide and tide until at last the sea gave him up, like all its secrets, like all its dead.

Perhaps he went in at Middleton, where the fairy seaplanes roared through the spray in the wake of the Great War. Certainly the tide, steady, kind, buoyed him up, sliding him eastward under the stars. He watched them for a while, in their canopy above him, through his dull and sightless eyes: Orion the Hunter striding north, the Plough arching through the night fields, the Sisters huddling together and shivering with the cold. Then the tide chose the time and turned him with the lapping waves to float face down into the blackness. Did his dead, deaf ears hear the church bell of drowned Atherington echo from the deeps off Climping Sands? Did he trawl its narrow, twisting streets and bob above its salt-grey roofs as the waters rolled him once more? East, east, ever turning as the tide took him, past the sail boards chained for the night at Goring-by-Sea, listening as the waves rippled like mocking laughter, lapping at his anorak, breaking the surface in the star-kissed night.

The Adur might have claimed him as the breeze stiffened

suddenly from the south and blew him shoreward, but it changed again, with all the contrariness of fate and carried him out once more, his white hands trailing in the weed of the estuary. The shabby old irons of Brighton Pier held him for a moment as he bumped among them, like shaking hands with old friends at a party. The barnacles cut his skin as he took his leave, as if offended that he should go. And the ten-times fingering weed wiped the bloodless wounds and sent him on his way.

As dawn broke grey and level to the east and the little terns, flitting in black and white, darted down to see who it was, this stranger rolling in their surf, Tom Sparrow drifted to the Leighford beach, at Willow Bay where men say Cnut sat defiantly in the sand and ordered back the sea. And the sea had changed Tom Sparrow. There was still the fine froth around his nostrils and mouth to tell an uncaring world that he had drowned. There was no dilution of his blood because the salt of the water in his lungs had a higher osmotic pressure and could not pierce his breathing membrane. But his blood was high in chloride as his legs felt the sand. Each lap of the water carried him higher up the beach, and it was summer, so his dead, white skin hung from his body like a shroud.

At last he lay in the snaking line of weed, black and rotting. A balloon of a man, swollen with the gases that death is heir to. And that kindly tide had rolled beside his head a piece of cork to his left and an empty washing-up bottle to his right. The flies came early to see him and they found him first. The heavy, fat-fed flies of summer droned around his corpse and settled there and stayed, fighting with each other for the choicest cuts, the sweetest morsels, buzzing and bickering with each other in the morning air.

The *Leighford Clarion* carried the story. ‘A body was discovered at Willow Bay last Thursday by local fishermen. The coroner, Mr Malcolm Davis, has been called in and newly appointed police surgeon Dr James Astley expressed his opinion that the body had been in the water for at least thirty-six hours. Police sources have revealed that the body is that of Mr Thomas Sparrow, sixty-one, who was well known in the local gay community.'

The rest was silence. Tom Sparrow had come home.

Metternich, the black and white ex-male of the genus *felix domesticus* had noticed something about his master, the pink, still vaguely male of the genus *Homo sapiens* called Peter Maxwell. He'd noticed that whenever a certain sharp, repetitive tone hit the ether, the idiot would trot to the white thing in the hall (there was one in the lounge, too) and pick it up. Then he'd start talking to himself. All rather sad, really.

That Saturday was no exception. Maxwell was not, unlike his cat, the domestic type, but needs must when a lack of jobbing gardener drives and he'd been forced to mow the lawn himself. This was particularly irksome to Metternich because not only did he have that great juggernaut snarling through *his* undergrowth, but the bloody thing had just minced beyond all recognition the half mouse he'd been saving for supper and was now demolishing the only hiding place in the garden. Did the man have no survival instinct at all?

The roar of the juggernaut had done its best to drown out all other noise, so it was a while before Maxwell heard the phone and hared off, as usual, up the garden path.

'Lord Lucan,' he hissed breathlessly, flicking bits of green out of his eyelashes.

'Bwana?' a dark brown voice crackled over the airwaves.

'John Irving, you old brown bomber!' Maxwell collapsed onto the bottom stair of his less-than-elegant town house and sat there, rivulets of sweat staining his shirt. 'How's Gonville and Caius's token black?'

'Up shit creek, actually. That's why I'm ringing.'

'Look, if it's that fiver you lent me the day they killed JFK . . .'

'Ha, ha. I've bought my freedom since then, Bwana. No, no, this is historical shit.'

'Ah,' Maxwell nodded sagely, 'the worst kind.'

'You're obviously still at Leighford,' Irving checked the number he had just dialled.

'Does the Pope shit in the woods?' Maxwell asked him. But since he knew John Irving's speciality was Afro-Caribbean history, he wasn't holding out much hope for an answer.

'Still teaching at Dotheboys Hall?'

'Please,' Maxwell hauled a towel off a side table and began to mop his fevered brow, 'Leighford High School is probably in the top thirty-eight thousand schools in the country. We haven't been Ofsteded yet, but the Headmaster's Auntie once patted David Blunkett's dog, so we'll be all right. And anyway, you Dodo, I teach in a mixed school – it's Dothechildren's Hall, if you don't mind.'

'Well, pardon me all to Hell, Bwana. What do you know about the army in, say, 1804?'

'British?' Maxwell checked.

'And French.'

'Regular or Irregular?'

'Er . . .'

'Ah,' Maxwell nodded, trying to do that thing where grownups rest the receiver in the crook of their necks, 'I see what you mean about historical shit.'

'I'd better come clean,' he heard Irving say. 'I've been commissioned – and please don't ask me how; it had a lot to do with too many dry Martinis at last year's May Ball – to act as historical adviser to a film company.'

'Excellent!' Maxwell smiled.

'Yes. Right.'

'Better than casting pearls before the usual swine, surely, John?'

'In a way,' Irving agreed. 'But there's the rub, Bwana. Said film company were going to make an epic on the slave trade – hence my involvement.'

'First-hand experience,' Maxwell clicked his tongue in admiration, suddenly realizing his turn-ups were sprouting grass, 'How is Mr Wilberforce, by the way?'

Irving ignored him. 'Then the buggers changed their minds. Now it's a sub-Catherine Cookson bodice ripper – out of Barbara Cartland by way of Julie Birchill.'

'Well, that's a winning combination,' Maxwell was extracting the burrs of summer from between his teeth.

'It's set at the time of Napoleon's invasion plans. 1804. The French landed a ship on the south coast apparently, but the local Dad's Army saw them off.'

'Wrong on almost all counts,' Maxwell was delighted to report, 'which is more or less what I'd expect from a Caius man.'

'Really?' Irving's professional heart was sinking by the minute.

'Well, the ship's right. And yes, they were French. But the year was 1797 which makes it just a soupçon too early for Bonaparte. And it was Pembrokeshire, not the south coast. Fishguard to be precise. The people who saw the French off were a bevy of Welsh fisherwomen. Apparently the French said later they mistook their black hats and red shawls for the regular infantry. Might have gone better for them if it had been infantry.'

'Well, it's definitely the south coast,' Irving stood his ground.

'You always did swear black was white, Jonathan. . .'

'No, I mean, I'm sure you're right, Bwana. It's precisely because of that rightness that I'm ringing your white ass. What I mean is that irrespective of little things like historical accuracy and a nod in the direction of truth, the film company is coming south anyway. To Willow Bay. Know it?'

'Like the back of Mrs Sheridan.'

'You bitch!' Irving screamed over the phone.

Maxwell held the receiver for a moment at arm's length while his silent laughter subsided, 'Still carrying a torch for your old bedder after all these years, Johnnie, me boy?'

'That was a long time ago, Bwana,' Irving told him. 'And I *was* pissed.'

'You must have been,' Maxwell conjured up the homely face of the blowzy old girl who did for John Irving, the wide-eyed Nigerian at Cambridge, just off the banana boat. 'And now you're Dr John Irving, Fellow of Gonville and Caius, author of . . . how many learned tomes is it now?'

'Sixteen. Seventeen if the OUP ever get their arses in gear.'

'And despite the fact that you fell in love with the first white woman you saw and that I've been blackmailing you ever since, you still need a favour, eh? Hello?'

For a moment, Maxwell thought the line had gone dead; then he heard Irving say, 'Well, bearing in mind the film company will be down the road from you and you're the sort of historian who knows which end the powder goes in a gun, I naturally assumed . . .'

'So I'll be . . . what? Historical adviser to the historical adviser?'

'Ah, well, I can't guarantee you billing, Bwana,' Irving blustered, 'but there'll be a drink in it for you, rest assured.'

'And when is Mr DeMille arriving?' Maxwell asked.

'Whitsun,' Irving told him, 'er . . . week after next. Can you do it?'

'Week after next,' Maxwell peered at the school calendar swinging in the breeze by his open front door, 'Whit week. Always cunningly timed to coincide with the start of study leave for A level and GCSE – just so the buggers don't get too complacent. You couldn't have timed it better, Jonathan. It's that nirvana of the academic year which we teachers look forward to for twelve months – the exam classes have gone. And week after next is for ever. Leo Tolstoy wrote *War and Peace* in less time than that.'

There was a pause. 'No, he didn't.' And John Irving hung up.

# Chapter Two

Is it the smell you notice first? Or the noise? Perhaps it's the litter, when a gust of wind reminds you that an average school, corridor by corridor, contains eighteen square miles of rainforest – or rather its equivalent in Snickers wrappers. Peter Maxwell had waded through all that waste for years on his way to the chalk face. The corner of his vastly experienced eye caught the ill-written poster that told him that a particularly talentless trio of Year 11 students with the unsavoury, but apposite, name of Afterbirth were playing at the Three Tuns tomorrow. He tore it down.

'Christine!' he bellowed to a hapless student turning the wrong corner at the wrong time. 'What is this?'

He held up a second poster which he'd spotted with his other experienced eye, the one in the back of his head.

'It's our Young Enterprise poster,' the freckled-faced kid had passed the test with flying colours.

'Is it, indeed?' Maxwell nodded, sweeping off the shapeless tweed hat he wore, summer and winter, man and boy. 'Read it to me, would you?'

Christine winced. There were kids coming and going everywhere. That spotty little shit who fancied her sister. And Mr Latymer who was all hands. Oh, God, no! Jez Harrap, the sex god, was coming down the stairs, biceps rippling under his T-shirt, the one that proclaimed he was hung like a mule. But 'Mad Max' Maxwell had given her an order. She really had no choice.

'Welcome to "Way Out",' she murmured, hoping Mr Sex-on-a-Stick couldn't hear her, 'Leighford High School's Young Enterprise Company. They're going places . . .'

'They may well be,' Maxwell nodded, 'but not with spelling like that. "They're" is a colloquial form of "they are", which has fewer eyes in it than a cyclops. And not, as you have it here "their". Do go back to that sink of technology you call Business Studies and put it right, there's a good girl.'

'Yes, Mr Maxwell,' and, bright crimson, Christine took the proffered poster and almost collided with Mr Testosterone at the bottom of the stairs.

'Mr Harrap!' Maxwell's stentorian tones froze the come-and-get-me look on the lad's face and he doubled up along the corridor.

'Jeremy, dear boy,' his Head of Year's nose was inches from his own, 'What did I promise to do if I caught you wearing that T-shirt again?'

'I think you said you'd rip out my entrails and set fire to them in the quad, sir.'

'What a memory,' Maxwell marvelled, and he pulled back his cuff. 'Shall we?'

'Or . . .' the boy said quickly, 'I could go home and change.'

'Damn!' Maxwell clicked his fingers. 'Foiled again. Make it so, Mr Harrap,' and he gave the boy his best Captain Picard as he swanned off into Leighford's gloom.

It was definitely the noise in the staffroom; that's what you'd remember – those multifarious little whinges that make up an entire profession. Maxwell's finely tuned ears caught them all as he made his way through the less than happy throng that Monday morning.

'But I covered that lesson last week' . . . 'Who's had the bloody *TES* again?' . . . 'And then she called me an effing old tart.'

'She got that right,' Maxwell muttered; but not *too* loudly; after all, he was an ex-public schoolboy who had found himself in the shipwreck of life. He reached his pigeon-hole, stuffed with irrelevance and consigned most of it to the bin.

'Can you do an Assembly for me, Max?' he turned to the large, rather awful woman who ran Year 8.

'When, Grace?' he asked her.

'Well, I was hoping for Wednesday.'

'Ah,' he beamed, 'That's what makes you unique among teachers. Most of us hope for Friday. What do you want?'

'Oh,' she laughed, 'that's completely up to you. You're so good at improvisation.'

'Improvisation?' Maxwell looked aghast, his face turning the colour of his off-white shirt. 'What may appear to be improvisation to you, dear lady, is actually the result of meticulous planning, years of experience . . .'

'Oh, of course,' Grace's smile had gone and she was mottling crimson around the throat, the one where the crucifix dangled ostentatiously. 'Look, Max, I didn't mean . . .'

Maxwell's hand was in the air. 'No, no,' he said politely, 'of course not. No harm done, I'm sure, Grace. No umbrage taken.' And he brushed past her. 'Wednesday it is.'

'Oh, thank you.'

He all but collided with Sally Greenhow, the tall, skinny Special Needs teacher who had grown up at the Great Man's knee. 'You are an utter shit, Max,' she clicked her tongue.

'Morning, Sally,' Maxwell beamed. 'If I were more common I'd ask you how your belly is off for spots.'

'Poor Grace.' Sally looked at the huge woman's retreating figure.

'Poor Grace, my arse,' Maxwell said. 'She's about as much

of a Christian as I'm a born-again Conservative. *And* that's the fourth Assembly I've done for her this year.'

'You love it,' Sally reached for her own sheaf of papers. 'A captive audience of two hundred kids? It's your bread and butter.'

'It is,' he agreed, helping himself to one of the chocolate digestives put out for the Investors in People meeting later that day, 'as long as the rope on the captive audience is nice and tight,' and he flexed his jaw so that his jugular stood out and his skin turned scarlet.

There was the usual line of problems outside his office on the mezzanine floor. Monday always brought them out, like the rats following the piper of Hamelin. He could read their sorry faces yards away. Melanie had been thrown out of home again and had nowhere to go. Zak's dad, at least from the puffy look around the boy's eyes, had been having a go at him again. And judging from the purple tuft of hair sprouting from Adam Clarkson's head, he'd been sent to Maxwell by Mr Diamond, the Headmaster, for a damned good throttling.

'Good morning,' Maxwell bowed to all three. 'Luckily for you, I'm wearing my social worker underwear this morning. That little old thing called History teaching, for which I am paid and for which I was trained, will have to wait until after break. Who's first? Don't all shout at once.'

And it was after break that Helen McGregor came to see him. This was the thing about teaching on the eve of the Millennium. A man like Maxwell was social worker, policeman, drug tsar, priest. But every time he looked at a girl, especially one as dumpy as Helen McGregor, he prayed he'd never have to be a midwife. She sat opposite him on the soft, ribbed chair he'd picked up at a car boot, looking as anxious as ever under the unfashionable fringe. She'd looked just like that on her first day at Leighford High. Not that Maxwell remembered her then. He hadn't become aware of her at all until the day he'd found her on the receiving end of the treatment doled out by Maria Spinetti, the Godmother of Year 10. That day, on his rounds behind the bike sheds, he'd found her with a bloody mess where her lip used to be.

That was then. Now, Helen was one of his sixth formers. And Maria Spinetti was doing time – life with hard labour on a Tesco's checkout.

'Helen,' Maxwell had hoped for some opening gambit. He was to be disappointed. 'Is there something?' He glanced at his watch. 'It's just that I promised to give Year Eight my legendary Cromwell impression and it takes a while to stick the warts on.'

Helen was fighting with her plain, brass ring. 'Well . . .' It was a start.

'Yes?' Maxwell eased himself back in his chair, a man with all the time in the world.

'Well, I was wondering . . . that is . . . the History sets were wondering . . .'

'No, I'm afraid I can't sit the Module for you, Helen. It's not that I'm not totally corrupt, it's just that I can't disguise my handwriting seventeen different ways. As Sir Robert Walpole would have told you, had you read the book, "every man has his price – he just can't do calligraphy".'

A grin flitted briefly across the girl's stodgy face. 'No, no. It's not that.'

'Well, then . . .' Maxwell could hear Year 8 swinging from the chandeliers in H4 as he spoke.

'Well, the paper said there was a television crew coming to Leighford. They're going to make a series, right here in town. And . . . well, they were asking for extras.'

'Extras?' Maxwell tried not to show he was flabbergasted. 'I'm sorry, Helen. I didn't know you were a thespian. You weren't in *Hello, Dolly* were you?'

The girl blushed crimson. 'No, I'm not. It's just . . . well, it's only a walk-on part. You only stand there.'

'Yes, I see.'

The girl shifted uneasily. It was like sitting in Old Sparky as her wrists twisted on the arms and her throat felt tight and dry. 'It's Marc Lamont.' Her eyes dazzled at his name and she felt her heart leap.

'What is?'

'He's the lead.'

'Lamont?' Maxwell frowned. 'Do I know him?'

Utter disbelief crossed Helen McGregor's face. '*Brookside*,' she said as though the Red Sea had just parted for her. 'He was Dawson's brother.'

'Ah, *Lamont*,' Maxwell clicked his fingers. 'Of course.' He'd really have to tell his sixth form one day that he thought a soap was something you washed with in the morning.

'Isn't he lovely?' Helen sat there transfixed, the gorgeous actor smiling at her through the ether. Maxwell daren't mention Leonardo diCaprio or the girl might have fainted on the spot.

'Ravishing, Helen,' the Head of Sixth Form nodded. 'But I don't really see how I can . . .'

'Oh, but you're into films, Mr Maxwell,' she threw her arms around the room, waving frantically to the posters that lined the man's office wall – Paul Newman outgrinning Robert Redford in *The Sting*, Robert de Niro looking weird in front of his yellow cab in *Taxi Driver*, ten white-suited John Travoltas in *Saturday Night Fever*.

'Ah, yes, my dear,' he smiled, '*films*, I'll grant you. The silver screen. The one and nines. The roar of the popcorn and the smell of Pearl and Dean. But telly . . . well, if I have to . . .'

'But it's historical,' Helen was unbelievably persistent. 'It's what you love.'

Maxwell laughed. 'And you love Marc Lamont?' he asked the girl.

Anyone more sophisticated than Helen McGregor would

have checked him, told him, as far as they dared, not to be so silly. Instead, Helen McGregor just hugged her knees and nodded like a three-year-old.

'Well,' Maxwell was on his feet, 'I'll see what I can do. It does so happen that I'll be working with that very television crew of which you spoke. Perhaps an autograph . . .'

'Oh, yes.' Helen was with him, babbling, grinning. 'Yes, that would be wonderful.'

'Now, run along, Helen. You, I'm sure, have private study and I . . .' he sunk his head into his neck and sprouted metaphorical warts, 'must expel the Rump. I'm sure you can see yourself out.'

John Irving found himself wandering the windy corridors of Leighford High that Friday. Accustomed as he was to the oak-panelled halls of academe, with their debating and philosophical societies, handwritten posters announcing that it was Geek's 18th and Everyone was invited came as a bit of a shock. So did the single, ill-spelt note flapping in the May breeze that told him that Stacey did blow jobs to die for. In Cambridge, there was no need to advertise that sort of thing – it was common knowledge all along the Backs.

'Hello,' a voice hailed him. 'Can I help?'

The silhouette was darker than he was until it emerged into the light and then it was paler than death. 'Bernard Ryan,' it announced. 'Deputy Headteacher. Can I help?'

'What's that black man doing on the premises?' a familiar voice bellowed.

Ryan's jaw dropped. He'd always known Peter Maxwell was the last of the velociraptors, but this was incredible. Thank God there were no kids about to hear it.

'I think it's far too late,' Irving smiled at Ryan, 'to help, I mean. If years of medication and a spell in Rampton couldn't do the trick, well . . . what can any of us do?'

'John, you old bastard!' Maxwell shook the man's hand heartily. 'How the Hell have you been?'

'Pretty well, Bwana, thanks.'

Maxwell caught sight of Bernard Ryan for the first time. 'Er . . . Bernard. Bernard . . . the mouth. Close the mouth, there's a good chap.'

The hapless Head's deputy turned the gape into a smile. 'Ah, you two know each other . . . clearly.'

Maxwell patted the man's shoulder patronizingly. 'Coming on a treat in Business Studies. Well done. I wasn't expecting you until tomorrow, John.'

'Couldn't keep away,' said Irving. 'I've brought the script – *The Captain's Fancy*.'

'Aha. Excellent. Walk this way,' and he crouched low, eyes spinning in all directions, like Marty Feldman in *Young Frankenstein*.

'Not a bad time, is it?' Irving asked.

'Lord, no,' Maxwell straightened. 'I've just got to teach the Year Nine Set From Hell – got the reading ages of three-toed sloths, all of 'em – then I'm all yours. I don't suppose you'd like to take them on? No.'

'Aren't you going to introduce us, Max?' Bernard Ryan called.

The Head of Sixth Form paused. 'No,' he said and swept out of sight.

They did a mean Chicken Chasseur in a Basket at the Weathervane. Mercifully, it wasn't one of those plastic places where children are allowed to run riot, that most damnable of twentieth-century inventions, the Family Pub. Those who frequented the Weathervane had been abandoned by their families years ago; wrecks of men who liked real ale and played dominoes for keeps. Maxwell settled back into the monk's settle in the corner and watched the head gleam on his pint in the dying rays of Friday's sun.

'Well, what do you think?' Irving tapped the dog-eared slab of paper resting alongside Maxwell's empty prawn cocktail bowl.

'Hm?'

'The script – *The Captain's Fancy.*'

'Well, it's crap, John.' He tweezered that annoying piece of lettuce out of his incisors.

'Ah.'

'God, you didn't write it, did you?' Maxwell said suddenly; he wouldn't have offended his old oppo for the world.

Irving laughed. 'No, no. The writer of the novel – and this bastardized version – is one Erika Marriner. I met her once at some publisher's bash. Insufferable. Gets all her history from the Ladybird series. Joe Public of course loves her. She's the new Catherine Cookson.'

'Goodie,' Maxwell clapped his hands in glee. 'Do television companies pay for tosh like this?'

'Eight Counties do. It's all about franchising and merchandizing and God knows what. I'm a bit out of my depth, frankly.'

'Your chicken, Mr Maxwell.' A scrawny kid with an annoying lock of hair over her face thumped the man's main course down.

'That's a lie, Donna,' Maxwell smiled and seeing the total lack of understanding on the waitress's face, added, 'But let it pass.'

'Was yours the steak?' she asked Irving.

It crossed Maxwell's mind to correct her with an order of hominy grits and chick-eyed peas with a side-helping of cornpone, but he knew he was wasting his time.

'Tell me, Bwana,' Irving reached for the condiments when the girl had gone, 'Do you know everybody in this town?'

'Everybody,' Maxwell nodded. 'From the Mayor to the bog attendants – or should that be the other way around? I have been at Leighford since before the Flood, John. If I haven't taught them, I've taught their fathers or their grandfathers and so on until the handle fell off.'

'We're going to have some problems with Eight Counties, Bwana.'

'Now he tells me,' Maxwell tackled the unidentifiable vegetables at one end of his platter. 'Politics?'

'With a capital "P",' Irving confided. 'I thought my colleagues at Caius were bitchy, but these people . . .'

'Ah, it's the artistic temperament,' Maxwell couldn't decide whether it was swede or carrot that tickled his taste buds.

'No, it's more than that.'

'Have you met Marc Lamont?'

'I have. We've completed most of the studio stuff. They were waiting for decent weather to do the location shots. Why do you ask about Lamont?'

'I've got eighty or ninety post-pubescent girls slavering to meet him.'

'They'll be disappointed.'

Maxwell raised an eyebrow. 'You mean, he's not as other heart-throbs?'

Irving chuckled. 'I don't know how many ways he swings, although there *are* rumours,' he said. 'No, I mean he's a bastard. Overexposed and overrated.'

'Ah, aren't we all. Who else am I going to meet on Sunday?'

'His leading lady is Hannah Morpeth – you know, the girl from the Morse episode where John Thaw's on holiday.'

'Oh, I know. Pretty girl. Big . . .'

'Potential, yes,' Irving winked. 'Her bum looks a bit big on telly. It's all right in the flesh.'

'Now, now,' Maxwell warned. 'I want none of that. You'll be drooling next "Where de white women at?" Remember to keep one foot on the floor at all times.'

'The point is, it's mutual hatred between those two. And I haven't even got on to Miles Needham.'

'Who he?' Maxwell drowned his scalded tonsils in the amber nectar.

'Director. One of John Birt's blue-eyed boys at the Beeb before he got greedy.'

'Not a nice person?' Maxwell asked, wide eyed.

'Bwana.' Irving leaned forward. 'Those two words cannot possibly follow each other from Sunday. Believe me, it's going to be murder. Still want to play?'

# Chapter Three

The headland drops away alarmingly at Willow Bay, out to the Shingle in the east. Here the terns dip and swerve, faster, more frantic, than the grey-backed gulls gliding on the breakers, riding the spray. To the west the sand blows sharp like needles off the dunes, the coarse grass swept flat in the winter winds. The end of May was kinder and the sky a pale aquamarine that morning when Maxwell tumbled out of John Irving's car and made for the beach.

They didn't, at first sight, look much like an army of invasion, the ragtag re-enactors who sat around on the sand, tucking into tea and sandwiches courtesy of Eight Counties catering. A tall, rather elegant man in a white roll-neck sweater was on his feet in front of them, the early morning sun dazzling on his Rolex.

'That's Miles Needham,' Irving muttered as they approached. 'Are you sure you've never heard of him? He got some award or other last year.'

'Of course,' Maxwell stopped in his tracks, 'How preternaturally stupid of me. He got Best Director at Cannes, didn't he? Some pretentious tosh by Somerset Maugham if I remember rightly.'

'Miles,' Irving called out, realizing they were within earshot, 'Miles, this is Peter Maxwell.'

'Ah, yes,' Needham turned from his troops to shake the man's hand, 'Delighted you're with us on this. You've read the script?'

'Yes.'

'What did you think?'

'Well . . .'

'Quite.' Needham read the signs quickly. 'All I can say in its defence is that it was a fuck-sight worse before I tinkered with it. Look . . .' and he took Maxwell by the shoulder, leading him away from the extras huddled on the sand, 'They're not very good, I'm afraid. I've had words with my casting man, already, but time is of the essence. How soon can you lick them into shape?'

Maxwell turned back to look at them. There were forty or fifty of them, mostly in their early twenties or late teens. To a man they were too tall and too well fed for the ragged armies of Revolutionary France or the British Yeomanry who repelled them.

'That depends,' he said cagily.

'Meaning?' Miles Needham didn't have the time to suffer fools gladly, 'expert' fools not at all.

'On how realistic you want this to be.'

'Well, totally, of course,' the director told him. 'But we don't have the time or the money to be picky. If a button's out of place or something, tough shit. I've got a pathetic budget from the powers that be. You'll just have to improvise. What about time?'

Maxwell looked back at them again. 'Any professional re-enactors here?' he bellowed over the lapping waters and rolling surf. A couple of hands went up, reluctantly.

'For what you want them to do, three days basic training,' he told the director.

'Three days. Angela!' Needham clicked his fingers and a harassed looking exec came running, clutching a clipboard. She was not unattractive in a harassed sort of way, her dark hair blown about by the wind. A mobile hung at her hip like a fashion statement. 'Angela, this is . . . sorry, I didn't catch your name . . .'

'Maxwell,' said Maxwell.

'This is Maxwell. He's our adviser on the battle scenes. Three days he says to get this lot into shape. Have we got that?'

'Two would be better, Miles,' she slipped a pair of shades up onto her head. 'Hello, Maxwell.'

'Angela,' Maxwell smiled and waved. Hers was the first human face he'd seen this morning.

'Can you do it in two, Maxwell?' Needham asked.

'I'll give it a whirl,' the historical adviser's historical adviser said.

'Right. Sort it, then, Angela. We're all at the Grand, Maxwell. I've got a fuck of a production meeting this morning, but I'll be back this afternoon to see how it's going. Anything you need, ask Angela,' and Britain's answer to Quentin Tarantino was gone over the dunes, John Irving striding to keep up.

'A man in a hurry,' Maxwell said.

'You mustn't mind him,' Angela defended, 'He's got a lot on his plate. I'm Angela Badham.'

'What are you, exactly?' Maxwell was trying to guess the girl's age. Twenty-four, perhaps? Twenty-five? William Pitt was already Prime Minister by then, but that was 1783; different days. And besides, William Pitt, for all the blue rinse, was a bloke.

'Oh, I'm Miles's assistant. Well, not that really. Sort of Johanna Factotum.'

'Ah,' Maxwell beamed, 'a Latin scholar. How rare.'

'Benenden,' Angela popped her shades back on. 'All seems rather a long time ago now. Maxwell, you mustn't be offended by Miles. He's not . . . well, he can be difficult, I know, but . . .'

Maxwell hated dark glasses. What he wanted to see was the girl's eyes, their softness, their glow. All he saw was a double image of himself, his hair madder than ever in the stiffening breeze. 'When do the costumes arrive?' he asked.

Angela consulted her clipboard, riffling through sheaves of paper. 'Tuesday at the earliest. Nathans and Bermans.'

'What about horses?'

'We've hired them locally. From a Mr . . . Ecclestone who lives at Merstone Farm.'

Maxwell vaguely knew it. 'How many has he got?'

'Twenty, he said,' Angela confirmed. 'But we haven't seen the quality yet. Does it matter if they're not all the same colour?'

'I've got my orders not to be too picky,' he chuckled. 'As long as we've got a grey for the trumpeter. It'll offend my sensibilities otherwise. Trumpeters always rode greys.'

'Would you like some coffee, Maxwell?' she asked him.

'I'd love some, Angela. And that's Max, by the way.'

'Max,' and she smiled at him. Maxwell had a knack of making women do that.

Working under Maxwell was a bit like working under Napoleon Bonaparte, with just a threat of Attila the Hun. First, that Sunday morning, with Angela's welcome flask contents in his fist, he gave the extras the gist of the speech the young General Bonaparte gave to the Army of Italy when he first took command in 1796. Then, instead of leading them into the beautiful, green fields of Lombardy, he led them to the shelter of the dunes where the discarded condoms lay; at least here he didn't have to compete with the roar of the surf. Then, like Bonaparte, he gave instant promotion to the men of talent, a great believer in the former Emperor's maxim that every extra carried in his holdall a statuette of a Bafta award. The two re-enactors became sergeants in the twinkling of Maxwell's eye.

'Bob, is it?' Maxwell asked the older of the two. Angela had already pointed him out.

'Don't you remember me, Mr Maxwell?'

'Er . . .' It was a question all ancient teachers dread. A thousand thousand children pass through their chalky hands and each and every one of them remembers 'sir'. 'Sir', as his memory fades and the blinds come down, remembers fewer each year.

'Bob Pickering. I didn't come into the sixth form. I left in '79.'

'I'm sorry, Bob,' Maxwell smiled, shaking the man's hand, searching the face. The sandy hair, the large grey eyes, he couldn't place them.

'Well, it's hardly surprising,' Pickering laughed. 'It's been bloody years.'

'Are you still local?' Maxwell asked.

'No. I live in Brighton now. Got my own metalwork business. You know, body-shop stuff. It's doing well. Me and a mate also run a shooting gallery on the pier.'

'Glad to hear it. So, you're also a re-enactor?'

Bob shrugged. 'I do my best. I joined the Sabre Society a while back. Now I'm with the Ninth Voltigeurs. As a matter of fact, it was you who got me into all this.'

'Was it?'

'It was a Wednesday. I shall never forget it. The room was . . . let me see . . . H4?'

Maxwell nodded, smiling. He'd placed many a corpse of delinquent children under those floorboards.

'You told us all about Napoleon; his white horse, Marengo; how he used to stand on the battlefield, have a ten-minute kip, then move on. Well, I don't mind telling you, Mr Maxwell, I was there. Bloody there, I was. I started reading up on the man and his times. Couldn't get enough of it. I make all my metal bits myself, you know, of the uniform, I mean.'

'Ninth Voltigeurs,' Maxwell quizzed him. 'What period?'

'1810 mostly. Course, I do whatever's required. I was with the 21st of the Line at the Jena re-enactment a couple of years back. Oh, and did you see *Sharpe's Waterloo* on the telly?'

'I did,' Maxwell nodded.

'I was on Maurice of Nassau's staff in that. Bloody nice bloke, Sean Bean. We had a kick about between takes. It's a bitch to kick a ball in hessian boots, I can tell you.'

Maxwell slapped the man's arm. 'I'm sure you can, Bob. Right, Maréchal de Logis it is. You don't mind playing a baddy?'

Pickering laughed. 'All depends on whose side you're on,' he said. 'And a sergeant's a baddy in any language.'

The other re-enactor stood half a head shorter than Bob Pickering. His name was Martin Bairstow and he too had been at Jena a couple of years back. Unlike Pickering, however, Martin's motives for buckling on stock and gaiters were entirely liquid. Jena, far from being a Prussian rout by the curly-headed Murat and his Cavalry of the Reserve, was one long *bierfest* for Bairstow. By the Thursday morning, he was so pissed he fell over his own musket and broke his ankle. Heigh ho, the fortunes of war. Bairstow said he could ride, so Bairstow instantly became a Troop Sergeant in the Castlemartin Yeomanry. Maxwell would get to his sabre drill later.

By mid-morning, Maxwell had the semblance of a unit. More like a young Dad's Army than the grumblers of the scariest nation-in-arms in the world, they stood to attention, turned right or left on command and even fired imaginary volleys from muskets of air in three rank formation.

There was always one, though, wasn't there? Giles Sparrow, one of Maxwell's Own from Leighford High, had sat up all night on the Saturday so as not to miss this. Unbeknownst to Maxwell, he'd been more than egged on by Helen McGregor. Angst-ridden in case she didn't make the screen test, she was determined *someone* she knew would get close to Marc Lamont. Perhaps it was Sparrow's youth, perhaps it was his course (GNVQ) but *something* certainly made him march out of time with the rest.

'Keep your heads up!' Maxwell snarled at them as they marched in column round the curve of the dunes and out onto the flat. 'By Tuesday, you'll all have a four-inch leather stock under your chin and a knapsack that weighs sixty pounds. Your musket will weigh another twelve and that doesn't include your water canteen, bayonet and sword. Keep those feet up. If the costumier gets it right, the boots they send won't be shaped left and right and nothing's going to fit you anywhere. By the time you've got your necessaries undone, you'll have wet yourselves. Keep time. Keep time. I'll get you a drum by tomorrow.'

'He's a miserable old bastard,' grunted Martin to Bob as they marched along the beach without musket or pack.

'Yeah! You'd better believe it,' chirped in Giles, stumbling over the driftwood that God had thoughtfully placed in his way. 'You should see him at school.'

Whit Monday was better. The props had arrived from Basingstoke and most of the morning was spent getting used to the weight of the cowhide packs and trying not to trip over the short, curved swords.

'Wear them high,' an exasperated Bob Pickering told his grumblers. 'High on the hip; that way you'll stay on your feet.'

'How many of these guns work, Bob?' Maxwell asked.

'They all do.' The Maréchal de Logis had checked.

'Amazing! Right.' Maxwell stood in front of the line of Marie-Louises, the raw recruits who, for today at least, were the invading French army. 'Today,' he said, 'we have naming of parts.' He held the musket across his chest. 'The script,' he told them, 'calls for three volleys to be fired. From what little I know of the film world that probably means about twenty takes, which means you'll have to do what I'm about to show you sixty times.' The drill-sergeant from hell caught a movement out of the corner of his eye. 'Giles, I hope you're concentrating,' Maxwell beamed. 'I shall be asking questions later. Now, there are twelve movements. First, the cartridge,' he fumbled in the leather pouch slung across his shoulder and produced one. 'I hope you've all got your own teeth, because you'll need them to do this,' and he bit the end off the paper. 'Any paper allergies, cut along to the regimental surgeon, who in 1797 wouldn't have the first clue what you were talking about, so there's a comfort, isn't it? Right, you've bitten off more than you can chew. Now pour the contents down your muzzle.' He dropped the musket butt to the sand and tipped the ball and powder into the tube. 'This is where we cheat,' he said. 'If this gun was real, you'd have to pour some powder into the priming pan – here – and close your frizzen. As this thing only fires blanks, that's not necessary. Now, push the ball and paper wad down with this.' He hauled the ramrod out of its pipes and poked it down the barrel. 'Now the fun bit,' Maxwell brought the musket upright again and half-cocked the serpentine. 'Half-cock – that's you, Giles,' he clicked again, 'Full cock – that's the rest of us.' He swept the weapon up to the level, pointing out to sea. 'I was always taught never to point one of these at anybody, but for verisimilitude, you'll have to. And, on command.' He lined up his sight with a windsurfer curling in to the bay. 'Fire,' and the gun bucked against his shoulder and the white smoke blew back in his face. There was applause and laughter. Maxwell's nose and eyes were a mask of black powder. 'Oh, yes,' he laughed with them, 'you'll get a bit dirty on this job.'

Indeed they did. For the next hour, forty-four angels with dirty faces slogged through the ritual of 1790s musket drill. Pieces of cartridge paper littered the dunes. Ramrods tumbled in all directions. Every so often there was a distinctly 1990s oath as a musket butt hit somebody else's foot. The most disastrous was the firing in three ranks, where the third rank fired too soon and there were scorched ears and chronic headaches.

'*Feu de billebaude!*' roared Maxwell over the noise. 'That's fire at will to you, boys!' But by that time, most of the will had gone and it was tea-up.

Maxwell squatted with his sergeants on a sweep of the dunes while the squaddies nursed sore thumbs and wiped the powder off their faces. 'Could be worse,' he said to Bob Pickering.

'It'll be better when we've got the uniforms,' the old grumbler told him.

It wasn't really. As Maxwell the consummate quartermaster had predicted, hardly anything fitted anybody. Historically, his heart fell in Tottingleigh village hall which had been commandeered by Eight Counties Television as a green room. Nathans and Bermans were splendid costumiers, but they'd been told 1810 for the epic in question.

'Jesus!' Bob Pickering muttered as the blue and white tailcoats were unloaded from the huge vans. Maxwell said something similar when the 1806 pattern shakos with their blue pompons and brass plates were delivered.

'What?' muttered Pickering, 'No striped trousers?'

'Never mind,' sighed Maxwell. 'This lot wouldn't know a *sans-culotte* from a CD – whatever that is.' He hauled out a rather handsome jacket with scarlet chevrons on the cuff. 'Yours, I think, Maréchal de Logis.'

When Miles Needham arrived for his daily inspection that afternoon, the lines looked pretty good. In fact, he and Maxwell, sauntering down the ranks like generals at a review looked decidedly out of place in their modern get-up; Needham in his Versace, Maxwell in his Man at C&A.

'Okay,' Needham nodded, endlessly signing bits of paper

on Angela's clipboard, as she hovered in the Great Man's wake. 'Can they move at all?'

'Well,' Maxwell hedged. 'French Light Infantry marched at seventy-six paces a minute. How does twenty grab you?'

'Let's get on, then,' Needham snapped, checking his watch. 'My so-called stars are arriving tomorrow. I want this thing wrapped up.'

Maxwell took his position on the flank of the front rank. Bob Pickering took up his at their head.

'Maxwell's Marauders!' Pickering bellowed, sword in hand. 'The company will advance.'

Tickled as he was by the name Pickering had suddenly dreamed up for the fighting men of Willow Bay, Maxwell instantly regretted giving their only drum to Giles Sparrow. The lad, already having visibility problems with the weight and outsizeness of his headgear, was stumbling over his gaiter straps. Only one thump in three hit the centre of the drum. Maxwell took it from him. 'Any drummers here?' he bellowed as the second rank got vaguely in step with the first.

A tentative hand went up somewhere in the middle of the line. Obviously not a regular, Maxwell noted; the boy had volunteered. 'I used to gig with a band in Hove,' the lad called.

'Right,' Maxwell sighed. 'Not exactly the Edinburgh Tattoo, but there is a war on. Change places, you two. Giles, get that man's musket.' After an initial kerfuffle in the line, the new drummer got into step and it wasn't at all bad, except for the odd fill and a tendency to slash the air with his sticks in a vain swipe at a high hat.

'Eyes left,' Pickering barked as the three ranks trudged past General Needham. Almost everybody obeyed that, but two or three of them collided with the rank in front.

'I think we'll skip the *Ordre Profonde*,' Maxwell called to Pickering. 'Too *profonde* for this lot by a long chalk.'

He turned to assess the reaction of the General and his Staff, but the General had gone, leaving an embarrassed Angela dithering on the dunes. 'Halt!' Maxwell bellowed and everybody gratefully took five.

The Head of Sixth Form ploughed back through the dry sand, past a variety of technicians tinkering with cameras and sound booms that looked like stuffed grey poodles on sticks.

'Been called away, eh?' he said to Angela.

'Er . . . I'm sorry, Max. Miles wasn't very impressed I'm afraid. Can you work on them a bit more?'

'We've got another three or four hours of daylight,' Maxwell said. 'But if you think they're bad on foot, wait till we get them into the saddle.'

The saddles were wrong, of course. So were the bits and bridles. All of it modern riding-school stuff by way of a Thelwell cartoon. But Maxwell estimated that about point nought eight per cent of the viewing public would know that, so it really wasn't worth making a fuss about. He also noted that the horses hadn't had their ears sliced off or the last two digits of their tails docked, which would certainly have been the case in the 1790s, the Cadogan dock being then in fashion. He shook his head and sighed at what a politically correct world he lived in now. They even advertised the fact on the telly – 'PC World', the irritating jingle ran. How green was his valley.

There was of course no grey for the trumpeter and no guidon for the troop. Still, the frogged blue jackets bore a passing resemblance to the Castlemartin Yeomanry and the Tarleton helmets didn't look *too* ridiculous with their leopardskin fur fabric effect.

'*Left* shoulder,' he growled at the Johnnie Raws who were getting hopelessly snarled up in their straps. 'Pouch belts are *always* worn on the left shoulder. One of the many things they got wrong in *Far From The Madding Crowd*. Still, with Julie Christie around, who was watching?'

Only twenty-one of the extras claimed to have had any riding experience and that would have to do. 'We might just get away with this, bearing in mind the script. Listen carefully. I shall say this only several times. This,' he took the bridle of the nearest bay gelding, 'is the head – that,' he pointed along the animal's flank, 'is the arse. Both ends can do you a nasty, but in the scheme of things, the teeth are arguably nastier than the shite. The point is, you won't have much warning of either. And any one of these things,' he crouched and hauled up the patient animal's forehoof, 'can kill you. At Waterloo, Wellington nearly had his brains splattered all over the place by his horse Copenhagen; but then, the bugger had been on his back for twelve hours.'

'Yeah,' grunted Martin Bairstow, 'I know how he feels.'

'The problem,' Maxwell drew the curved sabre he'd buckled around his hips, 'is that not only will you have to gallop on one of these, you'll also have to do it with one hand on the reins. None of you knows anything about riding long, with your legs straight in the cavalry tradition, so how the Hell you balance, I don't know. These are the words of command – "Walk, march, trot". Steve.'

'Yeah?' the drummer of Maxwell's Marauders shambled forward.

'Don't play the trumpet in that band of Hove of yours, do you?'

'Nah.'

'Well, pretend. I'm sure those clever technical people can dub you in later. After "Trot" you blow the bugle twice – once for canter, once for the gallop. All of you start off with your swords thus,' he rested the blade against his shoulder, 'at the slope. On the command "March", you bring it upright, like so. When you hear the second bugle call – whatever it sounds like – you extend your sword arm straight. That's all there is to it.

Right.' He sheathed his sword and stood aside in the puddles the receding tide had left. 'Prepare to mount.'

'Hang on,' Bairstow said. 'Aren't you leading this one, then?'

Maxwell looked appalled. 'My dear boy, I can't actually *ride*. You lads are on your own.'

It wasn't great, but the thunder of eighty hoofs along the level stretch of Willow Bay, albeit at a trot, had a thrill all its own. Bearing in mind that forty-four extras had to represent at least three hundred and that divided into two armies, this called for many takes and superlative skill on the part of the cameramen and editors. All that would start tomorrow. As it was, by the end of that Tuesday, Maxwell walked the circling tents of the Willow Bay Camp and Caravan Park, marvelling at the motley collection who were there to make a piece of entertainment.

Old hands like Bob Pickering and Martin Bairstow, re-enactors to their fingertips, sat in their Yeomanry jackets, smoking their clay pipes. There was a certain incongruity in the Carlsberg six pack lying beside Bairstow's sabretache, but you couldn't have everything. Steve looked an anachronist's nightmare too with a set of headphones over his *bonnet de police*, rocking his narrow head in time to some repellent piece of modern music. The horses had gone back to Merstone Farm for the night. No way, their owner had said, was he going to leave his animals tethered in the open, May or not, re-enactment or not, fortune though Eight Counties were paying him – or not.

Maxwell wandered the edge of the dunes. The crowd of curious sightseers had gone home now, but no doubt they'd be back tomorrow. Word was out that Marc Lamont would be there, so the teenaged groupies of Leighford High would take full advantage of the Whitsun hols to scream and tear their hair and dribble all over him. Hannah Morpeth would be there as well, so an awful lot of men with macs would, no doubt, be skulking in the dunes, Maxwell among them.

A sharp breeze had got up as dusk came to Willow Bay. The sea was a slab of silver under the stars as the drillmaster headed for White Surrey, the trusty bicycle that had carried its master on campaigns without number and was named after Richard III's courser at Bosworth Field. The wind sang lullabies in the tall spurge grass and the sighing sea pinks, but Maxwell picked out an altogether different sound – rhythmic, grunting. He turned a corner by the Park toilets and nearly fell over a couple writhing on the ground.

Even in the near darkness of the stunted oaks, he could make out the white piping of a trooper's jacket above a pale bum. Maxwell tapped that bum with the riding crop he'd somehow acquired during the day.

'Giles,' he said softly, 'I'm not sure Mr and Mrs McGregor would altogether approve.' Helen McGregor's startled face peered out from under the lad's braided shoulder, horror stamped in her eyes, her bra up somewhere around her ears.

'Ah, well,' Maxwell sighed, wandering off, 'camp followers will be camp followers, I suppose.' He was off duty. And Helen McGregor was a big girl now. That was fairly obvious.

The Victorians had built the Grand in the great days when Leighford was still competing with her sisters Bournemouth to the west and Brighton to the east. It was still the largest hotel in town, with three bars, not a bad tariff and a cybercafé for those sad bastards who filled their days with the spurious delights of communication technology and the superhighway that led nowhere.

Soft music was filtering through the hotel's PA system as Marc Lamont ordered his fourth gin and tonic of the evening. Outside, the seafront of Leighford was closing down, the coloured lights switching off as the drunks rolled home. Knackered bar staff in the Grand hoped to follow suit as soon as possible and stood looking at their watches and drumming their fingers on the mahogany. For a while before dinner, the front door was besieged by autograph hunters, groupies and the paparazzi of the south coast, carefully briefed by Lamont's travelling PR circus to give him the maximum of hype. Now, except for two or three painted trollops whose mothers had no idea where they were, belts for skirts and high, block heels on their fuck-me shoes, the Grand frontage was deserted.

Marc Lamont was blond this week. He'd come up the easy way. His dad was something on the production side in the old days of Thames TV; there were all sorts of rumours about money having changed hands at RADA. There were rumours too about Marc and Helena Bonham Carter, which came as a surprise to many, none more so than Miss Bonham Carter. You only had to look at Marc Lamont to know that there was only one person in the world he loved – himself.

'It's not going to be *too* early tomorrow, Miles, dear, is it?' he turned to his director lounging on the sofa next to his.

'Eight,' Needham told him. 'I want to catch *something* of the early light. Seven would be better.'

Lamont snorted. 'In your dreams. When does little Miss Tightbum join us?'

There was a silence.

'I think Marc means . . .' Angela thought she ought to break it.

'I know what Marc means,' Needham hissed. 'Hannah is not required until after lunch. We're doing the battle scene first. Your death.'

'You wish.' Lamont felt the ice cube hit his teeth. 'Angela, have you changed those boots yet?'

'Yes, Marc. They're ready.'

'And what about that poncy helmet thing?'

'Well, we've had it adjusted,' the flustered amanuensis told him, adjusting her shades and reaching for her clipboard.

'Is that some sort of dildo?' Lamont leaned forwards to her, an eyebrow raised in a vain attempt to become the Dirk Bogarde of the '90s. 'I never seem to see you without it in your hot little hand.'

The men just had time to see Angela's face darken and her lips crumple before she snatched it up and stalked out of the lounge.

'You really are a prize shit, Lamont,' Needham growled.

'You've got too many pussies on your team, Miles,' the actor told him. 'If there's one thing I can't stand, it's prima donnas.'

'"Prima donnas", he said.' Needham threw his shirt at the nearest chair. '*He* couldn't stand prima donnas. What a fuck that man is!'

The girl on the bed raised herself up on one arm and stretched out the other. 'Miles, it doesn't matter.'

'Doesn't matter?' he gulped down the contents of the glass in his hand. His eyes flashed anger in the dim light of the bedroom, 'I tell you, Hannah, somebody should kick that little prick's head in.'

'Well,' she laughed, peeling off her black negligee so that her hair cascaded over her breasts and her nipples rose in the half light, 'isn't it his death scene tomorrow? There's your chance.'

For a moment, Needham hesitated, then he kicked off his trousers and whipped down his boxers. Then he grinned. 'You're right,' he said, hauling back the covers and sliding in beside her. 'How much would it cost, do you think, for props to tinker with a musket so that it *really* blew the bastard away?'

'That's too quick,' the girl ran her fingers over her lover's chest, tracing circles around his nipples with her long, pointed nails. 'I thought you'd want him a piece at a time.'

'Even better,' Needham nodded against the headboard. 'Starting with his nuts.'

'These?' she fondled him playfully.

'Assuming he had any.'

'And then,' she started stroking his erection, 'we can start work on Barbara.'

She felt him stiffen in both senses and he shifted awkwardly, trying to pull away. 'Not tonight,' he said, 'I really don't want the why-don't-you-leave-her routine, tonight, Hannah, if that's all right.'

She half smiled in the half light and launched her naked body across his.

# Chapter Four

'Krispy Krunchie Wheeto Bites?' Maxwell perused the range of breakfast goodies for his friend, displayed as they were along the counter.

Irving sighed. 'I think I'll stick to the orange juice.'

'Wise,' Maxwell poured for them both and they took their chilled glasses back to their table. 'Comfy here at the Grand, John?'

'It's not bad,' Irving told him.

'Porn channel any good?'

'I wouldn't know,' Irving raised a contemptuous eyebrow. 'I spent most of last evening revising my article for Cornell University on Toussaint L'Overture's social policy.'

'Ah.'

'Morning, Mr Maxwell.' A chirpy waitress had appeared at the great man's elbow.

'Sasha, I didn't know you worked here.'

Irving groaned.

'Full English, is it?'

Maxwell looked John Irving up and down. 'Contrary to appearances, yes,' he said. 'Easy on the mushrooms.'

'Toast?'

'Absolutely. And a bottomless coffee pot, please.'

And the girl made her exit.

'Tell me, oh wise pundit of historical institutions,' Maxwell leaned across the table to Irving, 'why is it that hotels the country o'er give you your toast, which is traditionally eaten *after* the full English, *before* you get said full English?'

'Ah,' Irving winced as the orange juice seared his nerve endings, 'mankind has pondered that one for . . . oh, Jesus!'

Maxwell followed the man's staring eyes to the other side of the dining-room. An apparition in a tartan scarf and beret was shooing away a member of the hotel staff and making a beeline for their table.

'You're John Irving,' the apparition shrilled, pointing at him like one of Lord Kitchener's posters. Even the moustache bore an uncanny resemblance. Irving struggled to his feet. 'Good morning,' he said.

'Well, I want an explanation,' the apparition said. 'Am I to have it?'

'Won't you join us, Ms Marriner?' Irving hoped for a less than positive response. 'May I introduce Peter Maxwell? Bwana, this is Ms Erika Marriner.'

'Really?' Maxwell was on his feet too – ex public schoolboy and all. 'Charmed.'

'Bwana?' the old girl's hearing was like a needle, ga-ga though she probably was. 'He called you bwana.'

'An old term of familiarity,' Maxwell smiled.

'Well, it's quite overtly racist. Have you no respect for yourself, Dr Irving? I was told you were a Cambridge don.'

'It's a little in-joke, Ms Marriner,' Irving told her. 'Mr Maxwell and I go back a long way.'

'Really,' she sat down heavily, rearranging scarves, shawls and handbags in a flutter of fuss. 'I'm afraid I must have words with you, Dr Irving.'

'Is that another full English?' Sasha had arrived with two steaming dishes.

Erika Marriner bridled. 'Three pounds of assorted grease, you silly goose? Certainly not. Get me two Ryvitas and a glass of water. And charge it to Eight Counties Television.'

Maxwell grinned at Sasha and crossed his eyes behind Ms Marriner's ginger head. 'What an interesting tartan,' he said quickly as the old girl spun round with the speed of a cobra to stare at him. 'The clan Marriner?'

'The clan Campbell,' she corrected him. 'I'm currently writing a novel on the '45. I believe in living my books, Mr Maxwell. My research,' she turned her basilisk stare on Irving, 'is of course immaculate. So,' she rummaged in the tapestry portmanteau on her lap and hauled out a copy of the lamentable script of *The Captain's Fancy*. 'Here,' her cadaverous finger stabbed page thirty four, 'it says "Jemima pulls him to her and unbuttons his necessaries".'

'Does it?' Irving had to ask.

'I was told you were the film's historical adviser.'

'So I am.'

'Well, I've just seen the rushes or whatever these wretched film people call them, at Basingstoke. That slip of a gel, what's her name . . . Hannah Something, the one playing Jemima . . . she undresses Captain Fitzgerald in the twinkling of an eye. You do know, do you, that an officer's necessaries invariably had sixteen buttons?'

'Peeing must have been murder,' Maxwell shook his head in mid-sausage.

'Do you have any connection with this project?'

Maxwell swallowed quickly. 'I am supervising the battle scene,' he told her.

'And are you familiar with officers' necessaries?'

'Moderately,' Maxwell nodded. 'But more importantly, Ms Marriner,' he craned his neck to check page thirty-four's stage directions, 'I think it most unlikely that a refined young lady of Jemima's station in life would have done any pulling and unbuttoning in 1797, don't you? It was rather more of a man's world then, Ms Marriner.'

Ms Marriner was on her feet. 'How dare you? Are you sitting there and telling me that I have no sense of period?'

'Merely an observation.' Maxwell sipped his coffee while John Irving was stuffing bacon in his mouth to stop himself laughing.

'I wasn't happy about this from the start,' she growled, and spun on her heel. 'I'm going to see Miles Needham. Believe me, he – and you,' she pointed at Irving again, 'have turned my masterpiece into a charade. Heads aren't just going to roll,' she leaned towards the breakfasting pair, 'they're going to bounce!' And she swept past Sasha, scattering her Ryvitas in all directions.

'Mad as a snake,' Irving muttered.

'God save us from writers of historical fiction,' Maxwell smiled. 'Sasha, darling, never mind the nasty lady, freshen this coffee pot, could you, there's a sweetheart?'

The police car was parked at a jaunty angle above the Shingle when Maxwell and Irving arrived. A solitary copper, all flat cap and attitude was standing in the middle of a knot of people, making notes. There were other vehicles lower down – all of them marked with the Eight Counties logo. And a line of roadies was holding back the crowds, all nattering and laughing excitedly, waiting to spot a famous face.

'Can I have your autograph, love?' a middle-aged woman with a Sheffield accent accosted John Irving. 'Right here. Could you put "To our Janice. Love Rudolph."'

'Rudolph?' Irving frowned.

'Well, whatever your real name is then. I think you're ever so good in "The Thin Blue Line". Better than that Atkinson bloke.'

'But . . .'

'Come on, Rudolph,' Maxwell flicked out his pen. 'For your fans.' And he winked at him. Irving sighed and scribbled something on the woman's pad.

'Ooh, ta, love,' and she showed it joyfully to the cloth-capped man she was with.

'There,' Maxwell relieved Irving of his pen, 'it doesn't take much to make people happy, does it?'

'Mr Maxwell?' the pasty-faced policeman was suddenly in front of them. 'May I have a word?'

'Of course,' the Head of Sixth Form nodded. 'John. I'll be along.'

A pale sun was glinting on the bayonets of Maxwell's Marauders as they laughed and joked with the crowds under the headland of the Shingle. Television company cordons had been placed to hold the people back and technicians in headphones wandered aimlessly here and there, checking light and sound levels.

Maxwell found himself on higher ground, leaning against the constable's car.

'Mr Maxwell, do you know a girl called Helen McGregor?'

'Yes,' the Head of Sixth Form told him. 'Why?'

'She reported a prowler last night. A Peeping Tom.'

'Where?'

'Over there at the camp. She said you were here late.'

'That's right. I was.'

'What time would that be?'

'Oh, let's see . . . er . . . perhaps ten, ten thirty. The sun had certainly gone down.'

'And you didn't see anyone – in an anorak perhaps? Or a Barbour?'

'No,' Maxwell frowned. 'Is Helen all right?'

'Oh, yeah,' the constable flipped his notebook closed. 'She's fine. Tell me, you're her teacher, right?'

'One of several,' Maxwell nodded. He thought it might be sensible at this stage to spread the blame.

'Would you say she was . . . emotional? Over-excitable?'

Maxwell shrugged. 'She could be,' he nodded. 'Why?'

'Well, nobody else seems to have seen this prowler. She

says he was just standing there – up on the ridge of the headland. But no one else we've talked to saw a thing. You were the last one around as far as we know – who's not sleeping on site, that is.'

'She's certainly very excited to be involved in all this.'

There was a roar from the beach and female shrieking that drowned out the wheeling gulls. Maxwell and the officer turned to see a tall, scarlet-coated actor walking in a knot of admirers and waving to the surging crowd.

'Marc Lamont,' Maxwell said.

'Yeah, well,' the constable tucked his pencil away. 'Some of us live in the real world. Thanks, Mr Maxwell,' and he clambered into his car.

Down on the beach, Helen McGregor was already wearing her Welsh fishwife's costume. She'd passed her screen test because Miles Needham had said she looked horrendous enough to pass for an historic hag and she'd smiled delightedly at him. She pushed forward now with the others, her bright eyes fixed on the holder of her heart. There was some woman fussing around him, a peroxide tart old enough to be his mother and he was laughing with her.

'Marc!' she screamed. 'Marc! Over here!' But her screams were drowned by all the others and some of her oppos from Leighford High had unrolled a home-made banner that read 'We Love You, Marc' and it was signed by all the girls Helen hated. All she could do was stand there, swaying with the hysteria of the crowd, staring at the sun flashing on the gorget at his throat. She couldn't hear the crowd now. She couldn't see the peroxide tart any more. All she saw was the blond curls under the black hat, cocked fore and aft, the blue eyes steady and bright and looking directly at her. Then, the moment that made her life. As if in a dream, she saw his lips move. 'I love you, Helen,' and the crowd carried her away, like a helpless weed on a running tide.

* * *

Half a day's march and three volleys later, the company was glad to break for lunch. The sun was high and the Marauders sweated in their serge and their stocks. One more take and it would be time to switch the uniforms to play the Castlemartin Yeomanry. Mr Ecclestone had started bussing his horses in. Miles Needham had the full attention of Marc Lamont under his parasol under the lee of the dunes. Maxwell couldn't catch much of it, but both men's colour was high and he saw Lamont haul off his cross-belt and throw his sword into the sand before he strode off, followed by a flapping Angela and other production team lackeys. A further cohort stayed with Needham. After all, leading men came and went. As soon as their hair or teeth started to fall out, they were history. Directors went on for ever.

The extras left their sandwiches – with the accent on the sand – as a sleek limo crested the edge of the Shingle.

'Cor, it's her!' Giles Sparrow, ever the most articulate of men, was on his feet first, throwing off his crossbelts and staggering across the sand. The other invaders were with him, headed by Martin Bairstow, interspersed with the ragged Welsh women, Helen McGregor positively dribbling, among them.

'Hannah!' the lad roared, waving his cap as though young General Bonaparte himself had appeared on the horizon. Helen caught him a nasty one around the ear with her shawl, but he wasn't about to be deflected. The production team lackeys formed their second cordon of the day as Hannah Morpeth emerged from the car in jeans and sweater. She ignored Lamont completely and made for Needham and the brass hats around him.

'That'll be another two hours for costume and fucking make-up,' Lamont snarled to Angela, 'especially make-up. Let's go!' he bawled, snatching up his bicorn hat and striding for his horse. 'You – Maxwell, is it?'

The Head of Sixth Form turned to face him. 'It is.'

'We're wasting time here. I want to do the death scene.'

'Now?' Maxwell blinked.

Lamont stood nose to nose with his man. 'I don't need lip from technicians,' the actor growled. 'Get your fucking idiots lined up. Give me a fucking volley.'

'Mr Lamont . . .' John Irving didn't care for the man's tone.

'Don't bother me now, nigger,' Lamont stabbed his man in the chest with a white-gloved finger. 'I don't honestly have time for it.' And he marched away.

'Oh, John,' Angela, the pacifier, was at his elbow. 'I'm so dreadfully sorry.'

Irving waved it aside. It wasn't the first time.

But retribution had caught up with Marc Lamont. Its name was Peter Maxwell and not even John Irving was ready for the man's speed. He caught Lamont's sleeve and spun him round, gripping his throat by his bunch of lace and the silver gorget below it.

'The only actors I know,' he growled with a gravel that sent ripples through Lamont's curls, 'are rather sad people who can't hold down a regular job. Dr John Irving holds higher degrees from Cambridge, Harvard and Yale. But I don't suppose that means much to you, does it, philistine? You probably think Yale is a kind of lock. You want a volley, *Mr* Lamont? I'll give you a volley.' And he threw his man backwards to sprawl awkwardly in the sand.

Lamont scrambled to his feet, dusting himself down. There was no entourage now. The chattering crowd had fallen silent as all eyes were on the pair centre beach. Helen McGregor's eyes were narrowed against the sun, her face a mask of whiteness, her fists clenched.

'I'm suing, Maxwell,' Lamont shrieked. 'As soon as this crap is all over. I'm suing the arse off you.'

Maxwell had already turned his back on him. 'Marauders!' he bellowed. 'Form up. Two ranks deep. Maréchal de Logis!'

Bob Pickering swung his spontoon onto his shoulder. 'Here, sir,' he responded.

'The line will advance, Maréchal de Logis. Let's give this . . . English captain a taste of French lead.' Maxwell was good at clichés.

The ranks thumped to attention as Pickering's spontoon pierced the sky. Giles Sparrow was last in the line, fitting his shako and balancing his musket on his knees.

'End of the line, lad, end of the line,' Pickering muttered, nodding furiously to the boy.

'The Twenty-Fifth will advance,' Maxwell roared, taking his place next to Sparrow. 'Double time.'

Yesterday the Marauders couldn't manage single time, but galvanized by the extraordinary scene between their drillmaster and Lamont, they rose to it. The beach re-echoed to the thud of their hob-nailed boots and the shouts of Pickering and Maxwell over the staccato tattoo of Steve's drum, keeping the line taut, the going fast.

'Watch your dressing,' Maxwell called. 'Steady, steady the Twenty-Fifth.'

Everyone was watching now. The crowds on the dunes, the ragged, red-shawled fishwives, the knots of technicians and Miles Needham, under his parasol.

'They're looking pretty good,' he muttered to someone next to him.

'Right wheel!' Pickering roared and the ranks swung on a sixpence to face the solitary scarlet-coated officer who stood unarmed before them. But Lamont was not going to budge. He was supposed to fall, mortally wounded in a skirmish, according to the script but after what had just happened, no way would he go to the sand again. He planted his legs apart and rested his hands on his hips.

'Twenty-Fifth!' Maxwell roared as Pickering whirled his spontoon to full height in both hands and darted to the right flank, 'on my command. Load!'

There was a fumbling of cartridges as teeth clamped down on paper and musket butts hit the sand. The ramrods came out almost as one and the muzzles came up to the level. Marc Lamont found himself swallowing hard. He was staring down the business end of forty-three muskets and every one was aiming directly at him.

'Fire!' Maxwell thundered and his voice was drowned by the crash of the guns. The crowd cheered wildly, the extras throwing their caps in the air, Helen McGregor among them. As the smoke filtered away across the levels of the Bay, Marc Lamont still stood there, his ears numbed, his jaw flexing. Helen McGregor breathed a sigh of relief.

In the silence that followed the fusillade, a single scream rose from the throat of Angela Badham. She was kneeling on the sand next to the fallen parasol. And she was cradling in her hands the bloody, shattered head of Miles Needham. Yards away, near the fluttering papers of Angela's clipboard, lay a piece of his skull and the lead ball that had killed him.

Sylvia Matthews had loved 'Mad Max' Maxwell for as long as she'd been the Matron at Leighford High. Whether he knew it or not, she couldn't tell. But she was always there, patching egos along with elbows, the Agony Aunt par excellence to the shattered generation who were the children of the Flower Children. Perhaps the years and the need to haul fainters around school corridors had put a little weight on her, but her face was still attractive and her heart was still pure and good and she wore it on her sleeve for Peter Maxwell.

They sat facing the television screen in Maxwell's lounge in Columbine Avenue.

'There was a tragic accident here today during the filming of an historical mini-series,' the link man was saying against the backdrop of the dunes and the Shingle that ran far out to sea. 'Mr Miles Needham, director of the award-winning *Purple Skies* at the Cannes Film Festival last year, was shot dead when a piece of action went wrong. Mr Needham, forty-five, was rushed to Leighford General Hospital but was pronounced dead on arrival. Tributes have been coming in from around the world. This is Nicholas Witchell for the BBC at Willow Bay, West Sussex.'

The television screen filled with the solemn face of Michael Buerke. 'Miles Needham's career began twenty years ago with the BBC,' he read from the autocue. 'Live from Hollywood, we have someone who knew him well. Sir Anthony Hopkins . . .'

Maxwell made the Welshman vanish with a simple flick of the remote. 'Accident be buggered,' he muttered.

'Max,' Sylvia sat on the sofa next to him, 'are you sure you're all right?'

'It can't happen, Sylv.' He threw his arms wide, then ran a hand through the thatch of his barbed wire hair. 'Yes, people have been killed by blank-firing guns – Brandon Lee a few years back – but that has to be at close range. Needham must have been . . . what . . . seventy, seventy-five yards away from the firing line. Nothing could have hit him at that range, not even a paper pellet.'

'I'm sure the police . . .'

He held up his hand. 'Let me stop you there, Matron mine,' he said. 'The police . . .' and he raised an eyebrow.

'All right,' she sighed. 'We've both had bad experiences of them. But *some* of them are all right, aren't they?'

Maxwell pondered for a moment, then he swigged the last of his Southern Comfort. 'One of them,' he said.

The police are good at keeping their private houses private. If they weren't, you'd be able to tell a copper's house by the shattered windows and shit-daubed doors. For all Home

Secretary Jack Straw supported the barrel, he also wanted to weed out the rotten apples. And a lot of people were prepared to believe the whole keg was contaminated. Roaring towards the Millennium, the boys in blue were nearly as unpopular as teachers.

The face behind the frosted glass was pretty, the eyes grey and clear, the hair a light chestnut. There was a tiredness around the mouth as she opened the door, but it vanished when she saw Maxwell.

'Mr Maxwell,' she murmured.

'Woman Policeman Carpenter,' he bowed low, doffing his cap.

She glanced at the bike leaning at a rakish angle against her wall. 'Have you got a licence for that?'

'How've you been, Jacquie?' he asked her, the dark eyes suddenly serious.

She smiled. 'I've been fine, Max. You were at the beach today. Willow Bay.' She held the door open for him.

'Bad news travels fast, as they used to say in the Westerns.'

'Lounge,' she pointed. 'First on the right.'

'Look,' he padded across her carpet, 'I'm sorry about this. I've really no right . . .'

'You look all in,' she ignored him. 'Drink?'

'That would be civilized,' he said and took the weight off his feet by courtesy of her settee. It was a homely enough flat, nothing out of place except for a copy of *Marie-Claire* abandoned in the corner and a pile of tatty police reports she was reading for her sergeant's exams.

She crossed to her drinks cabinet and poured for them both. Jacquie Carpenter was probably nudging thirty, her long, curly hair tied up in what Maxwell still called a pony-tail, her hips swaying slightly in her stone-washed jeans.

'It's not Southern Comfort, I'm afraid,' she turned to him, smiling.

'That doesn't matter,' he said, taking the glass, 'I'm flattered you remembered. What do you know?'

'Uh-huh.' She sat opposite him, shaking a finger. She and Maxwell had faced cases before, kept the watches of the night. She knew him of old and had twice put her career on the line because of it. Mad Max was mad, mad and dangerous to know.

'Let me rephrase that,' he chuckled. 'What do *I* know? On my command, forty-three blokes let rip with their replica Brown Besses this lunchtime – and a man died. How is that possible, Policewoman?'

She shook her head. 'I did the usual three days firearms training at Hendon,' she told him. 'I can only just remember one end of a gun from another.'

'The odd thing was . . .' Maxwell was suddenly kneeling on her floor, grabbing things off her coffee table. 'May I? The odd thing was, they all missed the bugger they were aiming at.'

'What do you mean?'

'Marc Lamont.'

'He's dishy,' she squealed, the woman suddenly peeping out from the policewoman.

'He's a shit,' Maxwell corrected her. 'But that's another story. Here's Lamont,' he placed a fig in the middle of a carpet swirl. 'Here . . .' he stretched out a line of nuts, 'my Marauders.'

'Your what?'

'Soldiers. Re-enactors. Fine band of chaps. Not the sort John Mills or Noel Coward would have approved of, but there you are. Different war; different time. Over here . . .' he plonked an orange near the coffee table leg, 'Miles Needham. So . . .'

'So,' Jacquie squatted over the scene of the accident, 'they missed Lamont and hit Needham. Well, fair enough. He *is* in a straight line. Anybody behind the line of your men?'

'What?'

'A sniper?'

'Ah, you've been watching too much *Sharpe*, Woman Policeman. Maybe one of Sean Bean's chosen men could have put a ball in Needham's brain at over a hundred paces, but he'd need a Baker Rifle and . . . look, what am I talking about? These are toys. They're all just replicas. Their firing mechanisms don't work. All you get is a flash in the pan, from the saying of the same name. You've got to shake the ball out later.'

'It must have been a hell of a thing to witness,' Jacquie said softly.

'I didn't actually see it,' Maxwell told her. 'It was Angela Badham's scream that alerted me in the first place. All that gunfire is deafening when you're standing next to it. By the time I'd got the smoke out of my eyes, Needham was lying on the ground. Mind you, the blood . . .'

'Head shot,' Jacquie nodded. 'It's always like that. I've only ever seen one.' She shuddered at the memory of it. 'Not nice,' she whispered. 'Not nice.'

'That's funny,' Maxwell said. 'That's exactly what John Irving said about Miles Needham.'

# Chapter Five

Jim Astley hauled off the rubber gloves and threw them into the bin. He was tired and his back ached and perhaps he'd dissected one body too many. In his darker days, he felt like a butcher, hacking and sawing his way through the shells of what once had been people. The growl and shudder of the circular saw as it sheared through bone, the rip of the zip that closed the body bags, the unutterable silence of the mortuary – sometimes the sounds came back to him in the cold watches of the night when things seemed distorted and warped and mountainous. Then he'd shake himself and his old snobbery would reassert itself. He was one of the chosen, the élite, a man with the skill of God. He looked at his own hands as he ran them under the hot tap, flexed the fingers, stretched the knuckles. Good hands. Safe hands. And he looked up into the mirror, wondering for a moment whose face stared back at him.

'Jim,' there was another face in the mirror, out of focus with his own until he peered closer and the closing of the door brought him out of himself.

'Henry,' the police surgeon nodded, and snatched a handful of paper towels from the dispenser before turning to his man.

Henry Hall was a Detective Chief Inspector, one of those

legendary band they still write novels about. He'd put on a little weight had Henry over the years that he and Astley had known each other. But he was a distant bastard was Henry Hall. Had the warmth of a refrigerator. The strip lighting reflected back at Astley in the man's glasses. His eyes were invisible. There were times when people only recognized Henry Hall by his three-piece suit. It was rumoured that rookies on his manor called him the Ice Man, but that was just a rumour – Henry Hall wasn't colourful enough for that.

'I was going to ring you. Want to buy me a cup of coffee?'

'My pleasure,' Hall nodded, a man who'd never had any pleasure in his life; and Astley crashed the door back in his own mortuary on his way up to the upper levels and the light.

Leighford General's staff canteen was like hospital staff canteens the wide world over – the coffee was lousy and the tea was worse. You had to press all the buttons yourself and it was of course pot luck whether there was jam in your doughnut or not. The All Day Breakfast oozed cholesterol and every corner seemed to belong to the smokers in a profession that buried thousands of cancer victims every year. Rhyme? Reason? Not in Frank Dobson's National Health Service.

Hall and Astley sat opposite each other by the window, the one that looked out on the building site that was earmarked for Leighford's Millennium project.

'Sugar?' Hall handed Astley a sachet.

'Never touch it,' the good doctor said and slipped a few drops from his hip flask into his coffee before consigning the thing back to the bowels of his white coat.

'So . . .' Hall stirred his tea carefully. 'What can you tell me about the late Mr Needham?'

Astley leaned back in his plastic chair, 'A well nourished male in his mid-forties,' he said. 'Certain evidence of the use of narcotics, but not a problem.'

'Not a junky?'

Astley shook his head. 'Social user,' he said. 'I would think it's de rigeur in television producers, isn't it?'

'I understand he was a director,' Hall said.

Astley shrugged, 'Director, producer. Who gives a shit, Henry? They all die, you know.'

'How exactly?' the DCI asked.

'Gunshot to the head,' the doctor answered. 'Quite unusual, though.' He rummaged in his pocket. 'You'll need this.'

Hall took the lead ball. It felt cold and heavy in his hand.

'It's distorted by the impact with the skull,' Astley told him. 'It would have been totally spherical when it left the gun. It hit Needham here,' he pointed to his own head, 'just to the left of the midline, shattering what dear old Henry Gray – he of the Anatomy – calls the frontal eminence. So we have a circular hole at the entrance wound with cracks radiating outward, like a pebble hitting a window, if you can picture that. The ball went straight through Needham's brain – I won't bore you with the various lobes – and exited here,' he pointed to the back of his head where the hair got thinner, year by year. 'The exit wound was massive. Your boys handed me two pieces of skull – and I found three others. I can't reconstruct the occipital totally. There must be tiny fragments in the sand, at the Bay. You'll never find those.'

'So this is an early bullet, then?'

Astley shrugged. 'You'll have to talk to Hendon about that. A conoidal bullet would have done more damage, especially from a high-velocity rifle.'

'Either way, Needham would have been dead?'

'Oh, yes,' Astley nodded. 'As a dodo. Who's in the frame?'

It was Hall's turn to lean back. 'That's just it, Jim. Except for the Kennedy killing – and maybe Anwar Sadat – I can't think of a more public murder. Or was it execution?'

'That's good,' Astley grinned his humourless grin.

'What is?'

'Murder. Your Inspector Whatsisface kept talking about an accident.'

'That's the official line at the moment,' Hall said. 'We're keeping all our options open.'

'Have you got a murder weapon?'

'Forty-three of them,' Hall told him. 'But that's being narrowed down as we speak. I haven't even got to go to Hendon. Hendon has come to us.'

The smoke curled up from a dozen half-smoked cigarettes across the flickering shadows of the slide projector. This was the Incident Room at Tottingleigh, the little village now absorbed into suburbia by Leighford's eastward sprawl. It was a series of prefabs, freezing in winter, sweltering in summer; cheerless all year round. DC Jacquie Carpenter hadn't felt much like lunch before she saw the photographs of Miles Needham's head. Now, she'd positively gone off the whole idea of eating – perhaps Thursday, when the memory of the shattered, bloody skull had lessened. DI Whatsisface – Dave Watkiss to everybody but Jim Astley – was on his feet with pointer in hand. Henry Hall knew how he'd be spending his lunch hour. The wolf pack with the slavering jowls known as the country's media were howling so loudly he'd relented and called a press conference. When a man as high profile as Miles Needham died, discreet inquiries were out of the question. 'The right to know,' the media shrieked. 'In the public interest,' the newshounds bayed. Softly softly went out of the window.

'The gun that killed Needham,' Watkiss was saying, 'was a ringer.' He held up the Brown Bess in the dim light of the incident room for the benefit of his shirt-sleeved audience. 'Light, George, please.'

There was a popping of neon strips and the fan of the projector died. Everybody moved, as instinctively you do when the light of your environment changes and they all looked at the gun.

'This is a replica flintlock musket. Film companies and re-enactors use them all the time. They're designed to fire blanks. Except this one,' he clicked back the serpentine, the barrel presented, across this chest. 'This one is for real. Except,' he eased the hammer forwards again, 'it's even better than that. Hendon have been over all the forty-three firearms used on the day in question. Forty-two of them were harmless. Oh, you could knock somebody's brains out with the butt, like a club. But the most you'd get from the mechanism is a black face or a nasty one if your finger got in the way of the gubbins. But this one, Hendon tells us, has a rifled barrel. For the uninitiated out there, that means the shot will fire further and straighter. Whoever used this gun wasn't play acting. He was for real.'

'Who is it, then?' a voice called from the corner, 'Whose gun was that?'

DI Watkiss loomed sideways, the Brown Bess balanced nonchalantly in one hand, and flicked on the projector switch. The fan whirred again and the lights went out. Then, all of them, from DCI to the newest rookie, hot and sweaty off the beat, stared into the vacant, boyish face of a murderer.

James Diamond, BSc, MEd was in some ways a clone of Henry Hall. Both university men, of an age, they had come up the soft way, via management consultancy training. Diamond had read Biology at Salford – a slim volume, men like Maxwell knew. And for some reason best known to Diamond, the man had a streak of ambition in him. Or perhaps he wanted to escape from the science lab benches, the roar of the bunsen burners, the smell of formaldehyde. Anyway, he was a Deputy Head, albeit in Wolverhampton, at thirty-one. He made Head at thirty-four, but that was only because the governors of Leighford High belonged in a home and the Chief Education Officer had recently escaped from one.

Maxwell commented loudly in the staffroom on the day the new Head arrived, misquoting General LaSalle – 'a headmaster who isn't dead by thirty is a blackguard.' Maxwell himself was Head of Department at twenty-six; Head of Sixth Form by thirty; a living legend by half past two. He'd christened Diamond 'Legs' after the '20s gangster of the same name in the hope that it would give the man some colour. It didn't.

And the colourless James Diamond sat pale-faced in his office that Monday morning after the Whitsun break as elsewhere in the building, sixteen quivering wrecks shambled into the Hall to face the baptism of fire that was their first written A-level paper. Maxwell would have liked to have been with them. He always had been, at the start of every A-level paper in every subject for a quarter of a century. Just a calming word, a merry quip. It slowed the heart rate, mopped the brow, gave hope to the hopeless. But not today. Today, there was something more serious.

'The police here have arrested Giles Sparrow, Max,' Diamond said.

The Head of Sixth Form sat upright on the Head's excruciating office settee. 'Say again,' he blinked.

Diamond licked his thin lips. He couldn't stand it if Maxwell was going deaf; the man was enough of a handful as he was. 'It's true,' he said. 'I got the call a few minutes ago.'

'From whom?'

'Inspector Hall at Leighford Police Station.'

'Is that where they're holding Giles?'

'I believe so.'

'Right.' Maxwell was on his feet.

'Where are you going?' Diamond had to ask.

'What's he been arrested for?' the Head of Sixth Form asked.

'Murder,' Diamond still couldn't believe it, even as he said the word.

Maxwell was at the door. 'Where are you going, Max? What are you going to do?'

'I'm going to Leighford Police Station, Headmaster,' he told him. 'Just passing by long enough to pick up the gelignite,' he lapsed into his Liam Neeson as Michael Collins, 'then I'm getting Giles Sparrow out.'

Diamond was on his feet, his mouth open. Maxwell paused in the open doorway. 'Wanna hold the match?' he asked.

Diamond could only shake his head. He'd never known how to respond to Mad Max Maxwell.

'No,' Maxwell smiled grimly. 'I didn't think so.'

Peter Maxwell had been to Leighford Police Station before, not once, but several times. It was unprepossessing red-brick Victorian, with no trace of Gothic. They'd even taken the blue lamp away and Maxwell couldn't do his Jack Warner any more. Trouble followed Maxwell like flies on a dung heap and he knew his way around. Even so, there was protocol and everyone had to go through the desk sergeant. In this case, on that Monday morning, the desk sergeant had the shoulders and the intellect of a brick wall and nothing was going to get past him.

'Mr Maxwell?' a voice interrupted the pair whose tempers were rising with the June heat.

'Yes,' the Head of Sixth Form turned. 'Who are you?'

'Malcolm Sailer. 'I'm Giles Sparrow's solicitor.'

'How do you know me?'

'Aha,' Sailer raised an eyebrow. 'You're a legend in your own lunch-time, Mr Maxwell. Shall we?'

'Yes,' Maxwell threw a withering glance at the desk man. 'I think we'd better. I could use some fresh air.'

Sailer had probably had hair once, but it had long since vanished with the worry of conveyancing and he flicked one of those annoying remotes that bleeped to tell his car that its master had returned. 'Pig ignorant, the police, aren't they?' Sailer commented as he sank into his plush upholstery.

'I always thought they were pretty wonderful, actually,' Maxwell beamed.

Sailer couldn't read his man any more than Diamond could and he let the comment go. 'Giles suggested I come and see you. This has saved me a journey. Can I drop you somewhere?'

'You can take me to the murder scene, if you will,' Maxwell said. 'I'll pick up my bike later.'

The solicitor rammed the automatic into drive.

'They've charged the boy with murder?'

'They have.' Sailer swung left out of the station car park. 'Late last night. I got a call from George Sparrow in the early hours.'

'You're the family solicitor?'

'After a fashion,' Sailer nodded. 'You know George is a farmer?'

'No,' Maxwell said. 'No, I didn't.'

'I handle the usual bits and pieces of the farm, sales of land, that sort of thing. I don't mind telling you, I'm a bit out of my depth on this one. Susan's distraught of course, as you'd expect from a mother.'

'How's Giles?'

'Holding up. Between you and me, Mr Maxwell, he's not very bright, so it may be he doesn't fully grasp the implications . . . but you must know that.'

'I don't actually teach the boy,' Maxwell told him. 'I don't think I ever have. But he's one of my sixth form – that happy band they call Maxwell's Own. That's enough.'

'DCI Hall wouldn't give me any leeway of course – not that I'd expect that with a murder charge. They'll be moving him to Winchester tomorrow. Giles said you were there.'

'On the beach? Yes, I was. Standing right next to Giles, as

it happens.' Maxwell watched the cars whip past, grockles on their way to fun and festivities, taking their kids out of school 'cos it was their right. 'I've never seen a man die before,' he said.

'Not very pretty, I don't suppose,' Sailer nodded. 'Here we are.' He hauled the wheel over and the Megane purred down the slipway that led to the beach. A young constable stopped him there. Beyond the lad a police cordon fluttered in blue and white to keep the curious away from Willow Bay. It all looked different now. While Sailer explained to the officer his reason for being there, Maxwell stood by the car, resting on the open door. The tides had washed away the bootprints of the Marauders, but Bob Pickering's flag of the Ninth Voltigeurs still flapped defiantly on his tent ropes above the dunes. Needham's parasol and chair had gone with Needham's body and the pegs that SOCO had placed to mark the spot had long ago been lifted. Only a knot of paparazzi stood on the Shingle, smoking and chatting, waiting for any news. Only the gulls, high in the cloudless weather, cried for Miles Needham.

'To whom have you talked?' Maxwell asked Sailer.

'Only Giles and his parents at the moment,' the solicitor told him.

'The re-enactors,' Maxwell pointed to the lines of canvas, 'they were all there. Let's have a word.' And he trudged across the sand. 'Why Giles?' he asked.

'His gun, apparently,' Sailer said, looking oddly out of place on a summer's beach, on a summer's day, in a dark, pin-striped solicitor's suit. 'Ballistics have confirmed it. There's no mistake. It was Giles's gun that killed the director. And I must presume that it was Giles's finger on the trigger.'

'It was,' Maxwell nodded grimly. 'And he was standing as close to me as you are.'

Sailer stopped. 'Haven't the police talked to you?' he asked.

Maxwell chuckled. 'If I know Henry Hall,' he said, 'he'll choose his time and place.'

The re-enactors weren't helpful. It wasn't that they didn't mean to be. It was just that they hadn't seen anything. Hadn't heard anything. And now, they weren't saying much either. Two or three of them, Maxwell had seen hanging around the hostelries of Leighford. Two or three more were old Leighford Highenas, who in their former existence had been seen hanging around the corridors of the school. But no one had seen Giles Sparrow anywhere near the props caravan or tinkering with the guns or checking wind speed and velocity or issuing death threats to Miles Needham. But, as Maxwell and Sailer both knew, because the re-enactors hadn't seen any of this didn't mean it hadn't happened.

They had made a policy decision at Eight Counties. The show must go on. Miles would have wanted that. They owed it to his memory. Some faceless suit of an accountant from the corridors of power was working on the BAFTA speech already. They were toying with bringing in Dickie Attenborough to cry for them.

So the Marauders stayed, except for the two whose jobs demanded they be elsewhere. Except for Giles Sparrow who was taken in a large police van with high slit windows to Winchester, to await what the Americans call due process and we call the full majesty of the law. The paparazzi were there, running alongside the van, pointing their cameras pointlessly in the slits, popping away for no purpose.

The wind was getting up, blowing stinging sand through the whipping lines as Peter Maxwell went back there. The starry lights on the Shingle twinkled and blinked as he tethered White Surrey to a guy rope and pinged off his cycle clips – nothing sleek and Lycra for Peter Maxwell.

'Mr Maxwell,' Bob Pickering was sitting beside his storm lantern, patiently rolling his own. 'Any news of the boy?'

'He's in Winchester gaol by now,' Maxwell eased himself down on Pickering's proffered bed.

'We've had Mr Plod around again. Cuppa tea?'

'I wouldn't say no, Bob, thanks. Who was it?'

'Inspector somebody – Watface, was it? I can't remember. They shove these bits of plastic under your nose, don't they? He had a girl with him – Carpenter her name was. Now I *do* remember that!' and they both chuckled.

Pickering was clattering about with his primus, rummaging in his baggage for cups. Above the open tent-flap the flag of the Ninth Voltigeurs snapped on its ropes every now and then. The last of the camp's children were being called in by their parents from the caravans across the grass.

'He's one of your lads, isn't he, Mr Maxwell?' Pickering asked.

Maxwell nodded. 'That's why I'm here,' he said. 'Nobody takes one of my boys away and throws away the key. Nobody.'

'But it must have been an accident.' Pickering's mournful face flared briefly in the matchlight.

Maxwell shook his head. 'How do you account for it, then, Bob? You're a re-enactor. Ever heard of a blank firer ripping off half somebody's head?'

Pickering shook out the match as the gas jet roared into blue-flamed life. 'No,' he said. 'No, I haven't. Pity we didn't leave young Giles with the drum,' he mused. 'He couldn't have done much harm with that.'

Maxwell nodded. 'What's happening with the production?' he asked.

'We've been told to stay put,' Pickering told him. 'They're bringing in a new director blokey tomorrow. Are you still on?'

'Not before four o'clock, I'm afraid,' Maxwell said. 'That's when the day job ends.'

Pickering looked out to the sea with the moon shining cold on its silver ridges. 'I hope they hurry up and get this over with,' he muttered. 'The heart's gone out of it now. Talking to the lads, all of them, we feel . . . well, lost in a way. It certainly hasn't worked out like I thought it would.'

'No indeed.' Maxwell stared at the same sea. 'No, you're right there, Bob.'

'Anyway,' Pickering sorted out his re-enactors' tin mugs, the sort they used to serve grog in in the good old days. 'We haven't got much of a choice. Mr Plod told us to stay put until certain inquiries have been completed. The two blokes who've buggered off were only let go after a lot of hassle. And of course, the police . . .'

'Know where they live,' Maxwell chimed in.

'Joseph Stapleton and David Wood,' Maxwell sat back in the large loft of his house at 38, Columbine. He looked up at the stars winking at him through his skylight and he placed the plastic soldier carefully in his saddle for the first time. He looked across at Metternich the cat, curled up on the basket lid in which Maxwell kept his socks and underpants. The black and white bastard was pretending to be asleep, but Maxwell knew better – the twitch of ears and whiskers, the occasional lash of the tail. Either the neutered tom with attitude was dreaming of demolishing a rodent, ripping through bone and sinew or he was perfectly wide awake and listening very carefully to Maxwell all the time.

'Stapleton and Wood. Wood and Stapleton,' Maxwell was musing, rocking back in his modelling chair and tilting the army forage cap he always wore when modelling forward over his eyes, 'Those were the two who left the Marauders, Count. Now, the question arises, is that coincidence? Or does one of them know something the rest of us don't? I remember Stapleton. Bit of a surly bastard, between you and me, Count.'

Maxwell lifted the white plastic rider on his white plastic charger. 'Who is this one, Count, I hear you ask. This is – or will be when I've painted him – Lieutenant Henry Fitzhardinge Berkeley Maxse – no relation. He had the misfortune to be Lord Cardigan's ADC – that's aide-de-camp to you, Count, a sort of military arse-licker. He'd dobbed about a bit had old Maxse: Grenadier Guards, Thirteenth Lights, Twenty-First Foot. He took up his position to Cardigan's left rear, in front of the Seventeenth. In the Charge he was wounded in the foot. Went on to become Governor of Newfoundland.'

And he crossed the room to place the 54-millimetre figure a little behind the Brigadier from Hell, sitting patiently on the plastic charger, Ronald, ready for the plastic Captain Nolan to deliver the fatal order from Lord Raglan – 'Lord Raglan wishes the Cavalry to advance' . . . For more years than he cared to remember, Peter Maxwell had been making his diorama of the Light Brigade, all 678 of them mounted and waiting for the charge into that terrible cul-de-sac of fire. He wondered if he'd finish it before the Great Modeller in the Sky told him to put away his glue and his brushes for the last time and call it a day.

Maxwell caught his reflection in the angled skylight and looked out to the black headland where he knew the Shingle lay and the dunes and the blood-red beach where Miles Needham had died.

'The police know where they live,' Maxwell reminded Metternich, 'Wood and Stapleton. I think I'll have a little wordette with Jacquie.'

Metternich suddenly raised his head. Maxwell caught the move. 'Well, who asked you?' he growled.

'What a gift!' Maxwell beamed, having opened the A-level

Physics paper. Hardly a single word of it made any sense to him, but he knew the value of psychology. You could feel the tangible relief as the fourteen Physicists in the Hall in front of him relaxed and hearts descended again from mouths.

'Right, Ms Greenhow is here to hold your hands,' he smiled at his colleague of the frizzy hair – 'and that was *hands* by the way, Harrap' – a ripple of guffaws spread through the examinees as they turned to look at the sex god, Mr Testosterone, who bowed in his chair. That's it, Sally thought, make 'em laugh, Max, you old bastard. What are we going to do if you ever retire?

'It's 9.15 by this clock,' Maxwell announced. 'Three hours of total incomprehension. Off you go and may victory sit on your helms.'

He winked at Sally who sat down in the time-honoured tradition of invigilators and used the Exam-board-given time to do some marking.

They were waiting for him in the grim corridor outside, Hall and Watkiss. In the dim light, they could have passed for undertakers.

'Mr Maxwell,' Hall said, holding up his warrant card.

Maxwell placed an urgent finger on his lips. 'Physics exam,' he mouthed and led the police away. 'My office, I think.'

Hall had been in this office before. Three years ago one of Maxwell's Own had been found dead and for a while the Head of Sixth Form had been in the frame. It seemed to be a habit of Maxwell's, turning up like shit on your shoes, always in the wrong place, always at the wrong time.

'This is DI Watkiss,' Hall introduced him.

Maxwell nodded. 'Gentlemen,' he offered them seats, while he perched on the corner of his desk. This wasn't the Incident Room or Leighford Nick. This was Maxwell's manor. He called the shots. He spoke the body language. He looked down on them both. 'I thought you'd have called for this before now.' He passed the slim file on Giles Sparrow across the desk.

Hall took it, opened it, skimmed it briefly.

'Exactly,' Maxwell said, 'it doesn't say in the Interests section "Killing people with replica guns". Bit odd, that, isn't it?'

'They tell me you're a military historian, Mr Maxwell,' Watkiss was watching his man carefully.

'I have my moments,' the Head of Sixth Form told him.

'I assumed that was why you were working on this film. We've talked to Dr Irving.'

'Have you?' Maxwell took back the returned file, knowing as well as Hall how useless it was in a murder inquiry. It carried Giles Sparrow's NFER score, the GNVQ Modules he'd completed, his allergy to eggs. Beyond that it could have fitted half a million other seventeen-year-olds, almost anywhere in the supposedly civilized world.

'Yes,' Watkiss told him. 'He was very helpful. Said you were very knowledgeable about guns.'

'Tell me,' Hall took over, for the moment playing the nice policeman. 'Did you know Miles Needham before last week?'

'No,' Maxwell shook his head.

'And what opinion did you form of him?'

'I didn't,' Maxwell said. 'I got the impression he wasn't the most popular of men. Seemed to have his arse in his hand most of the time. But I suppose these people are under a lot of pressure.'

'According to our information,' Watkiss said, 'you were standing on the left of the line, next to Giles Sparrow.'

'That's right.'

'Had you handled any of the guns yourself?'

'Not that day,' Maxwell told him. 'Although I had earlier, to instruct the others.'

'And which gun was that?'

Maxwell shrugged. 'As far as I'm concerned, when you've seen one Brown Bess, you've seen them all. Tell me, is there a Mrs Needham?'

Hall and Watkiss exchanged glances. 'Why do you ask?' the DCI wanted to know.

'Standard procedure, isn't it?' Maxwell beamed his gappy smile. 'Isn't that what you blokeys go for? Next of kin become automatic prime suspect? It all seems a bit trite to me, but then, what do I know? I'm not a policeman.'

Henry Hall got up, followed by his Number Two. 'No, Mr Maxwell,' he said, standing opposite his man. Maxwell stood up too so that they were head to head. 'You are not a policeman. I'd like you to remember that.' He strolled to the door, Watkiss trailing in his wake. 'And as for what you know – that's always something of a sixty-four-thousand-dollar question, isn't it? We'll see ourselves out.'

Maxwell paused by the film poster of James Stewart in *Rear Window* and took the man off perfectly. 'Well, Jim, what would you do, huh?' he croaked. 'Huh? Put your binoculars back and say "Murder? What murder? I didn't witness any murder. No siree Bob."' He paused and was himself again, 'Of course you wouldn't. You'd get out there and sort it, wouldn't you? Broken leg or no. There again,' a disquieting thought had struck Maxwell, 'you also, in your day, talked to six-foot invisible rabbits, didn't you?' He became James Stewart again as he reached for the phone. 'Aw shucks, what the Hell?' and he was still being James Stewart when the girl on Leighford's switchboard answered.

'Pennsylvania six five thousand?' he drawled.

'What?' the girl on the switchboard was about sixty years too young to make any sense of that.

'Sorry, Thingee,' Maxwell's own voice bellowed in her headphones. 'Wrong number. Get me the Grand Hotel, will you? I can't find my telephone directory.'

# Chapter Six

The more Peter Maxwell thought about it, the more it annoyed him that the Grand hadn't got its own bike shed. Still, he didn't want to make a fuss today, of all days, so he propped White Surrey against a wall and made for the lounge.

Angela Badham was waiting for him as he'd arranged. She'd aged ten years in the last five days and looked as if she hadn't slept for a month.

'Angela,' Maxwell smiled, 'it's good to see you. You must be all in.'

'Actually,' she climbed off her bar stool, 'I'm glad to have somebody to talk to – somebody outside Eight Counties, I mean. It's all a bit fraught at the moment.'

'Can I get you a drink?'

'Just coffee, please.'

Maxwell waved to the lad behind the bar. Neil Somebody-or-other, did Art A level at Leighford High a few years back. Had a perfectly horrible mother. 'Two coffees, Neil.'

'Coming right up, Mr Maxwell.'

He led her into the cosiest corner, deserted now before the influx of families for tea and they sat down on the mock velvet plush. 'I understand you're about to get a new director.'

'Grant Prothero,' she nodded, reaching into her huge

portmanteau for her umpteenth ciggie that day. 'Do you mind?'

He waved it aside. 'When does shooting restart – oh, sorry, that was a little tactless.'

'What? Oh, sorry.' Mots, however bons, tended to pass Angela Badham by these days. 'Er . . . Saturday, we'd hoped. The trouble is, of course, we're well into the tourist season now and keeping nosy bastards away will be a full-time job. Especially after the police press conference. Every ghoul in the county will be on that beach. My mobile hasn't stopped today.' She slammed it down on the table, fiddling with her lighter, trying to get it to work.

'Nasty things, mobiles.' Maxwell shook his head. 'I'd rather carry round my own telephone box. Angela . . .'

'Two coffees, Mr Maxwell.' The chirpy ex-Art student was at his elbow.

'Thanks, Neil.' And he waited until the boy had gone. 'Angela, you knew Miles Needham. Who'd want him dead?'

Angela snorted smoke. 'Who wouldn't?'

'Ah.'

'Look, Max, I know you feel involved, because of the Sparrow boy,' she leaned slightly towards him, 'but take my advice – keep out of it.'

Maxwell shook his head. 'I can't, Angela,' he told her. 'You see, it was on my command that Miles Needham died. It may have been Giles Sparrow's finger on the trigger, but I told him to fire.'

'Oh, that's silly,' she sucked desperately at the cigarette. 'You weren't to know . . .'

'. . . That somebody switched guns? No, neither did Giles Sparrow.'

'But the police . . .'

'Have done the logical, obvious thing,' he finished the sentence for her, leaning back, languidly stirring his coffee,

'They've followed forensics, swallowed science. Very narrow road, science,' he was talking to himself, really. 'That's why I never took it up. Too claustrophobic, myopic, whatever metaphor you want to use. I prefer a road with turnings, options, partings of the way. The only problem with that is, which one to choose.'

'Max, I can't help you.'

'Oh, yes you can, Angela.' The gravel in his voice caught her off guard and she found herself staring into the darkness of his eyes. 'I'd go further and say you must. You're the signpost, my dear; whether you know it or not. Now,' he reached out and patted her hand, 'tell me all you know about Miles Needham.'

All that Angela Badham knew about Miles Needham could have filled the twenty-six unindexed volumes of the Warren Commission. As far as Angela was concerned, he'd put the 'ph' into 'philanderer'. It was nothing as naïve as the casting couch, but a whole succession of young, nubile wannabees had duly displayed their bedroom skills along with their screen tests. Angela hadn't wanted to get too particular in terms of detail, but she understood that oral sex was very much the dead man's penchant and she said it with all the distaste of a Victorian school ma'am; so much so that Maxwell was expecting Angela to be talking about sheep sooner or later. Needham had been married three times and the odd thing was the total silence so far, of Barbara, his current wife. Angela assumed the police had spoken to her, but that was conjecture. The current Mrs Needham never came on set with her husband. They had a large house in Berkshire and Barbara Needham seemed to have a private life all her own. No one at Eight Counties knew much about her, but it was widely believed that she knew Miles played, as well as worked, away from home. As far as Angela knew, Barbara had not been in touch.

Enemies? Well, yes, there was a list longer than Schindler's. There were the actresses to whom he'd promised screen immortality as they clamped their lips around his manhood. Given the knives-outness of the film industry today, there were the mothers of all those actresses. There was possibly Barbara Needham herself. It was a rare kind of woman, Angela observed with a certain profundity, who sat meekly by while her lawful husband screwed his way through the female edition of *Footlights*. And then there were the men whom Needham had screwed – in the professional sense, of course – the producers, actors, cameramen, editors. The list of tea boys he'd offended would probably stretch from here to eternity. At least Maxwell could rule them out – they surely would have used poison. But, suggested Angela, if Maxwell was really determined to get his head kicked in, there was no finer place to start than with Marc Lamont.

Marc Lamont didn't want to talk to Peter Maxwell, but Peter Maxwell was 'Mad Max', not merely nor' by nor'west, but any direction you cared to name. And the lights were already dimmed on the last of the evening's diners at the Grand when he tracked him down.

'That seat's taken,' Lamont paused with the coffee cup inches from his mouth.

'Correct,' Maxwell beamed, 'by me. Tell me, Mr Lamont – you don't mind if I call you Mr Lamont, do you? It seems so much more apposite than Marc in the circumstances. And certainly, it's streets ahead of your real name, Fluck – I can see your problem there.'

'Was there a purpose to all this?' Lamont leaned back from the debris of his pears Hélène, 'If you're trying to get me not to sue the arse off you . . .'

'Oh, that,' Maxwell waved it aside, 'that should come home to roost at about the same time your Race Relations Board case hits the headlines for referring to a Cambridge lecturer as a nigger. But both of those will be long after the *Sun*'s headlines, "Fifty-three-year-old bloke, unfit, out of condition, flattens thirtysomething heart-throb Marc Lamont with the gentlest of pushes". Actually,' Maxwell started playing with a napkin, 'some of those words are rather long for the *Sun*, aren't they? And anyway, we've got more important problems.'

'We have?' For the life of him, Lamont didn't know why he just didn't get up and walk away.

'Miles Needham,' Maxwell's eyes had never left his man.

'I've talked to the filth already.' The actor sipped his brandy eloquently enough. 'I don't see why I should talk to you.'

'Humour an old man.' Maxwell winked at him and immediately launched into *Father Ted*'s Mrs Doyle: 'Ah, go on, go on, go on,' he shrilled.

'I think you're a fucking idiot, Maxwell,' Lamont murmured.

Maxwell leaned towards him and murmured in the same tone, 'And I think you're a fucking murderer.'

'Prove it!'

'Oh, now.' Maxwell lolled back in his chair, chuckling. 'You'll be calling me a lump of poo next. Let's both *try* to be grown up, shall we? You give me a challenge like that, Mr Lamont, and I may have to take you up on it.'

'Well, I'm pissing myself,' Lamont hissed.

'Oh,' Maxwell raised an eyebrow, 'now that's something I *hadn't* heard about you. Which of the many things I have was Needham holding over you?'

For a moment, Lamont looked about to turn and run; or burst into tears or all three. In the event he just sat there.

'Look,' Maxwell sighed, 'it's no secret that Miles Needham was the director from Hell . . .'

'You don't know the half of it,' Lamont growled, finishing his brandy. 'Vicious was his middle name. I've lost count of the people – good people, talented, hardworking – whose careers that bastard has ruined. But you were there, Maxwell. If I remember rightly, you'd just assaulted me and I tripped and fell . . .'

'Oh, yes,' Maxwell nodded. 'It's all coming back to me now.'

'I had my back to Needham. Inches to the right or left and it might have been *my* head all over the sand.'

'Oh, no,' Maxwell smiled. 'If somebody had wanted you dead, Mr Lamont, you'd be in a refrigerator now with a suitcase label around your big toe.'

'So you admit that little shit intended to kill Needham, then?'

'Giles Sparrow? Good God, the kid is seventeen. He didn't know the man. What possible motive could he have?'

'The police are holding him, aren't they?' Lamont asked, 'They must know something you don't.'

'Yes,' Maxwell nodded, staring into the flickering flame of the table candle, 'yes, that's the trouble. They probably know a great deal more than I do.'

'Why don't you pester Dan Weston?' the actor suddenly said.

'Weston? Who's he?'

'Props man for Eight Counties. He'd have been in charge of the guns. Haven't you met him?'

'No,' Maxwell shrugged.

There was a commotion behind him. Three Leighford High girls, barely recognizable in make-up and skirts the length of belts, were standing in a corner, giggling with a waiter and trying to writhe past him to get to Marc Lamont, autograph books waving in their scrawny little hands.

'Well, your groupies have arrived.' Maxwell stood up. 'By the way,' he leaned over the blond curls of his man, 'the one on the left has recurring impetigo and see that hot, nubile one, nipples like chapel hat pegs?'

Lamont found himself nodding.

'Bedwetter.' And Mad Max was gone.

In the cut-throat hierarchy that was Eight Counties television, not everyone stayed at the Grand. Needham's entourage and the leads, plus suits without number were there, but the hoi polloi, who pointed cameras and edited film and brewed the tea, they all stayed in assorted guesthouses in the town. And it was Maxwell's bad luck that Dan Weston, the props man, was staying at the Belvedere.

To be fair it didn't look much like the late Duke of Windsor's rather austere Art Deco pad in Berkshire, but then, Mrs Oldcastle, the landlady, looked more like a man than ever Wallis Simpson did.

'Look, if you're a bleeding reporter . . .'

'No, no, dear lady,' Maxwell tipped his hat with an old-world charm they hadn't seen in Brunswick Street since Ivor Novello visited, 'I work with Eight Counties Television. I need to see Dan Weston.'

'Weston?' She was spitting profusely, trying to remove a shred of tobacco from her lower lip. 'Oh, yeah. Miserable sod. Room Four. But,' and an iron bicep lay like a girder across her doorway, 'How do I know you're kosher?'

Maxwell pulled back and adjusted his bow tie. 'Madam, would you have me drop my trousers here, in Brunswick Street?'

'What?' The point was lost on Mrs Oldcastle; as was Mr Oldcastle, who got lost fifteen years ago on his way back from buying two chump chops from the Asda store down the road. To be fair, Mrs Oldcastle hadn't tried very hard to find him. 'Look, do you know what the bleedin' time is?'

'It's half past eleven,' Maxwell leaned out so that the light of the street lamp caught his watch dial, 'And it *is* urgent.'

For a moment, Mrs Oldcastle stood like Horatius defending his bridge, then she relented and proud Tarquin inched past her matronly bosoms (and they *had* to be plural) and knocked on the door of number four.

Dan Weston looked different in dingy lamplight. Maxwell recognized him from the beach at Willow Bay, but in the sunshine, the man habitually wore a hat. Now he was bare-headed and the lamplight gleamed on his bald, freckled head.

'It's late,' Maxwell said. 'I'm sorry to come so late.'

Weston was peering over his shoulder at the redoubtable Mrs O. who hovered there like something unpleasant out of *The Dark Crystal.* 'You'd better come in,' he said, and closed the door purposefully on the stereotype in the back passage. 'Bitch,' he hissed.

Maxwell had been in rooms like this before, on education conferences without number where crap was on the agenda and all sorts of hot air were generated by it.

'I'd offer you a choice of seats,' Weston said, 'but it looks like the Lloyd Loom or nothing.' The chair looked more like Lloyd Webber, but Maxwell sat in it anyway.

'It's good of you to see me,' he said.

'You're Maxwell, aren't you?' Weston checked, uncorking a bottle of Scotch deftly, with one hand. 'Snorter?'

Maxwell declined.

'Sort of second unit director?'

Maxwell laughed. 'If that makes me the Yakima Canutt of Leighford, I'm flattered,' he said. 'But no, I was just helping out an old friend.'

'Dr Irving,' Weston nodded. 'Nice bloke. Not as stuck up as you'd imagine. No chip, what with being black and all.'

'No chip,' Maxwell agreed.

'You've come about the musket,' Weston said and took a huge gulp from the bottle. For a moment, his vision swam and the Scotch stung a tongue already raw from days of drinking – how many, he couldn't remember. Maxwell sensed it too, the man's despair. But Dan Weston was rock steady on his feet. Only his head shook a little. Only his eyes gave away the disintegration of his soul.

'Mr Maxwell,' the props man looked steadily at the teacher, 'I don't know you. You don't know me. You've never been in my situation, so you can't know. It's like . . . Well, I can't describe it.'

'Let me help you,' Maxwell reached across and gently took the bottle. Keeping his eyes firmly on Weston's, he swigged heartily and swallowed deep. Then he put the bottle down, 'Twenty-two years ago . . . and four months and a little less than a week, I wanted to watch a rugger match on the tele. It was the Five Nations. The Welsh were all the rage then – John Bevan, Barry John, names of gold. We English had our hands full. And I wanted to watch that match. Cardiff Arms Park. I can hear the roars to this day – "Cwm Rhondda" belted out of twenty thousand throats . . .'

'I don't see . . .' Weston had lost the thread.

'Please, let me finish. My little girl, Jenny, was two and a half. She had a party to go to. Her mother put her into her best frock, tied her bow and brushed her hair. It was my turn to do the party run. I hated it. Standing there like a lemon making small talk while twenty screaming little maniacs ran around.' He smiled. 'The kids were just as bad. I didn't want to go. I wanted to watch that match, that bloody, pathetic match. So Paula took her instead. She didn't mind, she said. She'd be back later.' Peter Maxwell's face darkened in Weston's nasty little guest room. 'But she wasn't back later. A police car, of all things, ploughed into Paula's car on a wet road. They were chasing tearaways, she was going to a party. I was crashed out on the settee as Barry John did it to us all over again. Aptly enough, they were playing injury time when the doorbell rang. A pasty-faced copper, not much older than some of the kids I teach. There'd been an accident. Would I come to the hospital?'

His voice trailed away, then he passed the bottle firmly

to Weston, and cleared his throat. 'I've never driven a car since,' he said, holding his head high, 'or watched a game of rugger. And if ever, just once, somebody asked me to take their little girl to a party . . .' He forced down the iron lump that lay like dead memories in his throat, his heart, his soul. 'So, you see, Mr Weston, I know how you feel. Nobody's blaming you. Nobody except the worst critic you've got – yourself.'

Weston nodded, taking the bottle from him slowly. Maxwell held on to it, gripping it in the electric air between them. 'And that,' Maxwell told him, 'is not the answer. Believe me.'

Weston nodded again, putting the thing down on the table alongside the script of *The Captain's Fancy*, 'I checked the guns every day,' he said, trying to clear his head, sort his life, 'and the bayonets and the swords. Each musket was a blank-firer. It's not possible that one of them could have been used to kill anybody.'

'Who else had access to them?' Maxwell asked.

'The police asked me that,' Weston remembered. 'Over and over again.' He rested his gleaming head in his hands and leaned back quickly in the chair, trying to keep Maxwell steady in his vision. 'I don't know. Anybody, I suppose.'

'Anybody?' Maxwell hoped the net wouldn't be that wide.

'My Number Two, Mario, was off sick that day. I was on my own. I was getting the sabres ready for the Yeomanry shoot. I had my hands full.'

'And the muskets were kept where, exactly?'

'In the props caravan. Up on the level near the road.'

'Jesus!' Maxwell muttered.

'Exactly,' Weston nodded. 'You see what I mean about anybody?'

'You didn't keep the caravan locked?'

'Remember the party, Mr Maxwell?' the props man said solemnly. 'The one your little kiddie was going to? And the rugger match. How often in the last twenty-two years have you said "If only"? I think they call it being wise after the event, don't they?'

'I think they do,' Maxwell nodded.

'The only thing,' Weston took up the bottle again, then he put it down and rammed the cork back into its mouth, 'is that with Miles Needham, it couldn't have happened to a more deserving bastard.'

'Anyone, Count.' Maxwell lay in the Badedas suds, his hands clasped across his chest like some medieval knight. The only thing wrong with the image was that he was stark naked with a glass of Southern Comfort between his fingers. He was staring up at the steam that swirled above his head. 'Anyone. Can you Adam and Eve it?'

Clearly, the cat could. He thrust out an elegant leg, offside rear and licked what on Peter Maxwell would have been his popliteal fossa.

'Dan Weston was hectically busy. His number two wasn't there. He hadn't locked the props caravan. He estimated there could have been anything up to an hour that it was totally unattended. And by the time you add up all the extras and technicians and Joes Public in the area, well, Dan Weston's right . . . anyone.'

He closed his eyes. It was well past two and he had a full teaching day tomorrow, but he couldn't sleep. He sipped the amber drink, felt it warm his cockles. 'No, you see, that doesn't help, Count.' The cat looked at him in mid-lick. He hadn't said a word. 'I know not everyone had a grudge against Miles Needham, but I've found precious few who haven't. Whaddya think?' He turned to the abluting animal, raising one tired eyelid, 'Get on with Lieutenant Henry Fitzhardinge Berkeley Maxse and get out to Glove Farm before breakfast? Yes. You're absolutely right. My thoughts exactly.'

Glove Farm lay on the downs high over the sea where the gulls and rooks fought each other in the clear air and dawn was still aurora on their wings. The trees slanted up from the sea where the winds of eternity had battered them to their bidding. It was strangely silent at this altitude, the hiss of White Surrey's tyres invading the privacy of the morning. Maxwell pedalled past the silver silos standing sentinel in their mist shrouds. There were still cobwebs dancing gossamer in the stunted hedgerows as he swung out of the saddle and leaned the bike against the rough bark of the cedar.

The farmhouse was Georgian, he guessed, with a lot of Victorian afterthoughts, B&Q make-do and EU money. The fields were laden with the greasy smell of rape and linseed. The yeomen farmers who had withstood the blast of the ages had sold out to Brussels, bowed to Maastricht. Once they fired arrows at the Belgian buggers; now they just took their money. He didn't have to hit the dulled brass knocker before the dogs told the house there was a stranger in the yard. He saw the nets shiver to one side and a ghost of a face peered out.

'Mrs Sparrow?' he tipped his hat.

'Yes?'

'Peter Maxwell, from Leighford High.'

The woman was tight-lipped and her eyes red-rimmed. She looked a stranger to food and sleep. 'Oh, yes, Giles has talked about you. What do you want?'

'I'd like to see him,' Maxwell said. 'But the police have told me that's impossible. So I've come to see you instead.'

She shook her head. 'Won't do no good,' she said, the door only half ajar. 'He's confessed.'

'What?' Maxwell stood rooted to the spot.

'Well, no, not exactly,' Susan Sparrow corrected herself. 'But he's told the police he aimed deliberately at that Needham bloke. And my Giles don't miss. Not ever.'

'He doesn't?' Maxwell blinked.

'His dad taught him. Ever since my Giles was little. Shooting's been second nature to him. Twelve bore, .303, you name it, Giles's shot it.'

'But he didn't know it was a real gun, Mrs Sparrow,' Maxwell persisted. 'Did he?'

Peter Maxwell had never seen a look so strange cross anyone's face before. 'I hope not, Mr Maxwell,' she said. 'As God is my judge, I hope not.' And she closed the door quietly in his face.

On his way back, down the long drive that led to Glove Farm, he passed the first of the day's paparazzi arriving by the car load. They watched him carefully and one of them took a photo of him, just in case.

'Who killed Diana?' he shouted at them. It wasn't a question worthy of Peter Maxwell, but the chill reaction of the farmer's wife had unnerved him. Who'd have thought that the harmless kid in the frame was Davy Crockett, Annie Oakley and Sergeant Yorke all rolled into one?

'Still at life's door then, John?'

Irving lowered his paper. 'Max, Bwana,' he almost smiled. 'Joining me for breakfast again?'

'Just coffee,' Max said to the Grand's waiter, astonishingly, one he didn't know. 'A little darker than this gentleman here.'

The waiter's eyes widened. He was under twenty-five. He couldn't remember a time before the Flood, when political incorrectness ruled OK and Posh Spice was an expensive brand of aftershave. He got away before the fists and lawsuits flew.

'What news, oh eminence noir?' Maxwell asked.

'Max, you look like shit.' Irving folded his paper and flung it aside. 'You're not working today, are you?'

'No, just teaching,' Maxwell told him. 'What's the scuttlebut on Miles Needham?'

'I thought you'd dug up all the dirt there was.'

Maxwell shook his head. 'I've got a feeling I've only scratched the surface,' he said.

'What about your friend in the police?'

'Ah,' Maxwell patted the side of his nose. 'My copper's nark. Well, her hands are tied . . .'

'*Her?* You dark horse, Bwana!' and Irving downed the last of his scrambled eggs.

'Giles Sparrow, it turns out, was a crack shot.'

'Never!' Irving swallowed his coffee quickly. 'Doesn't that make life a little difficult for the boy?'

'It does,' Maxwell nodded, mechanically taking the coffee pot from the waiter. 'I've got to talk to that solicitor bloke again. I got nowhere with the parents.'

'They're not likely to be very forthcoming,' Irving commented. It was no more than the truth. 'Listen, Bwana. Something's come up. I've got to get back to Cambridge. You don't really need me any more, do you? I mean, this new director is as much of an unknown quantity to me as he is to you.'

'Yes, of course,' Maxwell risked his upper lip in the hot, brown cup. 'No probs as I believe the Young People say. Will you be back?'

'What?' Irving seemed preoccupied, elsewhere. 'Oh, yes, yes, probably. I've got your number. Must dash.'

Maxwell was in the middle of a sentence when his old oppo from the Granta days was gone. He'd left his newspaper, his glasses case and an awful lot of crumbs. Maxwell grabbed the case and made for the foyer, but John Irving had merely hovered for a moment in front of the revolving doors and had dashed through them, nearly knocking over a woman in his haste.

Maxwell steadied her as she tumbled into the foyer. 'Oops,' he said. 'Are you all right?'

'Oh, yes,' she said, regaining her dignity and her composure with a speed that astonished. 'Thank you, I am,' and she swept away from him to the counter.

'May I help you, Madam?' the receptionist asked with a sienna voice.

'I hope so,' she said. 'My name is Barbara Needham. You have a room for me.'

# Chapter Seven

Grant Prothero had pulled his team together as best he could. June's long-lighted days gave him time to drill his men, practise his shots. The Fencibles and the Castlemartin Yeomanry were down by three men, the two who had homes to go to and the third who was in custody, charged with murder. Even so, Maxwell would have been proud of them and Bob Pickering had them fine-tuned by evening, film in the can, mini-series in the bag. There were just three more days to go, Prothero estimated and then *The Captain's Fancy* could have its soundtrack dubbed in and all the hype could start. The credits team was already working on the stark 'For Miles Needham', plain white on a black drop. But publicity like that could go either way; and whichever way it went, the paparazzi were there that Thursday evening under the purple-orange of the sunset as they took down the arc lights. A veritable army of Eight Counties men with shoulders like wardrobes kept them back, away from the action.

He saw her sitting on an upturned keg, staring at the ocean. She was Hannah Morpeth, the darling of the '90s, with a string of lovers and public spectacles in London's and New York's hottest hotspots behind her. But that evening, sitting there with the gentle rush of the sea, she looked lost, a little girl again, her sandcastle overturned and no one to play with.

'You know,' Maxwell approached from the Shingle, padding softly through the sand, 'Jemima Nicholas was rather a mannish lass.'

'Who?' Hannah Morpeth was far, far away.

'Your character,' Maxwell sat on the sand and crossed his legs at the ankles. 'Jemima Nicholas. The Welsh called her Jemima Vawr – Big Jemima. She was a cobbler, biceps like Sly Stallone's. I don't see you fitting that pattern.'

'Who are you?' Hannah Morpeth had a way of looking at men that sent shivers across the darkness of their souls. Her long pale auburn hair blew across her face and just for a moment, even Mad Max was caught in the magic of it.

'Oh, I'm sorry,' he said, reaching out a hand, 'I'm Peter Maxwell. I'm working with John Irving on the historical accuracy bit.'

'Oh, right. Look, do you have a cigarette?'

'No, I'm afraid I don't. How's it going? I mean . . . You were there when Miles Needham died.'

'Yes,' she said, suddenly looking out to sea where the glow of the sun was spreading over the watery ridges like molten gold. Then she turned back, 'So were you, weren't you?'

Maxwell nodded. 'How well did you know him?' he asked.

'I'd never worked with him before,' she said, her jaw firm, her eyes clear. 'I think as directors go, he had huge talent.'

'Nothing more?'

'What do you mean?'

Maxwell sat upright, clasping his hands, choosing his words. 'Hannah,' he said. 'You don't mind if I call you that?'

'I'd prefer it to Jemima Vawr,' she almost smiled.

He did too, 'Hannah. The boy in custody, Giles Sparrow, he's one of my students at Leighford High.'

'Really? I see.'

'No,' Maxwell said. 'I'm not sure you do. You see, Giles didn't do it.'

'But the police . . .' she frowned.

'. . . Are taking it all too literally,' he interrupted her. 'It's too obvious. Too pat. No one was more surprised than Giles when Miles Needham went down, believe me.'

'How do you know?'

'I've spoken to his solicitor, his mother,' Maxwell sighed and rested his elbows back on the sand again. 'I'd talk to his fairy godmother if I thought it would help me make sense of all this.'

'Why?' she asked, genuinely bewildered.

'Why?' Maxwell wasn't just sitting up now, he was standing. 'If you have to ask that, Hannah, then I'm asking the wrong person the wrong questions.'

He didn't know after that what to make of her. Could it be that the Face of the '90s was just that? A pretty bimbo with no heart? Or was there more to her? Something that Maxwell hadn't seen, perhaps would never see?

'Well, it's not your problem, is it?' she asked.

He squatted down beside her again. 'Yes,' he persisted, 'it's everybody's problem.'

She turned away, watching the gulls fighting at the water's edge. 'You didn't know Miles,' she said.

Maxwell sank to the sand again. 'But neither did you,' he said. 'You just told me, you'd never worked with him before.'

The girl looked at him wistfully. 'That's right,' she said, 'I haven't. Look, Mr Maxwell, I don't know what the Sparrow boy's agenda was. Maybe he's a gun freak. You hear about it all the time.'

'But this isn't Hungerford, Hannah,' Maxwell said, 'it isn't even Dunblane. If Giles Sparrow had popped off an M16 in all directions, I might buy it. But a musket? Do you know how long it takes to reload? No, I've got to look elsewhere.'

She smiled across at him, that distant, enigmatic smile, like a living Giaconda. 'Well, Mr Maxwell,' she said, 'it looks as though it is your problem after all.'

* * *

Peter Maxwell hated answerphones. He hated faxes too, but that was because he'd gone through a spate of technophilia early in 1996 when he'd fired off faxes from school in all directions, only to discover they hadn't arrived at their destinations because he'd put the paper in the machine upside down. Some of the younger wags on the staff tried to rechristen him 'Mad Fax' or Mr Faxwell at that point, but they lost their nerve and their careers continued.

'This is Jacquie Carpenter,' he heard the disembodied voice say. 'I can't come to the phone right now. Please leave your number after the long tone.'

It beeped at him viciously. 'Jacquie? Maxwell. You're probably out stepping aerobically or whatever young police things do of an evening. Look, can we talk? I tried to chat to Hannah Morpeth today, but talk about a brick wall . . . I need your input, as I think the jargon ran about 1986. I'll be here – all night unless my luck has changed radically. Bye.'

Her long pale auburn hair lay across her face and her face was on a pillow; and the pillow on a bed; the bed in a hotel bedroom at the Grand. Hannah Morpeth had never been asked to play a corpse before and now she'd be stereotyped; she'd play that part for ever. Her blue silk negligee was thrown open, her lacy bra ripped where something sharp and steel had thudded through it, slicing the pert breast below. In that one sudden thrust, her heart had broken – more than ever it had over the death of Miles Needham. And it would never break again.

The dead girl's photograph flashed up onto the screen. Seconds before, Henry Hall's Incident Room team had seen a very different Hannah, laughing with David Jason on the set of that sit-com; flirting with Sean Connery at the BAFTA awards; sparring with Kate Winslet in a photo opportunity with Leonardo diCaprio. Now her dead eyes stared back at them all, dull, robbed of life. 'Where were you?' she seemed to say, her head tilted to the right in the harsh, unflattering flash of the police photograph. 'Why aren't you bastards ever around when we need you?'

'She had a minder,' DI Dave Watkiss was on his feet, 'Buster Rothwell. Goes wherever she does.'

'Except her hotel room,' a voice called from the smoky, blind-drawn room.

'That's right,' Watkiss nodded. 'He left her at about eleven. Swears she was tucked up by then.'

'In fact, her bed hadn't been slept in,' Hall chimed in from the corner. 'Reg.'

Another slide clicked into focus. The girl lay on her back, with one arm trailing, her right hand nearly on the floor. Her legs were slightly parted and one breast, her left, was naked to the nosiness of the world, the savage, careless intrusion of scenes of crime. 'Notice the bed hasn't been disturbed. Neither had anything else in the room. No lamps overturned, no mats crumpled. Nothing.'

'Whoever killed her knew her.' Watkiss underlined it so that there should be no misunderstanding. 'She trusted him.'

'Him, sir?' it was appropriately Jacquie Carpenter who asked the question.

Hall got to his feet. 'That's what Dr Astley reckons,' he said. 'It would have required quite a bit of force to make that wound. But we're not wearing blinkers here, everybody. A single thrust delivered with both hands by a woman might have the same effect. It depends on the weapon to an extent. Have you got the info there, Dave?'

Watkiss riffled through his notes. 'Astley can't decide on the actual murder weapon yet. Knife certainly and not razor sharp, but the blade was long and straight. The point was used to nick her clothing first – causing the tearing you see there. Then – wham, bam, thank you Ma'am. One single thrust that pierced her left lung and the left ventricle of her heart. Death would have been very quick.'

'The bastard missed her ribs, then?' Somebody was wrestling with the wound dynamics.

'Oh, yes. It was neat. Like a . . . well, almost like a contract hit, in a way.'

There were murmurs around the room; heads nodded together, eyes swivelled, shoulders shrugged. Hall calmed it down.

'Before we rush out in search of the Godfather,' he said with his humourless delivery, 'Let's keep it all in some perspective. This woman knew and worked with Miles Needham.'

'Different M.O.' somebody observed. There were more murmurs.

'Agreed,' Hall nodded in the half light, 'but the same show. Jerry.' A burly sergeant half rose in the corner. 'From tomorrow, you and your people are all over Eight Counties Television. Their budgets, their personnel, their brand of coffee. If somebody in that company breaks wind, I expect to be informed.'

'Right, sir.' Jerry Manton had a reputation as a corporation killer. Something to do with his training as an accountant put the frighteners on an awful lot of suits.

'Paul.' A tall, angular copper with a shaved head nodded. He looked like Alexei Sayle on stilts. 'The Grand. I want plans of that hotel from the time the bloody thing was built.' It was not like Henry Hall to swear, even mildly. His team knew it, sensed the air. Hall had been with the Chief Constable all morning, almost since they'd found her. But Hall didn't need the Chief Constable to spell it out for him. Miles Needham was a celebrity among the cognoscenti, with his own luvvies. But Hannah Morpeth was a star. They'd already had to clear away the cellophaned bouquets from the pavement outside the Grand. She was a second Diana and the nation would cry all over again. 'I want to know every stair, every passageway. No one leaves. This is right from the top. I don't care how many feet you tread on. Reps, conference attenders, families with kids and grannies – nobody goes home. Look at their security system especially. If they've got cameras, I want the film and I want it by morning. Got it?'

'Clear as a bell, guv.' Paul Garrity was a young copper of the old school. He'd watched *Minder* as a kid. Engage him in conversation for long and he'd start talking about getting on the blower, getting the wheels out and watching out for shooters. He'd been a stranger to the Queen's English for years.

'Jacquie,' Hall turned to the girl on his left, 'I want you to get to know Hannah Morpeth like your twin sister. Men, money, career, the lot. I want to know who she played tig with at school and who gave her her first break.'

'Right, sir.'

'Enemies, ladies and gentlemen.' Hall waved to Reg to kill the pictures of the dead. 'That's what we had in the death of Miles Needham. And that's what we've got in the death of Hannah Morpeth.'

'What about the kid?' somebody asked. 'What about Giles Sparrow?'

'What indeed? I did put that question to Chief Inspector Hall,' Malcolm Sailer, the solicitor, was sipping the sherry Peter Maxwell had brought him in the snug of the Head of Sixth Form's local, which he had rechristened the Alcoholics' Arms.

'And?' It was Maxwell's second Southern Comfort of the day. Things were not going well.

'You must realize how the law works, Mr Maxwell,' Malcolm Sailer wasn't so much a legal eagle as a booby. 'There may well be a connection between Hannah Morpeth's death and Miles Needham's, but the fact that young Sparrow couldn't possibly have killed the girl doesn't mean he didn't kill the director either.'

'But, logically . . .'

Sailer's smile stopped him.

'What?' Maxwell asked.

'You're an historian, aren't you, Mr Maxwell?'

'Of sorts,' Maxwell nodded.

'And if I remember my old A-level course to any extent at all, it's all about human nature, isn't it? People don't behave logically. They never have. Murderers don't. And neither, for all they'd disagree, do the police. Anyway, any amount of philosophy about it isn't going to change things. Henry Hall isn't about to let the boy go. He wants more answers first.'

'Yes,' Maxwell swirled the burning liquid around his tonsils, 'so do I.'

Hannah Morpeth's agent was used to giving out publicity information on her. But this was different. The chit of a girl with the warrant card sitting opposite him was asking all the wrong questions. No, Hannah had not been to RADA. She'd been to Rose Bruford. Where was that? Sidcup, when the agent last looked. Men? That wasn't the agent's province. Enemies? Well, naturally, sugar. Every other woman in the industry. Was that any help at all?

Peter Maxwell was marking books and on his fourteenth version of the thoughts of 10B1 as to why people supported the Nazi Party in 1920s Germany when the doorbell rang at 38, Columbine. To be honest, he was grateful. It's a depressing business when it's confirmed over time that a whole generation of kids doesn't know an apostrophe from their elbows and half of them think that the late Führer's name was Hilter.

The mountain, so it seemed, had come to Mohammed. And the mountain, beyond the distorted reed-glass of Maxwell's front door, was DI Dave Watkiss, flashing his warrant card by way of introduction.

'I believe you know DC Carpenter,' he said, jerking his head in the direction of the girl next to him.

'I have had that pleasure,' Maxwell said, trying to read in Jacquie's face how he was supposed to play this one.

'May we come in?' Watkiss asked. His guv'nor had briefed him about Peter Maxwell, new to the manor as Watkiss was. Here was a tricky bastard, liked tilting at other people's windmills; saw himself as the Miss Marple of Leighford High School.

'*Mi casa, su casa,*' Maxwell bowed. 'It's up the stairs. Lounge off. Is this a social call, Jacquie?'

She flashed her clear grey eyes at him. A flash that said, For fuck's sake, shut up, Max. A nod was as good as a wink to Peter Maxwell.

'You left a message on DC Carpenter's answerphone,' Watkiss said. 'What was that all about?' Watkiss had flopped down in Maxwell's chair. The black and white cat, Metternich, couldn't decide whether he should leap onto his lap, claws akimbo or just fart and walk out. For the moment, he'd skulk under the coffee table, with his metronome of a tail, and see how it went.

'So,' Maxwell sat opposite the Inspector on the settee, 'George Orwell was right, then.'

'Heh, heh,' Metternich sniggered. He had no idea what his master had just said, but he knew body language like the back of his paw. Maxwell was preening himself; Watkiss squirming. Mad Max, one; Sussex Police, nil. Still, it was early days.

'Meaning?' Watkiss was a man unafraid to show his ignorance.

'Big Brother,' Maxwell enlightened him. '1984. Of course, George got his dates wrong, but, hey,' and he'd lapsed into his legendary Tony Blair, 'who doesn't? Tell me, Inspector,' he was himself again, 'do you steam open DC Carpenter's mail and check her undies drawer?'

'Now, look . . .' A vein throbbed in DI Watkiss's temple. He almost caught the smirk on Jacquie Carpenter's face, but not quite. Then he relented. Hall had warned him there'd be moments like this. 'Don't rise to it,' the DCI had advised, 'He's clever and he uses words like a sniper uses bullets. Keep your head down. Keep digging. Sooner or later . . . if you're lucky . . .'

'You said on the answerphone,' Watkiss persisted, 'That you'd talked to Hannah Morpeth.'

'I think if you play the tape again,' Maxwell said softly, 'Which is no doubt logged as Exhibit 453B, just in case, that I said "I *tried* to talk to her."'

'Are you denying you talked to her?' Watkiss's head was dangerously above the parapet again.

'No,' Maxwell shrugged, 'just being pedantic, really.'

'So you did talk to her?'

'There were an awful lot of television technicians and paparazzi on the beach who have no doubt already confirmed to you that I did.'

'What time was this?' Watkiss asked. Jacquie Carpenter was making notes.

'Sunset,' Maxwell remembered, 'I don't know. Nine thirty. Nine forty-five?'

'She died three hours later,' Watkiss volunteered. 'You were one of the last people to see her alive.'

'I suppose I was.'

'And you see,' Watkiss was leaning forward, that vein throbbing again, 'I was one of the first people to see her dead.'

Maxwell sat back, shaking his head. 'And that's the bitch of it,' he said, gazing steadily into Watkiss's eyes. 'What we're both looking for is the man who fits both criteria – the one who was the *very* last to see her alive and the very first to see her dead.'

'What we're *both* looking for?' Watkiss didn't like the sound of that.

'You've got one of my lads in choky, Inspector, one of my sixth form. "Trelawney he's in keep and hold, Trelawney he may die, Here's twenty thousand Cornish bold will know the reason why."'

He'd done it again. Watkiss had inched himself above that parapet and his ego lay spattered all over Maxwell's living-room like the head of Miles Needham all over Willow Bay.

'I can't leave it there,' Maxwell said. 'It's not in my nature. Hannah Morpeth was . . . shall we say, unhelpful? She seemed out of it, on something, I think the Young People say. Well, it isn't surprising. God knows what sort of life it must be when you can't scratch your bum without some magazine buying the exclusive rights. And she *was* standing nearer to Miles Needham than I was. My God,' Maxwell was sitting up, staring first at Watkiss, then at Jacquie, 'is that it? Is that why she died? Did she see something on that beach because of where she was standing? You must have talked to her as well. What did she say?'

At a signal from Watkiss, Jacquie Carpenter snapped shut her notebook and the police persons stood up. The interview, Watkiss informed him, was over – for now.

There was suddenly an atrocious, if fleeting, smell. Metternich had made up his mind.

The Grand had more ways in than the Maze prison – and a corresponding number of ways out. Hannah Morpeth's room, still sealed off that Tuesday with SOCO coloured tape, was on the fourth floor. There were two lifts for guests and a third for hotel staff. And at each end of her corridor, a stairway linked to the three floors below and the two above. Almost the entire floor had been booked for a fortnight by Eight Counties Television and everyone had been interviewed at least twice by Henry Hall's band of coppers over the death of Miles Needham. Now they were interviewed again. The same questions, tapes and ticking clocks; all the paraphernalia of an Incident Room mobbed by the morbidly curious hoping to catch sight of the fleetingly famous.

The Eight Counties Newsroom was disappearing up its own arsehole with the hysteria of it all. Death on its own doorstep, murder in the media, killings on the cutting-room floor. It was a three-ring circus – the *Mail* carried four pages on the shy little girl who had been a superstar – hardly any of it sounded familiar to Jacquie Carpenter; the *Express* concentrated on Miles Needham; the *Independent* got an exclusive from Sir David Puttnam, lamenting on the talent lost to the British cinema.

'Anybody, guv?' Paul Garrity was dog-tired, but tried not to let it show in the presence of his DCI. The detective-sergeant hadn't had much sleep in the last twenty-four hours and dawn, twilight and the summer sun had come to have little meaning for him. 'Video cameras only operate on the ground floor. Everything else is a dummy.'

'Pointless!' Hall threw his pencil onto his desk. It didn't clatter, because wherever it had landed, it would have hit paper. He seemed to remember leaving a wife and three kids somewhere. No doubt when something surfaced, he'd remember where. 'Why can't these people spend a bit of money where it matters? More security and a little less wall-to-wall walnut burr wouldn't come amiss. You've seen the tapes?'

'Yes, guv,' Garrity opened a black-bound file. 'We've counted forty-one different people entering or leaving the Grand's front door between the time Hannah Morpeth returned from her day's filming and the time of death. We can account for thirty-eight of them – all hotel staff or guests. Sixteen are Eight Counties people. Here are the stills of the three we can't identify.'

He slid the photographs across the piles of paper. Hall shook his head. Each one had the same camera angle, looking down on the reception desk.

'That's the night porter on duty,' Garrity pointed to the blond blur behind the counter. 'This one here is his assistant. In this first shot, you've got what appears to be a woman entering at . . . what, ten forty-three, according to the timer.'

Hall nodded. 'Tall,' he said. 'Middle-aged. What's she carrying, Paul? An umbrella?'

'Looks like,' Garrity said and caught the look on his boss's face. 'Yeah, I know. It hasn't rained since 1957 and she's carrying an umbrella.'

'I'd give my eye teeth for a look at that umbrella's tip,' Hall was talking to himself.

'The second one is eight minutes later,' Garrity pointed to the next photograph. By this time, the night porter's assistant had gone and his back was turned as a vague figure crossed the corner of the surveillance screen. 'We think it's a man. But that hat . . .'

'Disguises like that went out with Sherlock Holmes,' Hall frowned. 'Damn. We need more frames on this. Any record of these people leaving?'

'None,' Garrity shook his head. 'We've run these tapes so often we're in danger of wearing them out. The third one's the most infuriating of all. Look.'

Hall did. It was eleven twenty-three. 'That's Buster Rothwell, Miss Morpeth's minder, going off duty. He's about to bump – literally – into this bloke.'

Hall tried to make out the anoraked figure sauntering across the foyer. 'Youngish,' was as far as he could get.

'That's what Rothwell reckoned,' Garrity confirmed. 'He doesn't remember too clearly. It was a fleeting moment. But he thought curly hair under a hat and he didn't know him.'

'That anorak? Looks pale.'

'Yellow. Traffic wardens, council workers. Yachties. They're as common as buggery. No mileage there, I'm afraid.'

Hall screwed up his face, thinking, analysing, trying to dredge from somewhere some sort of organization out of the chaos of his case. 'And none of these were seen coming out?'

Garrity shook his head. 'Not so far. We've run the tapes up to lunchtime the following day. No one resembling any of these appears again.'

'What about the porter? What does he remember?'

'Woman A,' Garrity pointed to Umbrella Woman, 'Wanted to see a Miss Kenrick.'

'Guest?'

'Yes. Room 86. Third floor.'

'And?'

'The night porter rang through. Miss Kenrick wasn't answering. Woman A disappeared.'

'Disappeared, Paul?'

'I know, guv,' Garrity had voiced all the uncertainties to himself long before he'd gone in to the guv'nor. 'The night porter remembers she stayed in the lobby for a bit, thumbing through the "Places to Visit" stuff. When he looked next, she'd gone.'

'But not out of the front door?' Hall checked.

'No. But that's the bugger of it, guv. There's no working camera on the back or side entrances, nor the kitchen access. She could have slipped out of any of those. And more's to the point, anyone could have slipped in.'

'Figure B?' Hall took his man further on.

'Night porter didn't see him.' Garrity shook his head. 'He was doing his returns.'

'Yes,' Hall knew the feeling, 'it's all about paperwork in the end, isn't it?'

'He seems to be heading for the lifts,' Garrity went on. 'But that way, he could have veered into the Huntsman's Bar, the Kiddies Room or the West stairs.'

'And assuming no one saw him combing Barbie's hair in the Wendy House, we're none the wiser?'

'No, guv.' It was a lame response from Paul Garrity, but

then, he'd just witnessed a moment unique in his dealings with Henry Hall. His DCI had just cracked a joke. It was precisely because of responses like this that Henry Hall didn't crack them very often.

'The anorak in Frame C. Would Rothwell know this man again?'

'Well, he says there was something familiar about him, but he couldn't say what. Not on the company's roll, he's sure of that.'

Hall sighed. 'All right, Paul. You've done well. We'll just have to hope that SOCO come up with something from the murder room. Keep on to these three. They may be complete red herrings, but I don't like loose ends.' He metaphorically kicked himself, thinking how Peter Maxwell would have grimaced at the mixed metaphors there. Now why, Henry Hall wondered, as Paul Garrity saw himself out, should he be thinking of Peter Maxwell?

'Well, I can't understand it, Max.' Becky Evans was in full flight in the Great Man's office, the girl from the valleys with a voice like a circular saw. 'She was such a little mouse. What the Hell is the matter with her?'

'Love, Rebecca,' Maxwell said.

'What?'

'All right, then,' the Head of Sixth Form conceded, 'You're under forty – lerv. Better?'

Becky Evans was the Head of Art at Leighford High. Maxwell reminded her on every conceivable occasion that there weren't any great female artists. But as he was a public schoolboy himself, he said it *so* politely. A few years back, he'd said the same thing to the Head of Domestic Science, that there weren't any great female chefs either. He couldn't say it any more because the old battleaxe had retired and anyway, so had Domestic Science. It was called Food Technology now, whatever that meant. Maxwell was waiting for the day when they introduced History Technology into schools. That day he would quietly take a rope from the gym and hang himself from the Leighford High flagpole, the one where the Head hoped the Investors in People flag would fly one day soon.

Becky Evans was indeed under forty, but not by that much. And she stood in Maxwell's office that morning wearing her pastoral hat as Helen McGregor's Form Tutor.

'I haven't seen her for days. I followed the oracle, sent out the three-day absence letter, heard nothing. Then I rang. No reply.'

'Mum works,' Maxwell nodded. 'Dad was some surfer back in the summer of '79 – they took the Year of the Child very literally. Helen and Mum live with Gran, I think.'

'Well, it's obviously a man she needs,' Becky Evans wasn't one to stand on female chauvinist ceremony.

'Yes,' Maxwell agreed. 'Marc Lamont.'

'What, the actor?'

'Helen is seriously smitten, Rebecca,' the oracle explained.

'Well, I'd heard she was working with the television people, but I didn't believe it. Such a mouse. No acting ability at all, has she?'

'Not that I know,' Maxwell shrugged. 'Mind you, she looks the part of a homicidal Welsh fishwife running screaming along Willow Bay – oh, begging your pardon, of course.'

'That's not the point.' Becky Evans was used to slurs against the Welsh – they usually involved sheep. 'She ought to have been here.'

'But I'm sure I saw her in the corridor this morning.'

'Oh, you did,' Becky was striding across his County Hall carpet, waving her register to stave off the hot flush she felt creeping insidiously up from both breasts, 'That would have been just before she called me a fat slag and told me to fuck off – I'm toning it down, of course, Max, to save your blushes. I'd only asked her where she'd been.'

'Where is she now?'

'God knows. Flounced out of the Art Room like she was bloody Greta Garbo.'

'Well, that's perfectly understandable, Rebecca,' Maxwell said softly. 'She wants to be alone.'

Helen McGregor was still alone when Maxwell found her. The girl was sitting with her back to one of the old oaks that ringed Leighford's playing fields, like a child in a Maxfield Parrish poster. It was the end of another glorious day and children called to each other and laughed as they scattered and wandered home over the golden grass. Maxwell checked his watch as the roar of a TR7 made him turn. Four o three. Right on time, the Head of Media Studies was out of there, with the bats from Hell flapping in the debris of his exhaust. Maxwell had seen Helen from the window of the Science lab where he'd been covering for that silent non-event who taught Physics.

'Doddle,' he snarled at the hapless Year 12 students who fell to his charge, 'A-level Physics. Doddle. Latent heat of fusion of ice; coefficient of linear expansion – what could be simpler? *And* you can take all kinds of aides-mémoire into the exams with you. A-level Physics? Don't make me laugh.'

She didn't run when she saw him; didn't move at all. Only her face darkened. Only her knuckles whitened.

'Hello, Helen,' the Head of Sixth Form sat down beside her and plucked a shoot of wild barley from the grass by the hedge. He champed on one end of it and lay back, gazing up at the high mares' tails through the spreading branches of the oak. 'Filming over?'

She nodded.

'How do you feel?'

'What do you mean?'

'Now that it's all over.' He rested on one arm beside her, 'It's been a very long time since I trod the boards, but I still remember the feeling when the curtain came down at the end of a run. Empty. Desolate, sometimes. There's a hole in your life.'

'You pushed him,' she said suddenly.

'What?'

She turned to face the man for the first time. He was vulnerable, lying alongside her like an old friend – or a lover. Maxwell knew that. He and Count Metternich had invented body language. He could have done this in his office, he behind his desk, she on the carpet. But that wasn't his way. At least, not today it wasn't.

'Marc,' her face was like thunder. 'You went for him. And pushed him over.'

'Helen . . .' Maxwell was searching for the right words.

'Why?' she snapped. 'Why did you do that?'

'He wasn't very nice to a friend of mine.' Maxwell put it in terms the girl could understand. It was the language of the playground and some people never left it behind.

'So?'

'The friend was too nice to say anything. I decided I should.'

'You didn't have to push him, did you?' The tears were very near.

'No.' Maxwell was sitting up, both hands in the air, seeking for a reconciliation that would get this girl back on the straight, the narrow. 'No, that was wrong.'

'But what I don't understand,' she was on her feet now, her lips quivering, her shoulders tensed, 'is why you had to kill that Miles Needham too.'

Then she ran. And he was too old, or too tired, or too world-weary to give chase. He watched her until she'd run beyond the hedge that led to the road. He'd catch up with her tomorrow, ask her what she was talking about, sort it all out. Then he turned in the afternoon sun back to the gilded grot that was Leighford High, that place of tomorrows.

# Chapter Eight

Martin Bairstow sat shivering on the edge of the dunes, his anorak hood pulled up, his teeth chattering. Where had this bloody weather come from suddenly?

'Time to pull up stumps then, Bob?' he called to the man along the lines from him.

Bob Pickering straightened by his tent flap and sniffed the wind. He'd got a little workshop back home. Work piled up to buggery, he shouldn't wonder. The unplanned extra days may have taken their toll already.

'Reckon you're right, Martin,' he nodded and was just about to start hauling his Voltigeur gear with its burnished buttons and buckles when a police car snarled to a halt on the road above him.

'Oh, fuckin' 'ell,' Bairstow grumbled every bit as realistically as one of the Emperor's *grognards*, famous for grumbling all the way to the Neva and back again, ''Ere we go again.'

The raindrops started as the slim figure of Jacquie Carpenter dropped below the headland. They were large and almost hurt after the long, dry days.

'Gentlemen,' she flashed her warrant card, 'can I have a word?'

'In here,' Pickering said as the wind drove in from the sea in one of those freak storms which make the great British summer what it is, 'more room in here.' He made some space on the camp bed and stashed his gear on the waterproof floor. 'Cup of tea?' he asked the girl.

'No thanks,' she smiled. 'You'll be thinking of pulling out, then?'

'Bloody right.' Bairstow wrestled with the flap as the rain bounced on the sheltering canvas. It wasn't six in the evening yet, but the black clouds that rolled out to sea had brought the night with them.

'I can't force you to stay,' she said, 'but if you can, it would help. Mr Hall's inquiries haven't finished yet.'

Bairstow looked at Pickering. 'Look, luv,' he said, sliding back the yellow hood for the first time, 'You must be even more aware of this than we are, but two people have been killed in the last week. Shot, stabbed. Fuckin' hell! It's like Friday the bloody Thirteenth out 'ere. And we're cut off out 'ere, you know. Weird bloody place, Bob, ain't it, at night? Out 'ere. Now, I'm not normally funny about places, and that. But I don't like this bit o' beach. I sensed it when I come 'ere, didn't I, Bob? I told you, didn't I? Sort of . . . I don't know, sounds and that.' He looked at their faces in the dim light of the tent. 'Well, I dunno,' he rubbed his chin, screwed up his face, 'Nah. I gave that detective blokey my address. You know where I live,' and he laughed, nudging Jacquie in the ribs. 'Nah, I'm outa it. See you, then. I've got a scooter to load up.'

And, like Captain Oates, the intrepid Sergeant Bairstow vanished into the weather.

'What about you, Mr Pickering?' Jacquie asked. 'Will you stay?'

'Filming's over,' the ex-Maréchal de Logis said. 'Nothing to stay for now, is there?'

'Except a little thing called murder.'

He looked into her grey, bright eyes. Quite a little cracker, this policewoman. Streets ahead of that DI Watkiss who had interviewed him earlier. 'Are you getting anywhere with that?' he asked.

She shrugged. 'We're doing what we can,' she said. 'It'll be quicker if everybody co-operates.'

He smiled. 'I've got a business,' he said. 'It's not much, but it's bread and butter. You know, gotta keep the old wolf from the door.'

'How well do you know Martin?' she asked, peering out of the tent flap where she saw him wrestling with his ropes.

'I don't,' Pickering told her. 'Are you sure about that tea?'

'No, really,' she smiled.

'No, I only met him when we both arrived. He's a re-enactor too, like me, only between us his heart's not in it. You've got to love it. The sound of it all. The bugles, the thud of the drum, the rattle of the muskets.' He caught the look on the girl's face. 'All right,' he chuckled, 'I suppose I come across as a bit of a weirdo to you, right?'

'Not at all,' she smiled. 'It takes all sorts. I know a man whose loft is full of little plastic soldiers. He's spent a quarter of his life making and painting them. And he's one of the finest, most fascinating men I know.'

'Mr Maxwell,' Pickering nodded.

'You know about his collection?'

'He used to teach me – oh, longer ago than I care to remember now, to be honest. I expect he's forgotten all about it, but I haven't. Do you know, I was there when he bought his first one.'

'Really?'

'Yeah.' Pickering sniggered at the memory of it. 'He took us on a jolly to Brighton. Showed us all the historical sights. And there used to be this model soldier shop and he bought this kit. That was Captain Nolan, who, Mr Maxwell told us, carried the fatal order that led to the Light Brigade's rather nasty end. Fancy that. Do you know, I'd forgotten all about that until just now. Isn't it funny what memory'll do?'

There was a silence.

'Can I ask you a question?' he said.

'Of course,' she told him.

'Do you think that kid killed Needham?'

'Mr Hall . . .'

'No, no.' He waved a finger to stop her. 'Never mind him. Do *you* think Giles Sparrow did it?'

Jacquie Carpenter was used to being put on the spot. Usually by Peter Maxwell. This was a little different. There was something safe about Bob Pickering, something sure. His large, strong hands, his steady grey eyes, she felt somehow at home. Even in that freezing, wind-whipped tent. 'No,' she said, gazing into his open face, 'no, I don't. But I need all the help in the world to prove it.'

There was a cough and a rattle as Bairstow's Lambretta struggled for life and he purred away, across the soaking grass and past Jacquie's car.

Well,' she said, the noise having shattered the moment, 'I'd better be going. We've got your address.'

'Yeah.' He saw her out. The rain drove steadily from the west now, stinging the sand and Jacquie's face alike. For a moment, she looked at him, then turned to go. She'd nearly reached the car when she felt his hand on her shoulder. She started with the suddenness of it and the cold.

'Have you got Martin's address?' he shouted above the wind.

'Yes, of course. Why?'

'He left this behind,' Pickering was holding a canvas bag in his hand. 'Can you send it to him? He'll need that for his next re-enactment.'

'What is it?' she shouted back, trying vainly to keep her hair in place.

'Dunno,' he yelled. 'It looks like an old-fashioned surgeon's kit.'

'Clean as a fucking whistle.' Jerry Manton plonked the coffee in its plastic cup by Paul Garrity's elbow.

'What is?' Garrity's eyes were glued to the flickering screen in front of him.

'Eight Counties. I can't find a decimal point in the wrong place.'

'You can't have looked then.' Garrity broke off from his vigil to scald his tongue on the cup's contents.

'Yeah, I know,' Manton lolled back in the chair, tired, cold. Incident Rooms when the team had gone home were desolate, loveless places. Only Manton and Garrity were still there under the harshness of the strip lights. 'But if the guv'nor wants all the i's dotted and the tees crossed, he's going to have to call in the Fraud Squad. If anyone was on the fiddle at Eight Counties, I haven't sussed it. What have you got, Paul?'

'No bloody sugar, that's for sure.' Garrity's screwed-up face said it all. 'Apart from the three wise monkeys we can't identify on the video tapes, zip. Course, there's absolutely no way of knowing when Hannah Morpeth's killer got into the hotel. It could in theory have been hours before, maybe even the previous day. This is weird, though.'

He ran the tapes so that people scurried backwards and forwards across the lobby like an old Mac Sennet take. 'Here.' He pointed to the frame as he froze it. 'Who's this?'

Manton peered closer. Hours of spreadsheets had seared themselves on his eyeballs and he wasn't focusing. 'Elvis?' he speculated.

'John Irving, the historical adviser bloke working on the shoot.'

'Seems in a hurry,' Manton observed now that the frames were moving at the right speed.

'Correct. He goes through that revolving door like a bat out of Hell and nearly knocks over this woman.'

'Oh, yeah. What was that film where they all get stuck in a door like that?'

'Dunno.' Garrity wasn't a film buff and if he had been, the last twenty-four hours staring at this footage would have cured him of that. 'And this. This is Peter Maxwell, that smart alec from up at the school, the one the DI warned us about.'

'Oh, yeah,' Manton remembered watching the celluloid Maxwell jerking his way towards the door, steadying the woman and leaving the frame. 'Didn't like him, did he?'

'He did not,' Garrity sharpened the focus on the woman crossing to the reception counter. 'Unlike Mrs Fabulous.'

'Who?'

'Jacquie Tightarse Carpenter.'

'Oh?' Manton was a sucker for gossip and he sniffed it now in the air of the Incident Room. 'What have you heard?'

'What have *you* heard?' Garrity was a cautious man.

'DCI wouldn't mind slipping her one,' Manton observed, 'unless my encyclopedic knowledge of human nature is missing a few pages.'

Garrity nodded. 'Well, he's not alone there.' He lowered his voice lest Incident Room walls have ears. 'They say she's got the hots for Maxwell.'

'Never!' Manton didn't buy it, sitting upright again. 'He's old enough to be her father.'

'I didn't realize incest was on the menu,' Garrity sniggered. 'No, apparently, he rings her up. Goes round her place.'

'Never!'

'Has your CD got stuck, mate?' Garrity asked, risking his tonsils again with the coffee.

'Well, bugger me sideways. Who's that woman, by the way? On the hotel video? The one Maxwell caught.'

'Ah,' Garrity tapped the reverse button, 'that,' he almost

pressed his nose to the screen, 'is Mrs Barbara Needham, wife of the deceased.'

'What's weird then?'

'You what?'

'What's weird? You said "This is weird, though." What is?'

Garrity rewound the tape again. 'John Irving. Who interviewed him?'

'The DI, I think. Why?'

'Refined sort of bloke? Gentle?'

'The DI? Do me a favour!'

'Irving,' Garrity was fiddling, running the tape forwards and back, trying to find the exact spot, 'cultivated sort of cove. Cambridge professor and all that.'

'So?' Manton was lost.

'So,' Garrity pointed triumphantly at the screen, slowing the motion down, 'Look what he does. He hares across the foyer as if his arse is alight. Swerves. See – looks as if he's about to go another way. Then carries straight on and hits the door. There!' Garrity's finger hit the freeze-frame.

'What?' Manton was looking at Barbara Needham, hurtling towards Maxwell's open arms.

'He's looking back.'

Garrity was right. At the bottom left-hand corner of the screen, John Irving had half-turned, looking back into the foyer.

'See, he's looking back. He knows he's hit her and yet,' he clicked the frame on again, 'he keeps on going.'

Manton shrugged. 'He's in a hurry,' he said, 'that would explain it.'

'Yes, it would,' Garrity agreed. 'He also knows Maxwell's there to catch her. Even so . . .'

'What?'

'A cultivated, nice bloke like him. Wouldn't you think

he'd play the white man, so to speak? Nip back, see if she's all right?'

'Maybe,' Manton slid his chair back. 'Maybe not. Come on, Paul, call it a day, old son. You'll be spotting suspicious-looking cockroaches next.'

The summer came back to Leighford the next week. Hordes of holidaymakers who'd done EuroDisney and couldn't afford the Algarve swarmed south in search of sun, sea and sand. Leighford was like comfort food – steamed pudding, spotted dick, tapioca – all the smells and tastes of yesteryear. There was the inevitable Chinese in the High Street, the de rigeur Doner Kebab down the Front and the trail of litter which led inexorably to KFC. Dear dead old Colonel Sanders wasn't boasting about his famous eleven secret spices any more, probably because the place was staffed exclusively by Old Leighford Highenas who couldn't count that far.

The morbidly curious vied with each other to plant their deck chairs and windbreaks on the Very Spot where Miles Needham had died. Those who were rich as well as morbidly curious and could afford the Grand's inflated prices padded past Hannah Morpeth's room whispering to each other as at a shrine. 'It happened in there, you know.' And the management of the Grand were not reletting that room that season, hoping it would all go away, resisting pressure from the local crime writers' circle to open it up for tours.

The morbidly curious Peter Maxwell found himself on the floor above Hannah's, staring into the fish eye lens that he knew was staring back at him.

'Yes,' a disembodied voice called.

'Mrs Needham? My name is Maxwell. I'd like to talk to you about your late husband.'

Silence.

'Mrs Needham?'

'Are you a reporter?'

'No, I'm a teacher. I was historical adviser of sorts on *The Captain's Fancy*. May I come in?'

Another silence. The door was cardboard and ply by the look of it, but it might as well have been solid steel. Peter Maxwell had no warrant card to get him into places, no statutory right of entry. Nor had nature given him the brass neck acquired by journalists, nor the enormous feet to block the closing of a door.

It opened. Sesame. Maxwell took off his hat. 'Mrs Needham, Peter Maxwell.'

Her handshake was firm and her eyes were dry. Mourning became Barbara Needham like it became Electra, the black dress lacily echoing her raven hair. 'Yes,' she said. 'We met a couple of days ago in the foyer. You were kind enough to pick me up.'

'Indeed we did,' Maxwell remembered. 'And I want you to know I don't make a habit of that.'

'You'd better come in.'

Barbara Needham's room was the most en suite he'd ever seen and the sun twinkled on the sea through the open windows. With that fickleness of the British seasons, the cold snap had gone and the gold and the blue of summer was back. She led him out there onto a balcony. 'Would you like some coffee, Mr Maxwell? I was about to have my elevenses.'

'Thank you,' he said and sat down on the warm wrought iron work. 'Mrs Needham, may I say . . .'

She held up her hand, dazzling gold in the morning sun. 'Mr Maxwell, you can spare me the platitudes. My husband was a shit. I suppose I knew that when I married him. It's funny,' she sat down and poured coffee for them both, 'Loveless marriages are supposed to be a Victorian thing, aren't they? Dynastic arrangements. Well, let me tell you they aren't. You see, for all his arrogance, Miles was something of a rough diamond. A local boy, I believe.'

'Local?' Maxwell asked in mid sugar cube. 'To Leighford?'

'Not exactly,' the widow told him. 'Bournemouth. But I knew he came out this way often as a young tearaway.'

'You've known him long?'

'Most of my life, it seems. We married in '90. Before that there was, in reverse order, Cynthia, a ham actress who screwed her way into his affections. Perfectly ghastly. And before her, Elaine, I believe. They met at university.'

'Where was that?'

'Perhaps university is a misnomer.' Barbara Needham, needless to say, took her coffee black. 'Kingston Polytechnic.'

'How old was Miles?' Maxwell asked.

'Forty-six,' his widow said, 'though he was already starting to shed a few years. *Marie-Claire* had him down to thirty-five I noticed a couple of months ago. And he certainly wouldn't be the one to correct them. Tell me, Mr Maxwell, why are you so anxious to know about my husband?'

'I was there when he died, Mrs Needham,' Maxwell said, looking into the woman's bright, dark eyes. 'And one of my boys is accused of killing him.'

'Your boys? Do you mean your sons?' she frowned.

'No,' Maxwell chuckled. 'My students. My sixth form. I told you – I'm a teacher.'

'Oh, yes. The Sparrow boy. Did he have any reason to kill Miles?'

'Not that I can see,' Maxwell sighed, watching the grockle children squealing at the water's edge and the windsurfers soaring further out. 'Giles Sparrow is an ordinary seventeen-year-old; none too bright. But murderous? I don't think so. Then there's Hannah Morpeth.'

'Ah, yes.' Barbara Needham looked as if she'd just swallowed a lemon. 'My part of our domestic alliance was that I gave Miles refinement, taught him which knife and fork to use. Bedroom antics were never really part of it.'

'I see.'

'Mr Maxwell, I married Miles Needham for his money. I have an addiction for it. The price I had to pay was his infidelity. While I was cutting a swathe through New Bond Street with his plastic, he was getting sucked off by anything in a skirt. It wasn't much of a price, really. And now I've got it all.'

'Really?'

'My husband had his faults, Mr Maxwell. He was arrogant, offensive, deeply homophobic and occasionally racist, but he was, even I must agree, bloody good at his job. He made, if you'll excuse the less than bon mot, a killing every time he went to work.'

'So you won't miss him, then?'

Barbara Needham looked out to the horizon where the line of sea and sky was shrouded in the June haze. 'Him, no. His money, no, because he left it all to me in some fit of conventionality. There are things I'll miss . . . but I'll get over it. Or perhaps I won't have to. We'll have to see.'

'Will you be in Leighford long?' Maxwell asked.

She gave him an old-fashioned look as a gang of lager louts sang and bawled their way along the beach far below them, ''Ere we go, 'ere we go, 'ere we go.'

'No longer than I have to be,' she smiled. 'I'm waiting for them to release my husband's body for burial.'

Maxwell glanced out at the yobboes kicking a can to each other. 'Football,' he muttered. 'The Sport of Things. Mrs Needham,' he turned to her again, 'if anything occurs to you – any reason you can think of why anyone would want to see your husband dead – will you contact me?' and he passed her his address and phone number on the back of an old Leighford High report form.

She looked at him, the shambling, yet somehow attractive teacher sitting opposite her. 'Yes, Mr Maxwell,' she said. 'Yes, I will.'

* * *

There is a story concerning the late Duke of Wellington. Stormed at with shot and shell from Assaye to Waterloo, the great Duke never turned and fled in the face of the enemy in his life – except once. He was an old man, nearing the end of his life and he was visiting the Great Exhibition, wandering its upper corridors as gobsmacked as everyone else. A group of working-class gits recognized him – 'Oi, it's 'Is Grace the Dook o' Wellin'ton' they said, and they gave chase. The old man's nerve broke. Fearing they would snatch hairs from his head as souvenirs, he turned tail and fled the gallery, the gits floundering in his wake.

In the life of Peter Maxwell, the gits had lessened to one – hardly a git at all, but a rather refined old boy called Dr Nicholson, who had been a teacher himself when they still called such people schoolmasters. Dr Nicholson meant well – as did Wellington's admirers at the Exhibition – but he bored Maxwell rigid because he was old and retired and his day lasted at least twenty-four hours longer than Maxwell's. So it was that Peter Maxwell met his Waterloo – or rather, ran from it – that Monday. He urgently had to see the school matron while Paul Moss, the Head of History, coped with and glazed over in front of Dr Nicholson.

'So there it is, Sylv,' Maxwell rested his back against the paper-thin wall that divided matron's sick-bay from her office; coffee, pep talks and morning-after pills in one; the dying room in the other. 'Barbara Needham obviously couldn't care less. But then, Angela Badham said as much. I shouldn't be surprised really. It's just that I'm an old-fashioned sort of cove. When a man gets his head blown off by person unknown, I expect just a little bitty tear from the wife. Or am I out of touch?'

'The "person unknown" bit, Max.' Sylvia Matthews was refilling her coffee machine. 'Any news of Giles?'

'Not a dickie bird. Glove Farm is like something out of

Mervyn Peake meets Miss Haversham – all cobwebs and off-the-wall people. Sailer the solicitor is seriously out of his depth as he himself admits and the boys in blue are their usual mind-your-own-business selves.'

'What about Jacquie?'

Now, Peter Maxwell was usually very good at nuances. Thirty years at the Chalk Face had taught him a few dodges. He recognized the arched eyebrow, the sideways glance, even the edge in the voice. But with Sylvia Matthews it was as if all this passed him by. It wasn't that Sylvia hated Jacquie Carpenter – though when she was nine she might have done – it was that she loved Peter Maxwell. And Peter Maxwell seemed to be spending more and more time with the girl he called Woman Policeman Carpenter.

'Funny you should mention her,' Maxwell stretched out with both feet on the desk. 'As soon as the damn bell *sans merci* goes, I'm outa here, as our American cousins have it and I'm pedalling round to the dear girl's lock-up. I want to know more about those two Marauders who left.'

'But they've all gone now, haven't they? The television people pulled up stumps ages ago.'

'All except Bob Pickering,' Maxwell nodded. 'I noticed his tent is still up on the Shingle. The Voltigeur flag's still flying.'

'Why hasn't he gone?'

'Bob?' Maxwell mused. 'I don't know, really. I think in a way, he feels a bit like me, really – responsible.'

'That's silly, Max,' Sylvia scolded as the coffee machine bubbled and hissed at her elbow, 'for both of you. All right, so you were supervising the battle sequences. He was . . . what . . . a sergeant, or something?'

Maxwell nodded.

'Well, you've done nothing to reproach yourselves for, either of you. You know who I blame for all this?'

'You've got a suspect, Sylv?' Maxwell brightened immediately. 'Say on, Miss Nightingale.'

'John Irving.'

'John . . . Oh, come on, Sylv. Really!'

'No, no,' she said. 'I don't mean I think he did it. But he did get you into this in the first place.'

'And I could have said no at any time and he did warn me about Eight Counties. He actually said . . . Oh, God . . .'

'Max? What's the matter? You've gone a funny colour. Put your head between your knees.'

'No, no, I'm all right. He actually said at one point – "It's going to be murder".'

The door burst open and Tracy Wilmot stood there, in non-regulation trainers and unseasonal black tights, 'Miss Matthews,' she wailed through the wodge of chewing gum.

'Oh dear, Trace,' the Matron sighed. 'Who was it this time?'

'I'd rather not say, Miss. Nobody you know.'

'Married?'

'Yeah.'

'Mr Maxwell, would you excuse us? It's a girl thing.'

Maxwell was on his feet. 'You know, the more I think about it, Matron, the more I think you could be right. Know what the best oral contraceptive in the world is, Tracey?' he asked the girl as he reached the door. From the vacant look on her face it was clear she didn't. 'The word "No",' Maxwell enlightened her. Or at least, he'd like to think he had.

'Has he gone, Paul?' a terror-struck Peter Maxwell stuck his head around the Head of History's door.

'No, I buried the old bastard under the floorboards,' Moss beamed in mid-marking. 'You owe me one, Max.'

'Oh, ambience gris,' Maxwell salaamed to the younger man, 'I owe you thousands. You did tell him if he was seen on site again, he'd be shot, didn't you?'

'Of course,' Moss played along, 'But unaccountably, it came out rather like "See you again, Dr Nicholson. Thank you so much."'

'Curses!' Maxwell rummaged through the filing cabinet for the past papers he needed to terrify 12C with. 'And what did you have occasion to thank him for this time?'

'Items for the school museum. You know, the one we haven't got.'

'Ah, that one.' Maxwell knew it well.

'Pile of shit – over there,' Moss pointed to old newspapers and other ephemera neatly stashed on the corner of his table. 'Actually, I shouldn't knock it. Old Doc Nicholson just comes from a different world, that's all. I thought it was your world, Max?'

'What, you mean the one where kids had shining faces and brushed hair and blazers – and they actually wanted to learn? That one?'

'That's it,' Moss winked.

'That's the land of Never-Never, my boy,' Maxwell smiled, 'and it's getting more pie-in-the-sky with every day that passes. Bugger me!' He was running his eyes down one of the newspapers.

'Not now, Max,' Moss hadn't looked up from 9C4's solutions to the Irish question which he'd promised to submit to Mo Mowlam at the next conceivable opportunity, Good Friday Agreement notwithstanding. 'I've got my hands full.'

'Listen to this, Paul,' Maxwell sat in the only vacant chair. '"A body was discovered at Willow Bay last Thursday by local fishermen. The coroner, Mr Malcolm Davis, has been called in and newly appointed police surgeon Dr James Astley expressed his opinion that the body had been in the water for at least thirty-six hours. Police sources have revealed that the body is that of Mr Thomas Sparrow, sixty-one, who was well known in the local gay community.'

'Local gay community?' Moss echoed, leaning back and

putting down his red pen with relief. 'I didn't know we had one.'

'Neither did I.' Maxwell turned the paper over. 'But this is the *Clarion*, the *Advertiser*'s forerunner. Dated . . . June 1977. That was the summer before I started at Leighford. Ever heard of Tom Sparrow, Paul?'

'Christ, Max,' the Head of History clasped his hands behind his head, 'And with respect, of course, I was nine, living in Suffolk and having a passionate affair with my mountain bike. I didn't know what a community was, much less a gay one. Presumably though, he's related to Giles, this dead poof.'

Maxwell clicked his teeth, smiling. 'Ah, such a way with words,' he said.

Moss's face suddenly darkened. 'Now, Max, you're not off on one of your crusades again?'

Maxwell tucked the folded paper under his arm, 'When I am, Paulie, my boy,' he winked, 'rest assured, you'll be the last to know.'

The *Leighford Advertiser* had taken over the old Temperance Hall in the early '80s, back of the bus station. That Monday afternoon, the sun of summer still high over the newsdesk, White Surrey rested against the yellowed brick wall, its owner inside and making a nuisance of himself. He who had put the 'f' in technophobia, in that he always prefixed it with an 'f' word, now sat at the microfiche desk, his tired old eyes whizzing along the faint lines of somebody else's deathless prose from yesteryear.

'Bill Donlan,' a plumpish woman put a card down next to him. 'As far as I can tell, he worked on the paper then and was its principal reporter. That was his address five years ago. Course, he could be dead.'

Bill Donlan wasn't dead. But he lay as if he was, on a

hammock between two pear trees in the shade of his evening garden. Delicious smells of something tandoori wafted from the open kitchen door, where Mrs Donlan was being creative with the leftovers of the Sunday joint. Thank God for the Raj, Maxwell thought to himself.

'Oh, yes,' Donlan was less comatose when his mouth moved, 'I remember it very well. Twenty-one years ago? Is it really? Bloody Hell, I'd never have said that. Now then – can I get you a lemonade, Mr Maxwell? The wife does a lovely lemonade.'

'No thanks,' Maxwell sat upright in the excruciating cane chair under the tree's shade. His jacket and hat lay slung on White Surrey's handlebars around which the Donlan's dog sniffed and ferreted. 'Tom Sparrow.'

'Yes, Sparrow.' Donlan creaked on his taut housings as the wind ruffled what was left of his hair. 'They found him on a Thursday, I think, washed up on Willow Bay. Not a pretty sight. Not that we were allowed beyond the cordon of course. Dave May got a sneaky photo before Mr Plod took his camera away. Course, they were different days, Mr Maxwell. No body bags then – a rather nasty American idea, if I remember rightly. They just put the corpse on a stretcher under a blanket. And no FACE, no police PR in those days. We hated them and they couldn't stand us. Dave May certainly couldn't when they trod on his camera.'

'Was it an accident?'

'Course not. It was deliberate. Oh, I see – Sparrow; well – open verdict, according to the coroner. But I had my doubts.'

'Really?' Maxwell was all ears. 'Why?'

Bill Donlan looked at Maxwell through slitted eyes. 'I followed up on Tom Sparrow. Nobody knew much about him. We assumed he was related to the Sparrows of Glove Farm, but they had nothing whatever to do with him as far as I could tell. He used to hang around the loos in the Square and around Tottingleigh – a bit of a lavatory cowboy. Even so, he was harmless enough. Not a paedophile or anything like that. He lived alone in a basement flat in Gracechurch Street. Nobody seemed to know what he did for a living, but he always paid his rent. You'd often see him sitting on the old sea wall before they did the reinforcements, talking to people. Always had a little group of kids with him.'

'But I thought you said . . .'

'That he wasn't a paedophile. No, he wasn't. At least, there were never any complaints. When I say kids, I mean teenagers, really. Mind you, the world wasn't as mad as it is today. It's this computer rubbish, this Internet. Porn at the push of a button, interactive sex sessions and Christ knows what. No such things as paedophile rings in those days, Mr Maxwell.'

Mad Max leaned back as far as the rickety old chair would let him. 'So you think Tom Sparrow was pushed?' he asked.

'Let's just say he was a victim waiting for a murder to happen,' Donlan sucked his dentures as he ruminated. 'People's paranoia, Mr Maxwell, that's what it's all about. Don't trust a black – he's different, so he's trouble. And a poof? Well, you don't want to turn your back on one of those, do you, for all sorts of reasons. We've had black candles and white cockerels in Rochdale council estates and social workers and psychiatrists bleating along with all the rest. Whatever happened to the good old sense of fair play we British used to be so proud of, eh?'

'Out with the bath water, like the baby, Mr Donlan,' Maxwell nodded. 'Was there anything physical – forensic evidence, I mean – which added fuel to your murder theory?'

'For that,' Donlan propped himself up on one elbow, 'you'd have to ask Jim Astley, the police surgeon. He was a new bug then, fresh out of being a police surgeon somewhere else. I could never cotton to him. Sanctimonious old bastard, even when he was a young bastard. *But*, he's got one weakness, I think you'll find. Press the right button and he'll shoot his mouth off. Indiscretion is his middle name.'

Dr Jim Astley's middle name was actually Neville, but Indiscretion suited him better. His wife, a long-suffering woman who had long ago climbed inside a gin bottle to escape the world, told the tweed-hatted cyclist who appeared at her doorway as dusk fell, that he was in the pub. He was, holding forth at the bar on medical ethics to a group of florid faced gentlemen only marginally more pissed than he was.

'Dr Astley?'

'Yes,' the medic turned to face the same cyclist his wife had met.

'I'm Peter Maxwell.'

Astley's bonhomie had vanished. 'Yes,' he almost growled, 'I know who you are.'

'Might I have a word?'

'What about?'

'An old case I'm anxious to clear up.'

'I don't do urogenital stuff,' Astley mused, swilling down the last of his Scotch, 'and I *am* off duty.'

'And your glass is empty. Let me freshen it for you,' and Maxwell caught the eye of the barman and placed an order. He led Astley, still protesting, into a darkened corner, as far away from the rowdies in the main bar as he could get.

'Your wife told me I'd find you here,' Maxwell placed the Scotch down on Astley's beer mat.

'Really?' He took a sip, 'I'm surprised she remembered. Well, Mr Maxwell, it's been a while.'

'Nearly four years,' Maxwell nodded, savouring the fragrance of his Southern Comfort. 'Nearly four years since Jenny Hyde died. Since you found her at the Red House.'

Astley remembered the Red House too, and the girl,

another of Maxwell's Own, found strangled there. Her face, like all his dead, lay among his souvenirs.

'How the Hell have you been?' Maxwell asked.

'Mr Maxwell, I don't know you very well, but I do know you well enough to know that you don't give a flying fuck about my health. So let's get to business, shall we? What do you want?'

Maxwell smiled. 'Perspicacious as ever, Doctor,' he said. 'Tom Sparrow.'

'Who?'

'Thomas George Sparrow. Found drowned in Willow Bay in June 1977. You examined the body.'

'So I did,' Astley remembered. 'One of my first cases at Leighford. What about it?'

'What was the cause of death, do you recall?'

'Christ, Maxwell, that was over twenty years ago. You'd have to check the coroner's records.'

'I did,' Maxwell told him. '"Open verdict". That's legal-speak for "We haven't a bloody clue", isn't it?'

'More or less,' Astley nodded. 'There was water in his lungs, I seem to remember.'

'Meaning?'

'He drowned.'

There was a sudden roar of laughter from the rowdies at the bar. 'Come on, Jim,' one of them called. 'It's your shout!'

'Right. Hang on,' Astley waved at them. 'Why the interest, Maxwell? I know you. You're like a bloody terrier when you get your teeth into things – things I might add in which your teeth have no business being.'

Maxwell let the appalling sentence construction go. 'Do you know if the late Tom Sparrow was related in any way to Giles Sparrow? It's not a very common name.'

'As you say,' Astley nodded. 'And I really have no idea. You'd have to ask the Sparrows of Glove Farm. But I personally wouldn't do that, Mr Maxwell.'

'Really, Dr Astley. Why not?'

'Because it's none of your business, I repeat. As it is, I shall be reporting this conversation to Detective Chief Inspector Hall.' And he stood up to join his cronies at the bar.

'Shall you, Dr Astley? How unbelievably petty of you.' And Maxwell downed his drink and left.

# Chapter Nine

'Jacquie? Is that you?' The lights burned late that night at 38, Columbine and the noises of the night sounded eerie and distorted through Maxwell's open window. Metternich the cat lay in the shrubbery and watched his master in the lounge, that silly white thing glued to his ear again. And his lip curled at the silhouette that had made him a eunuch.

'Jacquie?'

'Hello, Max.' The voice was subdued. Distant.

'Can we talk?' Maxwell asked. 'I've been trying you all evening. I thought it was a case of answerphone shall speak unto answerphone. Except of course I haven't got an answerphone.'

'Max . . .'

'Stapleton and Wood – the re-enactors who left after Needham's death. I need their addresses.'

'I can't do it, Max,' the distant voice said. 'Not this time.'

'Is someone there?' Maxwell frowned, whirling from side to side of his lounge carpet. 'Is somebody with you?'

'Max, listen to me. DI Watkiss has had a word – upstairs. Hall himself. My career's on the line now, Max; I mean it. I just can't help any more. Not now. Not ever.'

And the line went dead.

'Hello?' Maxwell shook the receiver, willing the wires to reconnect. 'Hello? Jacquie?' Nothing. Just the flat-line hum. 'Oh, bother!' and he let the receiver fall onto the settee. Outside in the light of the street lamp, a boy and girl were walking past, wrapped in each other, laughing as youth will, carefree and in love. Maxwell poured himself a Southern Comfort. His lover. His wife.

'Here's looking at you, kids,' he gave them his best Bogart under his breath. Then a thought came to him. 'As one door closes,' he mused to himself, 'another opens.' And he rummaged through his back copies of the *Mail on Sunday*, strewn in a less than edifying corner of his lounge. Simon Heffer in full cry, the holiday of a lifetime somewhere unpronounceable, somebody else's thoughts on the probability of alien life beyond the galaxy. There – the two-page spread on Hannah Morpeth. And there it was, below the picture of the laughing girl photographed with Jeremy Irons, the name of the man he wanted.

Buster Rothwell, Hannah Morpeth's minder, took some finding. A call next morning to Eight Counties had tracked down Angela Badham and after some initial caginess, she'd given Maxwell Rothwell's number. After that, it was up to the Head of Sixth Form. A bit of judicious lesson-swapping with Anthea Edwards and Paul Moss of the History Department and a quick – 'I think that's two I owe you, Paul' – Maxwell was on the 12.45 out of Leighford and rattling north, where the brave curve of the railway ran below the Gothic splendour of Arundel castle.

He stoically bore the abysmal coffee that the funny little man in the buffet car sold him and he manfully fought the grease that threatened to trickle down onto his shirt from the all day BLT at which his taste buds were recoiling. But when a flash entrepreneurial type sitting next to him hauled a mobile from his inside pocket, Maxwell's composure cracked.

'Tell me,' he tapped the type on the shoulder, 'did you pay someone to ring you on the train just to impress little old me? Well, I have to tell you, you've failed. Ah, Guildford – gateway to even more suburbia.' And he placed what was left of his BLT in the entrepreneur's free hand.

Now, Maxwell remembered the '80s *Minder* series on the telly very well and the fact that Arfur had become a household word across the nation. But anyone less like Dennis Waterman's happy-go-lucky Terry McGann he had yet to meet. Buster Rothwell was a squat pug of a man – the sort dear old Geoffrey Chaucer used to call a 'thicke narre' – with a collar-straining neck that flowed like rock into his shoulders. His hair stood up on end like a newly hatched duckling, but cute was the last epithet that came to mind. At first, he didn't offer Maxwell a seat. All he offered him was a bunch of fives and it took all the Head of Sixth Form's charm to worm his way past the front door.

Buster Rothwell's flat had little to recommend it, except perhaps the rather impressive range of hardware displayed on the pine cladding.

'That's a rather fine Martini Henry.' Maxwell pointed to the rifle at the top.

'I presume you didn't come to admire my etchings,' Rothwell said. He was pure Essex by way of the Lea Valley.

'I came to enquire about Hannah Morpeth.' Maxwell turned to face him.

Rothwell gnawed his lip for a moment, judging his man, weighing the situation. 'Now, why did I know that?' he asked.

'Mr Rothwell, it's obvious to you that I have no right to ask you anything, but I'd like to know all the same.'

'That's right,' Rothwell nodded. 'I could throw you out any time. It'd be my right.'

'It would,' nodded Maxwell. 'But somehow I don't think you will.'

'Oh, really? Why's that, then?'

Maxwell crossed to the lowest gun on the rack. 'A Brown Bess,' he purred. 'What a beauty – quite a rarity too.'

Rothwell was at his elbow. With a deft movement, he took the musket by the barrel and slid it across his chest, presenting arms. 'Want to sniff it?' he asked. 'That's what they do in all the best Westerns, isn't it? And then come out with "This gun's been fired recently". Well, it has.' He slid the musket back into position on the wall, 'Not that you'd know that because I look after my guns. I shot a rabbit with it the other day.'

'In Guildford?' Maxwell raised a doubting eyebrow. Perhaps in Guildford they had them hopping alive around Sainsbury's meat counter.

'*Near* Guildford,' Rothwell said.

'Who do *you* think killed Hannah, Mr Rothwell?' the Head of Sixth Form asked.

The minder turned away and fell heavily into an armchair. 'Well,' he said, 'that's the sixty-four-thousand-dollar question, isn't it? Why do you wanna know?'

Maxwell risked sitting opposite him, gingerly among the Pumping Iron mags strewn on the sofa. 'A little thing called justice,' he said.

'You what?' Rothwell sneered.

'One of my sixth form is in police custody charged with the murder of Miles Needham.'

'Well, then,' Rothwell shrugged. 'You didn't do a very good job there, did you, eh?'

'I think you're missing the point,' Maxwell smiled. 'Whoever killed Needham also killed Hannah.'

'Well, it doesn't take a fucking genius to work that one

out, does it?' Rothwell rolled an eternal piece of chewing gum around his mouth.

'No,' Maxwell smiled again. 'I'm slumming at the moment. Humour me.'

There were many words Buster Rothwell did not know the meaning of – humour was one of them. But he was in an expansive mood that day. 'What do you want to know – exactly?' he asked.

'Tell me about Hannah Morpeth. How well did you know her?'

'I didn't,' Rothwell shrugged. 'I work for an agency. Just doing a job. After the army, it's all I could think to do. I'd only been with her a week.'

'And what impression did you get?'

'Of Hannah? Stuck-up bitch. Public school. Acting School. Looked down her nose at people like me. I remember thinking when I was introduced to her; I thought "I could rearrange your face, darlin'". That would be it.' Rothwell was gazing into the middle distance at the memory of it. 'End of a glitterin' career. It'd be easy.'

'You didn't like her?'

Rothwell focused on Maxwell again. 'You catch on quick, don'tya? Look, Maxwell, I was nothing to her. Just shit on her shoes, that's all. She was an arrogant piece of arse. Didn't know just how much she needed me, did she, till it was too late?'

'Tell me about the day she died.'

Rothwell leaned back, sighing. 'First coppers, then you. I must be a fuckin' idiot.'

'What time did you come on duty?'

'Lunch time. That's when she got up.'

'You were staying at the Grand?'

'Yeah. Some grotty little hole near the generators. Sounds like the engine room of the Titanic at night.'

'What was the day's itinerary?'

'You what?'

Maxwell felt at home. This was like talking to 9Z. 'Schedule,' he tried again, 'What happened during the day?'

'I drove her down to the beach.'

'Willow Bay?'

'That's right. I waited outside her caravan while she got into make-up and costume, then she did some filming.'

'Did anything unusual happen?' Maxwell asked. 'Anything odd?'

'No,' Rothwell shook his head and curled his lip. 'She had a phone call mid-afternoon. That seemed to shake her a bit.'

'Really?' Maxwell frowned. 'Who was it from?'

'Christ knows. It was to her mobile. You can't trace calls like that.'

'In what way was she shaken?'

'Dunno,' Rothwell grimaced, trying to remember it. 'She was a bit pale, I do know that. I heard her say "Well, she's got to be told".'

'Did that make any sense?'

'Not a lot,' Rothwell shrugged, 'You've got to realize a woman like High and Mighty Morpeth gets a lot of calls, from all sorts of people. She was having a tough time of it, as it happens.'

'She was?'

Rothwell hesitated for a moment. Then he leaned forward, all shoulders and attitude. 'Why should I tell you, Maxwell? What's in it for me?'

Maxwell leaned forward too, all hair and tenacity. 'How about a good night's sleep?' he asked. 'I'd guess probably the first since she died.'

Rothwell's face fell. 'You bastard!' he growled under his breath and leaned back. He gnawed his lip again, sensing the moment, weighing his options. 'All right,' he muttered, letting his head sink back for a moment onto the chair's head rest. 'I still don't know why the fuck I'm doing this. Look,

I ain't told the coppers, all right? And I don't want them to know.'

'I'm not exactly in bed with Mr Plod myself,' Maxwell assured him.

'Right,' Rothwell nodded. 'Well, what the fuck? Hannah had a stalker.'

'Did she now?' Maxwell sat upright. 'How do you know?'

'She told me. Oh, not at first. The first couple of days it was Miss Hoity-Toity, like I was a bad bloody smell.'

'And then?'

'It was the Wednesday,' Rothwell remembered. 'Just before breakfast. She had a letter – delivered to her at the Grand.'

'Did you see it?'

'Yeah. I thought it was a bloody joke. It was like one of them B Movies – you know. Death threats cut out of newspapers. I said to her "Is this a wind-up or what?"'

'And it wasn't?'

'No.' Rothwell was shaking his head. 'No, she cracked a little that day, Miss Frozen Arse. Got all tearful and asked me to help her.'

'What could you do?'

'Nothing. That was just it. I'm a minder – a bodyguard, if you like. I'm not a fuckin' detective. I told her to go to the filth with it.'

'And she didn't?'

'Said she couldn't,' Rothwell said.

'Did she say how long all this had been going on?' Maxwell asked.

'A few weeks,' the minder told him.

'Do you remember what the letter said?'

'Better.' Rothwell got up suddenly and crossed the room. From a drawer under a computer desk he pulled out a piece of paper with black letters badly cut out and pasted onto it with cheap glue. 'Have a look for yourself.'

'Mr Rothwell,' Maxwell said. 'Should you be in possession of this?'

'No,' the minder said sulkily, as if he'd been caught scrumping apples, 'but then I shouldn't have ignored that phone call on the beach either the day she died, nor knocked off without checking on her one last time at the Grand. Then there was the bloke in the foyer.'

Maxwell looked up sharply from the letter. 'What bloke in the foyer?'

'Anorak. The filth asked me about him.'

'They did?'

'They've got him on the hotel's security tapes – video cameras over the front door.'

'Who was he?'

'Dunno. He did look sort of familiar, but I couldn't place him. Curly hair. Gormless looking. I bumped into him going off duty. Course, there's nothing to connect him to Hannah. It's just the filth chasing their own tails. Couldn't catch a fuckin' cold, that lot.'

'Do you mind if I keep this, Mr Rothwell?' Maxwell asked.

'No,' the minder shrugged. 'I still think it was somebody's idea of a joke. That's why I didn't tell the law. Do you think it was real, then? A stalker, I mean?'

Maxwell shook his head. 'Let's say it narrows the options a little,' he said.

'Yes, of course I lied to him, Count.' Peter Maxwell was staring into his own reflection in the amber glass. 'It doesn't narrow the options at all. Well, here it is – see for yourself.'

If Maxwell wanted to play silly buggers with his cat's IQ, Metternich was certainly in no mood. He didn't even look up as his lord and master shoved a piece of paper in front of him. What would be the point?

'Quite,' Maxwell sighed. 'You're right, of course. Not

worth looking at, is it? A plain piece of eighty gram, bog-standard office stationery, just a millibit of a rainforest. However,' he angled the threatening letter to the lamplight in his midnight lounge, 'we shouldn't be *too* dismissive. If I gave this to DCI Hall – yes, I know I should – he'd have his lab boys test the glue. Pritt, I shouldn't wonder – bog-standard again. And of course he'd look for prints – and find mine. Which is precisely, cat o' my heart, why I'm not giving it to him. Now, the letters are something else. See these upper case ones, here, Count? Independent or I'm a Geography teacher. These . . . difficult. Could be Telegraph, Grauniad. It's difficult. Can we infer then, that our anonymous threatener is a broadsheet reader? Or are they a tabloid reader being ultra clever?'

He shook his head, then freshened his Southern Comfort. 'You see, that's the trouble with sleuthing, isn't it? So many variables; so little time. All right,' he kicked off his brothel creepers and padded across the hearth rug, 'Psycho-babble time. The note says "Darling Hannah, you won't be so pretty when I've finished with you. Your career's over, bitch. Enjoy life while you can. This is not a rehearsal." Not a rehearsal? Cliché, but it echoes her calling well enough. "Darling Hannah"? Does chummie know her? Wishes he knew her? Does he drool over her pictures? Has he asked for her underwear and a signed brassiere?' Maxwell raised a disapproving eyebrow at the sleeping cat. 'You don't want to be so cynical,' he said. 'The poor girl is dead, after all. "You won't be so pretty" . . . what's this, then? Fist? Knuckle-duster? Acid? The paper said she was stabbed. There was no mention of mutilation. But perhaps killing her was enough. Jacquie, Jacquie,' he muttered under his breath, 'where are you now I need you? Still,' he threw the letter onto the coffee table, 'The stalker got one thing right. Hannah Morpeth's career is over, all right.'

*   *   *

'Mrs McGregor?' Maxwell was balancing on one leg in his office, trying to close the door with the other.

'Yes?' a disembodied voice answered at the other end of the phone.

'Peter Maxwell here, from Leighford High.'

'Oh, yes.'

'Er . . . is that Helen's granny? Mrs Hetherington, is it?'

'Yes.'

'Ah. We haven't seen Helen at school for four days. Is she unwell?'

'Yes,' the voice came back after a moment's hesitation. 'Something glandular, the doctor says.'

'Oh, I'm sorry.' Maxwell moved the exam papers to find his chair. 'Is she up to any work? I'll send some home.'

'That'd be a comfort,' the voice said. 'Thank you,' and the line went dead.

Maxwell looked up at the unimpressed face of Becky Evans, Helen McGregor's long-suffering form tutor. 'Granny,' he said, 'Helen lives with Granny at the moment. Old girl sounds as incisive as a tapioca pudding. I expect Mum's gone busting down to Waikiki again to relive her youth – they get that way, single mums, when they stare thirty-six in the face.'

'I wouldn't know,' Becky Evans said stonily, ever the Buster Keaton of Leighford High.

'Heigh ho, Becky, me proud beauty,' Maxwell leaned back in his chair, catching sight again of the Year Ten coursework that lay like the weight of all the world on his wall shelf. 'There's not a lot I can do at this stage. Granny is in loco grandparentis; she's mentioned the doctor, who won't tell us anything even if I rang him; and she's chosen "glandular" which, along with back trouble, is the hardest symptom to refute this side of SAD and Gulf War Syndrome. In short, my dear, we're buggered.'

'I'll go and see her, then,' the girl from the valleys said. 'Put her on the spot.'

'Your prerogative,' Maxwell shrugged. 'I'd advise against it, personally.'

'Yes, well,' the Head of Art spun on her heel, 'Doesn't do to get too personal in this job, does it, Max?' and she was gone.

Maxwell found himself wandering the shore that night, where the wavelets grew less brave with the tide receding along the margin of Willow Bay. The sunset was golden again in that marvellous summer, the way Maxwell imagined it must have been in 1914 before they heard the guns in Flanders along this shore and fresh-faced boys lied about their ages and buttoned themselves in khaki when their womenfolk said 'Go!' When he told Year Nine about it, they all believed he'd been there, one of the doomed youth of 1914, doomed to spend eternity in the chalk-filmed corridors and classrooms of Leighford High.

A lone fisherman stood at the lapping edge, checking his line, taut in the shallows, swigging from a can of lager to stave off the dryness of the night. Squealing children ran home to the magic glow of their mobile homes where it was all microwaves and telly and sunburn cream. Bob Pickering's tent stood by itself now, a little apart from the others that had joined it on the ridge over the Bay. The flag of the Voltigeurs still flew there and the odd strain of a marching band wafted on the breeze from Pickering's portable CD player.

'"*Ça Ira*",' Maxwell popped his head around the flap, 'From the Greatest Hits of 1791 LP. Sorry to barge in, Bob.'

'Mr Maxwell,' the re-enactor was polishing his buttons. '"*Ça Ira*" it is. Funny how a tune can get you going, isn't it? And a bloody French one at that. I always think, when I play this tape how the armies of Europe must have shook when they heard that. The Old Guard, every man of 'em seven foot tall marching with a tread that came straight out of Hell.'

Maxwell nodded. What a waste. This man had a soul. Why, oh why hadn't he come into the sixth form all those years ago? Pickering switched off the CD.

'I thought you'd have long gone by now, Bob,' Maxwell took the proffered bed and sat opposite his Maréchal de Logis, cross legged as he was.

'The law asked me to stay.'

'They did?' Maxwell asked. 'Why?'

'Buggered if I know, really. This was . . . four days ago now. Mind you, it wasn't just me. It was all of us. I was all set to go when Martin did.' He jerked his head to where the other tents had stood. 'I s'pose I'm the only sap.'

Maxwell chuckled. 'It's the first two who went I want to talk to,' he said.

'What? Stapleton and Wood?'

'Yes. Unfortunately I haven't a clue where they live and my usual sources have dried up.'

'Brighton,' Pickering said.

'What?'

'Brighton – little place along the coast.'

'Bob,' Maxwell was sitting upright. 'You don't know *where* in Brighton?'

'My van's outside, Mr Maxwell,' Pickering grinned. 'We could be there in half an hour.'

Maxwell thought he knew his Brighton, the AIDS capital of the South. It was no longer the fashionable watering place of Prinnie's friends, promenading along the Steyne like walking wallpaper. And now that the permissive society had been launched, it wasn't even the place where 'Mr Smith' would take his secretary for a dirty weekend. Even the candy floss and Kiss-Me-Quick hats were a fading memory. After dark, they came out like lepers from a colony, studded and tattooed like the Vandals and Ostrogoths whose descendants they were, bent on destroying the sunlit civilization of the Roman day.

And it was to these alleyways that Bob Pickering took his car, spinning the van's wheel through his hands, snarling through the gears as he clipped curbs and cut corners.

'I don't believe it!' Maxwell gave Pickering his best Victor Meldrew as the van's handbrake croaked in the darkened cab. They were outside a pub called the Volunteer. 'They even named a local after you.'

'Good, innit?' Pickering chuckled. 'But it's not my local – it's theirs.'

'What – Wood and Stapleton? How the hell did you know that?'

'It's a small world, re-enacting, Mr Maxwell. Everybody knows everybody else.'

'What? They're re-enactors? You mean, full time?'

'Nah, no more than me.'

'But, when I first met you all and asked for volunteers . . . oh, shit!'

'Exactly,' Pickering wound up his window. 'First rule of pretend soldiery, Mr Maxwell – never volunteer. Just like the real thing. I did five years with the Hampshires – I know.'

It was Maxwell's shout. And shout he had to over the din of the DJ; some sad bastard slumped in a corner, wearing a Motorhead T-shirt and shades, slapping on the CDs with one hand, thumping some vague, unpredictable rhythm with the other. Three or four floozies were gyrating in the centre of the floor, on a raised dais, breasts flying in all directions, while men sat around trying to see up their frocks. Try as he might, Maxwell couldn't see a handbag anywhere.

'We're in luck,' Pickering bellowed in his ear. 'It's not the stripper tonight.'

'What'll it be?' Maxwell asked him, grateful for the smallest of mercies.

'Pint of Boddington's, please. Aye, aye,' and he nodded

to the far corner. Dave Wood leaned against a flock-papered wall, one raised arm propping up a cigarette machine. Across the table from him was Joe Stapleton, a half-filled glass in front of him, eyeing up the talent.

'Evening, gents,' Pickering slid back a chair and joined them.

'Fuck me!' Wood let his arm fall. 'Hello, Bob. How's the scrap metal business?'

'OK last time I saw it,' Pickering nodded, taking Maxwell's drink, 'I'm still at Leighford.'

'Fuck me!' said Wood again. It was obviously his party piece. 'Ain't you got no job to go to?' And he and Stapleton roared and slapped their thighs.

'You've met the Reeves and Mortimer of Brighton, Mr Maxwell?' Pickering re-introduced them.

'Fu . . .' Wood was about to say, but Maxwell leaned forward.

'It's a pleasure,' he said, shaking the man by the hand.

'Hello, Mr Maxwell,' Stapleton stretched a languid arm across, 'is this one piss of a coincidence or what?'

'More of a what, I'd say, Mr Stapleton.'

'Hello,' Wood slurred, 'he's after your body, Joe.'

Maxwell smiled. 'It's more Miles Needham's body I'm interested in, actually.'

'Ooh.' It wasn't a bad Kenneth Williams from Wood, though had Maxwell thought about it, it really had to be Julian Clary, given Wood's age. 'There you are, Joseph. Necrophilia. Mr Maxwell's one of those people your mother warned you about.'

'You left early,' Maxwell came straight to the point.

'We've got fucking jobs, mate,' Stapleton said. 'I like a laugh. Bit of telly. Few bob. But you can't doss around for ever.'

'Not unless you're self-employed, of course,' Wood grimaced at Pickering.

'That's right,' Stapleton agreed. 'Still, I'm sorry we came away now. What with that Hannah Morpeth getting hers.'

'Better than a play, is it?' Maxwell felt his hackles and a certain red mist rising.

'Nah, don't get Joe wrong, Mr Maxwell,' Wood defended his friend. 'It was bloody terrible, wasn't it?'

'The only bloody terrible thing,' Stapleton slurred, trying to focus, 'is that the little fucker who done it is still – what does the filth say? At large.'

'Really?' Maxwell leaned forward. 'Who's your money on, then, Joe?'

Stapleton looked at the men around the table. Dave, his old mucker – straight as a die and a good bloke. Pickering, bit of a hard nut; even in the pub's half light, not a bloke you'd tangle with; and Maxwell, mad as a bloody snake, with his poncey hat and bow tie. Christ, what a crew.

'Let me put it this way,' he said, having drained his glass, 'Who carried her photos in his wallet? Eh?' He was warming to his theme now, leaning forward, wiping the lager's froth from his lips. 'Who said – and I quote – "I could really give her one"? Eh, Dave? You remember?'

'About half the fucking extras at Willow Bay,' Wood blinked.

'Yeah, yeah, but who in particular? Maybe you couldn't see the look on his face from where you was sitting, but I could. I tell you, if I was her, that Hannah Morpeth, I'd have locked my bloody door, I can tell you. And I'd have had a chastity belt fitted.'

'Who are we talking about, Joe?' Maxwell wanted to know.

'Time at the bar!' their host's voice bellowed above Marilyn Manson.

Joe Stapleton leaned closer to Maxwell, his face a livid white under the DJ's spinning stars. 'That fucker Martin Bairstow, that's who.'

* * *

It was about that time that Jim Astley was padding his way up the stairs from the morgue. He was getting too long in the tooth for all this. And was he mellowing? In the old days, when he still had all his own hair and doctors were pillars of society, he wouldn't have done this, not even for Henry Hall; not even for Jacquie Carpenter.

She was waiting for him on the ground floor, in that polished silence that marks a hospital after hours where only the cleaners clatter about their business and the wards settle down for the night. A sultry night it was, the glass doors thrown back to let a little of the night in, a little of the light out.

'Dr Astley?'

He stumped past her, barely acknowledging the tired eyes, the drawn face of a young woman caught up body and soul in a murder inquiry. 'It's half past eleven,' he said. 'Time all good girls were tucked up safely in bed.'

Fat chance, thought Jacquie; she with still another three hours of her shift to go.

He paused at the door. 'By the way,' he said, 'You've got yourself a murder weapon. Six-inch blade, double edged, not as sharp as it might have been. That surgeon's knife's it, all right. Tell the DCI he'll get my report in the morning – *if* he can bear to wait. And if he can't – tough 'nanas. Good night, constable. Oh, by the way . . . would it be impetuous of me to ask whose knife that is?'

She shouldn't really have told him what she did. 'We have reason to believe,' the words hung on the near-midnight air, 'one Martin Bairstow.'

'Never heard of him,' Astley shrugged. 'But then, I'd never heard of Fred West once upon a time.'

# Chapter Ten

✦

'Well, I hoped you might do the tannoy again, Max,' Roger Garrett, Leighford High's First Deputy, was ever hopeful.

'The Summer Fête Worse than Death?' Maxwell opened one eye, dozing in his corner of the staffroom, relishing his only free period of the day. 'I should cocoa.'

'But it's tradition, Max,' Garrett wheedled. 'Schools are built on it, you know that.'

'Yes, I do,' Maxwell had closed his eyes again, his hands locked over his chest, his feet up on today's copy of the *TES* strewn over the coffee table. 'In fact, *I* told *you*. You realize this will cost you, Roger?'

'Really,' Garrett sighed. He'd fenced with Mad Max before. The old duffer had a riposte like a razor and a flêche to die for. 'Like what?'

Maxwell's eyes were open now, flashing, piercing. 'Like I have to be in Basingstoke by four of the clock. Cover?'

'That's pretty short notice, Max,' the first deputy hedged.

'I'm sure the Headmaster's free,' Maxwell hauled himself to his feet. 'Or perhaps even your good self. By the way,' he scooped up the *TES* and prodded Garrett's chest with it, 'great job in there, page eighty-three. Head of Bollocks in a third-rate comprehensive you've never heard of. Should suit a go-getter like you.' And he winked and dropped the paper into Garrett's hands.

Without Bob Pickering at his elbow, Peter Maxwell took longer to find his quarry this time. First of all he had to cope with the slow one from Leighford Central and was forced to eavesdrop on the sort of conversation only Alan Bennett usually listened to. It didn't help either that Basingstoke was a closed book to him. He'd been there once long ago, when he still had a lean and hungry look. He'd been in search of an eating place – anything would do – in the ghastly town centre and had been so busy looking right and left that he'd collided with a brick pillar; one of those pillars of society you hear about. The next few days were a painful blur as his head swam and his cheek throbbed, but he'd never actually forgiven Basingstoke, he realized, as he plodded the length of the interminable Alençon Link in search of Martin Bairstow.

Against all the odds, the man had a phone according to the Directory in the local library where there were more CDs than books and he lived at 63, Clifton Terrace. Shouldn't be *that* difficult to find. By the time Maxwell reached the Eastrop Roundabout, which was a sort of poor man's Circus Maximus, he'd realized he'd overshot and had had to retrace his steps. Number 63 was an ordinary-enough looking Victorian terrace, quite elegant in its day Maxwell supposed and now subdivided into flats according to the panel of buzzers next to the old brass bell pull. But Maxwell didn't have a chance to get close enough to see which was which. He veered away as, from nowhere, a white patrol car snarled to the curb outside and three uniformed policemen scrambled out, the fourth staying with the vehicle, resting his arm on the car's roof and muttering into a crackling radio intercom.

Maxwell crossed the road as nonchalantly as he could

and merged with the knot of onlookers that was gathering. In minutes the officers re-emerged and in their midst, a full head shorter, Martin Bairstow, his shirt undone, his jeans tatty.

'What's he done?' somebody shouted at Maxwell's elbow.

'Yeah. Leave him alone!' somebody else insisted.

'Bastards!' It was an old lady with a Sainsbury's trolley who was shrieking the loudest.

One of the officers ducked Bairstow's head in the time-honoured way and shovelled him into the vehicle. The car roared off, the man in custody lost in the press of shoulders inside it.

'Poor sod,' muttered one of the bystanders. 'I'm surprised he's not a black bloke.'

Dr John Irving sat in his Cambridge study that night, trying to concentrate, trying to get a grip. His publisher was pestering him again, and he had that New York lecture to give next month. But every time, his mind strayed back to the letter, the one he'd got that morning. In the end he snatched the glasses off his nose and threw them down in the pool of light from his lamp.

He leaned back in the padded swivel chair and rubbed his aching eyes. He slid open the top drawer suddenly and unfolded the paper there, sliding it under the light. Then he picked up the phone and dialled quickly, the number he'd learned by heart.

'Room 34, please,' he said as it answered, tapping the desk with the annoyance of the wait. A voice answered. 'It's me,' he said, as people do when they are the centre of their own little universe. 'I've had another one. What? Yes. This morning. Basingstoke postmark. Oh, it's a beauty,' and he slipped on his glasses again to read the badly cut out letters pasted onto the paper. '"Well, you black bastard. He's not cold and you're shafting his memory. Don't turn your back, nigger." That makes three. Yes. Yes,' he sighed. 'All right,' he listened solemnly, 'Thursday. Where? Yes, I'll find it. Ten o'clock.' And he hung up.

'I know,' DCI Henry Hall was the epitome of patience, 'But I'd like to hear it again. And slower, please, Mr Bairstow – for the tape.'

Martin Bairstow could bluster and hustle his way out there with the best of them. But that was out there, in the hurly burly and the noise, where it was lambrettas and re-enactments and piss-ups with the lads. Now all he heard in Interview Room Two at Leighford Police Station was the tick of Henry Hall's clock and the hum of Henry Hall's tape and the persistence of Henry Hall's voice. In a different light, at a different time he might have fancied Jacquie Carpenter, but in the harsh glare of the Interview Room, she looked blank and unfriendly. And anyway, he knew she was a copper.

'All right,' he sighed, leaning back. He hadn't made his phone call. Why should he? He hadn't done anything.

'What made you come to Leighford?' Hall asked, starting with the basics.

'The ad. The one in the paper. This TV company was asking for extras in this costume thing, re-enacting. Well, I was between jobs, so I thought, why not? A couple of hundred quid, a few pints, a few birds.'

'Any birds in particular?' Jacquie asked.

Bairstow leaned forward. 'You offering?'

Hall snapped off the tape. 'Mr Bairstow,' he said, 'my team and I are tired. We've knocked on a lot of doors, walked a lot of miles, talked to a lot of people. We don't really have time for the macho man image. And I, for one, won't have my officers spoken to like that. Do you own an anorak?'

Bairstow looked at them both. Coppers! 'Yeah,' he said. 'Some sort of crime, is it?'

'What colour is it?' Hall asked.

'Yellow. Why?'

'Would you have any objection if an officer from Basingstoke collected it from your flat?'

'You've gotta have a search warrant for that . . . haven't you?'

'If we don't get your permission, yes,' Hall told him. He flicked on the tape again. 'Let me outline the case against you, Mr Bairstow,' he said. 'There are two people dead. Let's take Miles Needham first. The man was killed with a modern working replica of a flintlock musket.'

'I didn't fire the fucker!' Bairstow blurted.

'Indeed not,' Hall nodded, his eyes invisible behind the lenses of his spectacles, 'but you camped less than three hundred yards from the props caravan where the murder weapon was switched for its harmless equivalent. You were there when the murder took place. You're an experienced re-enactor. Familiar with guns.'

'I didn't do it!' Bairstow spread his arms in exasperation. They never listened, did they? Coppers!

'So you say,' Hall said softly, noting something on his pad. 'So you say.'

'You were a fan of the late Miss Morpeth,' Jacquie took up the reins of the interview as if on cue, looking steadily into the man's eyes.

'Yeah – me and half a million other blokes.'

'We've spoken to others who were with you in the re-enactment,' she said. 'They all confirm it.' She flicked open a sheaf of papers – '"I'd like to get her on her own for five minutes", "Gagging for it, she is", "Over here, darling, I've got what you're looking for".'

'Oh, come on,' Bairstow shouted. 'I never said that.'

'We have witnesses who will swear on oath that you did, Mr Bairstow,' Hall assured him.

'And of course,' Jacquie leaned back, watching her man closely, 'we've got you on video.'

'You what?'

'At the Grand Hotel. A man answering your description was seen entering the foyer less than half an hour before Hannah Morpeth died.'

'Bollocks!' Bairstow shouted, but there was no conviction in his voice. The room seemed to close in on him.

'Tell us about the knife,' Hall said.

'What knife?'

'The replica surgeon's knife, the one from the surgeon's kit you left behind when you left Willow Bay.'

'I've never seen it before.'

Hall looked at Jacquie. 'You know, Mr Bairstow,' he said, 'I am not known by my colleagues as a humorous man, but I almost laughed just then. It was found by your scooter, it's got your fingerprints all over it and you've never seen it before.'

'Oh, the kit, yeah. I seen that,' Bairstow backtracked. 'But it's not mine. And I never handled the knife.'

'Whose is it, then?' Jacquie badgered him. 'The surgeon's kit?'

'I dunno. Eight Counties provided the props, didn't they? Ask them. Look,' he felt the sweat on his forehead, his upper lip, 'Look. Miles Needham. Hannah Morpeth. They were television people, right? That's what all this is about. Something to do with the television. Look,' he wasn't making any headway; he knew that by their faces, 'I only come here for the beer and the birds – *any* birds, not her. Christ, look at me. The likes of Hannah Morpeth, well, she wouldn't look at me twice, I know that. This . . . none of this, has got anything to do with me.'

'You won't mind giving us a blood sample, Mr Bairstow?' Hall asked.

'What? Why?'

'Just routine,' Hall shrugged. 'Elimination. You know.'

'No, no,' Bairstow clamped one hand over the other

in his lap to stop himself from shaking. 'Anything to help.'

'Of course,' Hall turned to switch off the tape, 'at . . .' he checked his watch, 'seven forty-three, interview over.' He flicked another switch on his right and the door opened, with a policeman behind it. 'Constable, Mr Bairstow will be our guest tonight. We'll need to see him again in the morning. See if Dr Astley's available to arrange a blood sample, would you?'

'Right, sir,' the constable said and Bairstow shambled to the door.

'One thing,' Bairstow said before the uniformed man took him away. 'What was he doing there?'

'What was who doing where?' Hall turned to face him.

'That historical adviser bloke. That Maxwell. He was there when your blokes came for me.'

'In Basingstoke?' Hall checked.

'Yeah. What was all that about?'

Hall looked at Jacquie. 'I've no idea, Mr Bairstow,' he said. 'But you may rest assured I'll find out.'

Maxwell strode the furrow out across the sloping fields that slanted to the sea. Across those cloudless skies a generation before, Spitfires and Hurricanes darted silver, outgunning and outmanoeuvring an airforce four times their size. They still found wreckage out on Harland Sands when the tide was low and the sea gave up its secrets. The historian in him thought he heard the snarl of their engines and saw their smoking trails. And the Romantic in him would have liked to have seen Farmer Sparrow's Clydesdales plodding through the plough-lines with their arched necks and feathered feet, proud heads nodding under jingling brass. As it was, all he could see was the clear blue and a 747 like a silver pinhead in the ether; and in the furrows, a clapped out Land-Rover resting at a crazy angle, its door open, its bonnet up.

'Mr Sparrow?' he extended a hand.

George Sparrow was a solid, no-nonsense farmer with the Sussex clay on his boots and the Sussex clay in his blood. His face was flat and the colour of leather, a wild grey beard ringing it. Only his eyes shone clear blue, like the sky. 'Who's that?' he stuck his head out from the uptilted bonnet of the Land-Rover.

'Peter Maxwell, Leighford High.'

Sparrow wiped a grimy hand and gripped Maxwell's. 'Morning,' he grunted.

'What news of Giles?'

'We've got a phone, y'know,' the farmer said. 'You could've rung.'

'Yes, I know,' Maxwell smiled. 'But I wanted to meet you face to face. I called at the farm. Your wife said you'd be out here.'

Sparrow squinted to the field gate. 'You on foot?'

'Bike,' Maxwell said.

'Well, he's all right,' Sparrow said. 'The boy. Well, as all right as you can be in Winchester gaol.'

'Your wife said she hadn't seen him.'

Sparrow turned back to his tinkering. 'I won't let her go. My Susan's not a strong woman, Mr Maxwell. I could see what it was doing to her, going every day to see him in that place. I put a stop to it.'

'They'll have to let him go soon,' Maxwell encouraged.

'They've charged him with murder, Mr Maxwell,' Sparrow said, straightening up. 'Glove Farm isn't what it was. I can't afford the bail.'

'But there's legal aid . . .' Maxwell suggested.

'That's charity.' Sparrow clattered about with spanners, twisting here, wrenching there. 'My family has had some trouble in the last few years, Mr Maxwell, but we don't take charity. Never have, never will.'

'I want to help, Mr Sparrow,' Maxwell looked steadily

at him. 'And I want to know about Tom – the Sparrow who was found drowned back in '77. Was he your brother? Uncle? What?'

'Know anything about engines?' the farmer asked, his face suddenly as black as the Land-Rover.

Maxwell shook his head.

'I thought not,' Sparrow said. 'You take my advice, Mr Maxwell. You keep out of what you don't understand. I wouldn't come up to the school and tell you how to teach the kiddies – any more than you'd come to the farm and tell me about the spring sowing. It's the same with this. Sparrow problem. That's an end to it.'

And it was.

Mrs B. hoovered around Peter Maxwell as he sat marking in his office at Leighford High that afternoon. He could always tell when she'd done that because of the trail of fag ash she left in her wake.

'You poor little bleeder,' she said, 'All that marking. It'll send you blind, y'know. Look at this,' and she held up a condom from the corridor outside, 'French bleeding letters. I dunno. When I was these kids' age, I didn't know what a letter was hardly, let alone a French one. Ain't you got no home to go to?'

Maxwell was used to Mrs B.'s strings of inconsequence. She did for him up at the school and, by mutual arrangement, at home too. Without looking up, he answered her mechanically, 'Yes, I know; good Lord, not used, I hope; didn't you?' He sighed and closed the exercise book, looking at the old girl for the first time. 'Yes, Mrs B., I believe I have.'

There were two old girls in Peter Maxwell's life. One was the chain-smoking cleaner with the heart of gold and the mouth of sewer, Mrs B. The other was Miss Troubridge, of 36 Columbine, a shrewish old duck with just a hint of the actress Mary Merrill about her. Maxwell shouldn't have been surprised to see her, secateurs in hand that afternoon as he swung out of White Surrey's saddle. The secateurs meant only one thing. Maxwell had had a visitor and Miss Troubridge wanted to know more.

'It's that nice policewoman, Mr Maxwell,' she confided so that most of Columbine caught it, snipping ineffectually at her privet. 'The one who's often hanging around. Pretty girl. Light chestnut hair.'

The pretty girl with light chestnut hair was walking across the grass as she said it.

'Ah, she's been waiting for you. How nice. Would you care for a cup of tea, my dear?'

'Thank you, Miss Troubridge,' Maxwell unlocked his front door and shepherded Jacquie Carpenter inside, 'I think I can run to a quick Tetley's. Bye.' And he rested gratefully against the glass. 'Jacquie, I've been trying to reach you.'

'I know, Max,' she said, looking up the stairs. 'Shall we? This is official.'

'Ooh, from the tenth floor, huh?' He broke into his Al Pacino as Serpico, but it was before Jacquie's time and anyway she wasn't, daren't be, in the mood. He led the way up into the lounge, scooping up film mags various as he went. 'Sorry about the mess,' he apologized, 'I hadn't expected the Spanish Inquisition.' But Monty Python was before Jacquie's time too and he let it drop. 'Drink?'

She shook her head. 'I'll come to the point,' she said.

Metternich the cat didn't need to be told. He stretched indolently on the settee, then half raised himself and stared at the detective, his tongue sticking out. In cat years, he was older than either of the humans in the room. In cat years he could remember when detectives wore trench coats and trilby hats and smoked pipes and called villains 'chummie'. Maxwell could too, but then Maxwell had to throw at least a glance in the direction of political correctness; Metternich had no such compunction. He lashed his tail once and left in search of those little hard brown bits that constituted his evening meal.

'Martin Bairstow,' Jacquie said, feeling the seat warm where the cat had been.

'Ah,' Maxwell was pouring himself a Southern Comfort.

'You were there, when he was taken into custody.'

'Was I?'

'Don't do this, Max,' she warned. 'Bairstow identified you.'

He put down the drink and held his wrists out, as though for handcuffs. 'All right,' he said, 'it's a fair cop. By the way,' and he launched into his Jim Carrey as *Ace Ventura*, 'I *was* the second gunman on the grassy knoll.'

She shook her head. Peter Maxwell was the most awkward man she'd ever met. How do you cope with a bloke who's fifty-three going on four?

'What were you doing there?' she asked him.

Maxwell sat down opposite her, staring into her steady, grey eyes. 'Sleuthing,' he said.

'Max,' she shook her head again, 'this isn't a game. Two people are dead.'

'I know that, Jacquie.' He was suddenly as serious as she was. 'That's why I was in Basingstoke.'

'Did you talk to Bairstow?'

'No,' Maxwell leaned back in his chair. 'Your boys got there first. What did you find out?'

'Come off it, Max,' she said. 'You know I can't tell you that.'

'You have in the past,' he reminded her.

'I know.' The response was sharp, sudden, then calmer. 'I know – and I shouldn't have. What . . . what is it about you? I can't . . .'

For a moment he thought she was going to cry, but she held herself in check and sat upright. 'I was sent here by

Chief Inspector Hall. He says that if he finds you've been interfering in the course of this inquiry again, he'll arrest you for obstruction.'

'Why did he send you?'

'What?'

'Why you?' Maxwell crossed one leg nonchalantly over the other. 'Why didn't he send Inspector Watkiss, or come himself?'

'I . . . I don't know.'

'Yes, you do, Jacquie.' He leaned forward suddenly, looking deep into her eyes. 'He sent you because he wants to know what I know. And he thinks I might tell you.'

'What do you know?' she blinked.

Maxwell leaned back again, as aloof as his cat. 'Tiddly squat,' he said, with open hands.

'I don't believe you,' she told him.

'What is it about you police persons?' Maxwell shook his head sadly. 'Is *everybody* guilty until they prove themselves innocent?'

'That's not fair, Max,' she argued.

'No, it isn't,' Maxwell nodded. 'And it's not fair that two people are lying on slabs in morgues and you've got the wrong bloke in the frame for it.'

'What do you propose to do about it?' she asked coldly.

'Whatever you let me do,' he said urgently. 'Look, Jacquie, I'm too long in the tooth to be a Special Constable or to retrain at Bramhill now. I haven't got the computer access and the miles of shoe leather and the forensic capabilities that you people have. All I've got is what they still call at the universities an enquiring mind. Oh, and one other thing – a sense of injustice the size of Jeffrey Archer's bank-balance. I'm not the kind to sit back and read about all this in the Sundays or hear it from Trevor McDonald on *News at Ten*. If the fray is thick, that's where you'll find me.'

'Hall means what he says, Max,' Jacquie warned. 'He'll pull you in.'

'I suppose you realize,' Maxwell's Bugs Bunny was legendary, 'this means war?'

'Why did you want to see Bairstow?'

'Are you asking me as a friend or as a policewoman?' he wanted to know.

'As a policewoman, for Christ's sake. It's what I am.'

'Not a friend?' Maxwell was probing.

'Max,' Jacquie leaned forward, holding both his hands in hers, the tears rimming around her eyes. 'I can't be both. Don't you see that? I . . .' And he stopped her with a kiss. She wasn't ready for it, but her lips opened instinctively, and she felt his hands, strong and warm, on her cheeks. She pulled back quickly, blinking away the tears.

'I went to see Bairstow,' he said softly, 'because I'd already been to see Stapleton and Wood. The picture they painted of him was of a sex maniac. Or at least a potential one. It didn't square with Miles Needham, but opened delicious possibilities for Hannah Morpeth.'

'Max . . .' she was staring at him, trying to understand what had just happened.

'Now it's your turn,' he said. 'You tell me why you wanted to see Bairstow.'

'The murder weapon,' she said. It wasn't her head thinking now, but her heart. There was an iron lump in her throat and she suddenly wanted to be held by this man, not just now, but for ever. This couldn't be happening. She couldn't allow it to happen. But how, she thought, as she gazed into those dark eyes, could she stop it?

'What?' he frowned.

'We have reason to believe,' she used the time-honoured police phraseology, 'that Martin Bairstow owns the knife that killed Hannah Morpeth.'

'Jesus,' he whispered.

'Max . . .'

'Jacquie,' he stood up, pulling her up with him, 'I'm sorry,' he said, 'I shouldn't have done that. Shouldn't have kissed you.'

'No,' she sniffed, the policewoman taking over again from the woman. 'No, I suppose not. I'd better go.'

'Hmm,' he nodded, 'I suppose so. Jacquie . . .' He caught her hand as she turned from him. 'Thanks,' he said.

She felt it all bubbling up again, this stupid schoolgirl well of emotion. She could have screamed, kicked the furniture, thrown things through the plate-glass windows. As it was, she just kissed Maxwell quickly on the cheek and hurried away down the stairs.

Metternich the cat sat on his haunches in Maxwell's kitchen, watching the girl's departure through the open door. *What*, he asked himself, was that all about?

'A knife, Bob.' Maxwell hugged Pickering's tin mug that Wednesday crouching under canvas as the long June day turned gold and purple into the short June night. 'Something about Martin Bairstow and a knife.'

The voltigeur sergeant looked blank for a moment. 'The surgeon's kit,' he said. 'That would have a knife in it, probably two.'

'What surgeon's kit?'

'Bairstow's. He carried it in his gear. Left it behind as a matter of fact when he pulled out. Or at least I assume it was his. Come to think of it, that's how the law got to know about it. That policewoman Carpenter was here the day he left. She got all interested in the kit and took it away with her.'

'Did she now?' Maxwell mused. Jacquie Carpenter hadn't strayed far from his mind since that afternoon. He was too old for this. In the seven ages of man stakes he'd long ago left off sighing like a furnace with woeful ballads.

Maybe there was still something of the soldier about him – certainly he still had a few strange oaths up his sleeve. But essentially he was the embodiment of justice and no one had wiser saws than Mad Max, even if some of his instances weren't all that modern. 'Why would Bairstow have a surgeon's kit? I hadn't got him down for a particularly serious re-enactor.'

'Nor me,' Pickering agreed. 'Still, you meet a pretty rum lot in the war game. I've seen that bloke around again, you know.'

'What bloke?'

'Well, I don't know whether you remember, but a couple of weeks ago, before Needham was killed, there was a bloke hanging around the camp.'

'That's right,' Maxwell clicked. 'Helen McGregor from my sixth form saw him. Some sort of Peeping Tom, wasn't he?'

'Probably,' Pickering said. 'Only she saw him that time, but she told everybody about him at great length. He's harmless enough, I should think. But it's camps like ours that attract them. That and the sea. Chance to see a bit of topless tottie. I'm glad you came along tonight, Mr Maxwell. I'm off home tomorrow.'

'You are?'

'Well, there's no point in staying, really, is there? The law don't seem to be doing much. It's just another summer holiday come to an end.'

'They've arrested Martin Bairstow,' Maxwell told him.

'Have they now?' Pickering drained his cocoa mug. 'And all on account of that knife. Funny, I never had Martin down for the murderous sort. Anyhow, I've got a business to run.' He stood up. 'Mr Maxwell,' he held out his hand, 'It's been great meeting you again.'

'You too, Bob,' Maxwell shook it. 'Here's to the next campaign.'

Pickering laughed. 'I don't think you've finished this one, yet, have you?'

'No, Bob,' Maxwell sighed. 'I don't think I have.'

Thursday morning was Sixth Form Assembly. Nearly a hundred and forty scruffy collections of hormones sat in the hall at Leighford High waiting to catch the pearls of wisdom scattered liberally by their Year Head, Mad Max. He stood before them on that hot, sticky day, reminding them that no matter how glorious the weather, no one was to sunbathe on the fields during private study and that young ladies should on no account expose their midriffs – or any other part of their riffs – lest it enflame the passions of the young gentlemen.

That over, Maxwell resisted the urge to lead them all in community hymn singing and stumped off to his first lesson. On his way he collided with Becky Evans hurtling to Art.

'Morning, Rebecca. No news of Miss McGregor, I take it?'

'None,' she told him as Maxwell took a child by the shoulders and planted it on the correct side of the corridor.

'You know the Headmaster's edict, Liam, as well as I do. Gentlemen dress to the left, especially in the main corridor.'

Liam looked a little sheepish and wandered off to start the rest of his life.

'I'm afraid I chickened out of calling round there,' Becky confessed.

'You were wise,' Maxwell sighed, 'I'll pay her a visit. She's had long enough.'

'What about the EWO?' the Head of Art suggested.

'Endlessly Whingeing Officer?' Maxwell looked dubious. 'Nah. Malcolm's a nice bloke, but he's also the softest touch south of Salisbury. Of course, Education Welfare Officers used to be kid catchers in my day –

but don't get me started on that or we'll be here 'til Christmas.'

He swept regally into Room H4 where a ragbag of intellectuals in Year 8 were whiling away the time flicking soggy bits of paper at each other.

'Strappado!' Maxwell roared. 'A method of torture much favoured by the late, great Monsignor Torquemada – he of the Spanish Inquisition. It consists of being hung up by your thumbs, toes or other extremities from the ceiling. You, Jason, will be my first victim of the morning. Off with your shoes! Now, there's a brave command.' And he fell back from the hapless Jason, gagging uncontrollably.

The eighth version of how Appeasement led to World War Two drove Peter Maxwell into a state of terminal depression. And by the ninth, penned by the almost unreadable Sabrina Marshall, he'd lost the will to live and had fallen asleep. For a moment, he was lost in a dark world of murder, and the ghost of Miles Needham, with shattered head, came wandering along the water's edge to talk to him. He heard the serpentines click back and the muskets thunder. And Hannah Morpeth, riddled with a thousand cuts smiled at him from police photographs he'd never seen. The bell was ringing madly, out of context with his dream. Like Pavlov's dog, he sat bolt upright, reaching for his chalk. Another day. Another lesson.

But it wasn't day. It was nearly one in the morning and the curtain by his open window shivered in the night breezes. And he wasn't at school, that Hell where youth and laughter go. He was at home, the febrile outpourings of futile minds scattered like confetti across his lap.

'All right, all right,' he called to himself. Metternich the cat was out on the prowl, adding more corpses to his terrifying tally as the most prolific serial killer on the south coast. Maxwell shambled downstairs in his stockinged feet, trying to focus on the dark shape distorted by the reeded glass of his front door.

'Bwana!'

'Christ, John,' Maxwell opened the door wide, 'You look as if you've seen a ghost.'

'No.' Irving was trembling, clammy, cold. 'Just a corpse. Can I come in?'

# Chapter Eleven

It was several Southern Comforts later that Peter Maxwell got any rational sense out of John Irving. He talked him through it, step by step, turn by turn. And dawn was already aglow over Leighford's gasworks and the new multi-storey Sainsbury's when Maxwell was ready to recap.

'Right, John.' His old oppo of the Granta days sat with a steaming coffee mug in his hand. Even he, used to the deceptive smoothness of the drink from the banks of the good ol' Mississippi, was beginning to see the world a little cock-eyed. Time to add a little calming caffeine to the equilibrium equation. 'From the top.'

The man didn't look much like a Cambridge don in the early hours, huddled on Maxwell's settee. His shirt looked as if it had been slept in and his jeans were dusty above the boots. 'From the top,' Irving said, running his fingers through the tight, jet curls and closing his eyes. 'I got this letter from Barbara Needham, out of the blue.'

'Addressed to you at college?'

'At Caius, yes. She asked to meet me as a matter of some urgency, tonight. Sorry, last night.'

'Where?'

'A place called the Shingle.'

'Out beyond Willow Bay,' Maxwell nodded. 'It's a headland. Well known trysting place for lovers.'

'Why do you say that?' Irving asked.

'Because it is, John,' Maxwell explained. 'Far enough off the beaten track after dark. Headily romantic, I should think, with the moon over the sea.'

'I wouldn't know,' Irving dismissed it.

'Neither would I. There never was a Mrs Irving, was there?'

The Cambridge man shook his head. 'There never seemed to be the time. Oh, Christ.' He buried his head in his hands.

'Take it easy, old man,' Maxwell said softly, holding his friend's arm. 'We'll get through this.'

Irving looked up at him. '*We*, white man?'

'That's the spirit,' Maxwell laughed. 'All right, so you got the letter. Do you still have it?'

'No. I binned it.'

'Why?'

'I don't know,' Irving flustered. 'Is it important?'

'I'm just putting myself in the place of Mr Plod, John,' Maxwell explained. 'I've had quite a bit of experience one way or another.'

'It won't come to that.'

'John,' Maxwell looked at him. 'A woman is dead.'

'Two women,' Irving reminded him.

'One at a time.' Maxwell held up his hand. 'Take me through last night. You got here how? Car?'

Irving nodded. 'The arrangement was to meet on the Shingle at ten o'clock.'

'Why the Shingle? Why not the hotel?'

'What?'

Maxwell was talking to himself really, but Irving would do as a sounding board. 'Barbara Needham was staying at the Grand. You'd stayed there too.'

'What's the significance?'

Maxwell shrugged. 'Damned if I know,' he said. 'All right, for reasons we can only guess at, she arranged to meet at a local trysting place, after dark, a man she didn't know.'

'She knew me in a way,' Irving said.

'She did?'

Irving nodded. 'When I first met Miles Needham that was almost the first thing he said to me. "My wife's a fan."'

'A fan?' Maxwell blinked. 'You dark horse, John. I had no idea the slave economy of Hispaniola had such pulling power.'

Irving ignored him. 'The name didn't connect at first,' he said. 'I ran an Open University course three years ago. Barbara Needham was on my books.'

'So you'd met her?'

'At the summer camp, probably,' Irving said. 'Though I can't say I remember her. The college was in the throes of all kinds of reorganization that year. My mind was on other things anyway.'

'All right. So she was a fan. But she hadn't seen you for three years, had presumably not been in touch in the meantime?'

Irving shook his head.

'So what did she want? Out of the blue, as you say.'

Irving was still shaking his head. 'The letter didn't say.'

Maxwell took him through it. 'What time did you get to Leighford?'

'Eight. Eight thirty,' Irving remembered. 'I'd stopped at Guildford for a bite to eat.'

'How did you find the Shingle?'

'That street plan thing, the one by the bus station.'

Maxwell knew it and nodded.

'I was too early of course, so I just drove around for a while.'

'How did she get there?' Maxwell mused. 'To the Shingle, I mean.'

'I don't know,' Irving said. 'I didn't see a car.'

'I don't know whether she came in one,' said Maxwell, 'to Leighford, that is. So you found the Shingle?'

'Yes. I drove out past that pub.'

'The Longshoreman.'

Irving nodded.

'Not a bad pint,' Maxwell informed him for the record. 'Crisps are a bit salty though, if you'll excuse the pun.'

'There were cars there,' Irving told him. 'Perhaps one of those was Barbara's.'

'It was dark by now?'

'Near as damn it,' Irving told him. 'I drove to the end of the road. It peters out about half a mile further on.'

'And there's a path that leads to the right.' Maxwell could see it in his mind's eye.

'That's right.'

'It actually forms a loop, but I doubt you'd have seen the left fork, especially in the dark. The land falls away quite sharply.'

'You seem to know the place damn well,' Irving observed.

'Ah, misspent youth,' Maxwell sighed. 'Besides, when you get to my age, a spot of mac opening in front of copulating couples has its attractions.'

Irving ignored him again. 'I couldn't see anyone at first. I took the seaward side of the headland.'

'Willow Bay would have been to your right,' Maxwell was helping the man retain his bearings.

'There was no one there,' Irving's face was a mask of concentration as he tried to focus on the nightmarish details in his head. 'I'd begun to wonder what sort of wild-goose chase I'd come on. Then I saw her . . .'

'John,' Maxwell broke the ensuing silence as softly as he could, 'John, I've got to know.'

Irving looked up at him through his pain, his isolation.

'You came to me, remember?' Maxwell said. There was no going back now.

'It was Barbara all right.'

'Even in the dark, after three years, you knew her?'

Irving nodded. 'It was her. She was lying on her stomach, but her face was turned towards me. I don't know why, but I looked at my watch.'

'What time was it?'

'Ten eighteen. It was almost as if . . . as if she was looking at me with reproach for being late. I didn't . . . see the blood at first.'

'John,' Maxwell's steady voice reached across the man's terror like oil on water, 'are you absolutely sure she was dead?'

'Oh, yes,' Irving muttered. 'I felt her pulse. There wasn't one.'

'John, I have to ask this – was she still warm?'

Irving nodded, shuddering at the same time. 'I don't think she'd been . . . interfered with, but I couldn't really tell. I . . . ran, Max, Bwana. I just ran and left her there . . .'

Maxwell's hand was on his friend's drooping head. 'It's all right, John,' he reassured him. 'Which of us wouldn't have done the same? The police will understand.'

'The police?' Irving's voice was stronger now and he was sitting upright, staring hard at Maxwell. 'You wouldn't go to the police with this, Bwana?'

Maxwell blinked. 'No, John, I wouldn't,' he said. 'But you must.'

'Oh, no.' Irving was on his feet. 'No. Look, Max, I'm grateful to you. I didn't know where else to turn. I panicked, so I came here. But I'm not involved, not in any way.' He was pacing the room like a man possessed. 'Someone else will have found her by morning. It's not my problem. Now I've got to get back home to Cambridge. I'm not involved.'

'John,' Maxwell was on his feet too, gripping the man's shoulders. 'John, you can't just walk away from this. What if you were seen up there on the Shingle? This isn't exactly the black market at midnight. You'll forgive my political incorrectness if I point out that you are a tad conspicuous? At last count, Leighford's ex-Nigerian population was somewhat in the minority.'

'I'll take that chance,' Irving nodded grimly. He put his coffee mug down on Maxwell's table. 'I'm sorry Max,' he said, 'I shouldn't have involved you.'

'Involved is my middle name, John,' Maxwell sighed. 'I'll see you around.'

Quite a crowd had gathered on the Shingle below the fluttering blue and white cordon. Mine host at the Longshoreman, ever an enterprising chap, was doing a roaring trade, dipping in and out of conversations as he pulled pints and microwaved bar food. But the topic in the conversations was all the same. Whose was the body carried into the ambulance at the end of the Shingle road? And how had it got there in the first place?

The man with the answers, but only some of them that Friday morning, stood on the sunlit headland as Peter Maxwell was cycling to school nearly two miles away. Jim Astley was unimpressed by Home Office directives to gown up in white as though for a nuclear explosion and wore his tweed jacket and flat cap. Henry Hall was of course in his suit, the return-of-the-three-piece that marked the new breed of managerial detective they were spawning these days.

'Early days, Henry,' Astley muttered to the man's unspoken question, 'but I'd say a heavy object, probably metal, driven diagonally across the back of the skull.'

'One blow?'

'Maybe two.' Both men watched as the body in question

was zipped up and lifted silently into the waiting ambulance by young coppers who would never get used to doing this. 'She's been dead for about nine, maybe ten hours.'

'Late last night,' Hall gazed out to the turquoise sea. It would be another scorcher, another day of ice-cream and hot dogs and sun-block. Not that he'd see any of that. 'Any sign of sexual assault?'

'Nothing obvious,' Astley said. 'I'll know more by tea-time. You do *have* tea, do you, Henry? And dinner and things?'

'It has been known,' Hall said, straight faced.

'Well,' Astley grunted, fishing for his pipe now that SOCO had done their grass-combing and all the photographs had been taken. 'I haven't had my breakfast yet this morning. Come to think of it, I haven't even had my morning shit. Plays merry hell with my bowels, Henry, murder.' And he crossed to his car. 'Oh, by the way,' he said, 'I don't know why mention of the word shit should remind me, but I meant to tell you next time we met, which is now; that teacher blokey, Maxwell . . .'

'What about him?' Hall asked. Peter Maxwell was just what he didn't need right now.

'He's been poking his nose in again. Buttonholed me the other night at my own bloody hostelry, fishing about Hannah Morpeth's death. Isn't there something you can do about that?'

'There is,' Hall nodded. 'Leave it with me, Jim.'

Astley grunted.

'Love to Marjorie,' the Chief Inspector muttered. He'd only met Dr Astley's wife once and he hadn't, if push came to shove, much enjoyed the experience. But wishing each other's wives compliments had become routine for these men at murder sites and he didn't have to hear Astley's words as he mumbled them over the roar of his ignition. 'My best to Helen.'

* * *

The SOCO boys had excelled themselves. By Astley's much vaunted tea-time, the slides had been processed and were flickering on and off the grubby screen in Tottingleigh Incident Room. Outside, the paparazzi, who had never really gone away, were back in even greater numbers. There would have to be another press conference. The Chief Constable, who was disturbed when Miles Needham died, and gravely worried at the death of Hannah Morpeth, was apoplectic come the end of this gruelling week and the steady rise of the body count to three.

'Public confidence,' he stressed to Henry Hall. That was the key. Without that, everything would fall apart. 'Catch him, Henry,' the Chief Constable had said, 'and do it quickly.'

For the time being however, Henry Hall would ignore all that and confine himself to the matter in hand, briefing his men and women.

'Barbara Jayne Needham, lady and gentlemen,' he had centre stage under the slides of the dead woman lying on the short, windswept grass of the Shingle where the gorse bush roots were home to the rabbits. 'Widow of Miles Needham who needs no introduction here. She was forty-four, living with her husband-as-was near Windsor. For the last fortnight less a day, she'd been staying at the Grand. Paul!'

Paul Garrity took over the limelight. He knew the hotel better than his own house by now. 'Mrs Needham had Room 34 on the fourth floor. She generally dined alone, and was away from the hotel on the nights of the thirteenth, sixteenth and seventeenth. The manager says she left all her things in the room. There was no suggestion she wouldn't be back.'

'And last night, Paul?'

Garrity checked his notes. 'Last night she had dinner at seven thirty. Stayed in the coffee lounge reading until a little after nine.'

'She ate alone?'

'As far as the waiters remember, yes. You've got to remember, everybody, she'd been there for two weeks; becoming a little bit part of the furniture. That makes our job more difficult. Some people had got so used to seeing her around they couldn't tell you whether she was there or not. Other people started talking to her – "good morning", "good evening", pleasantries like that. Any one of them could have been her killer.'

'What time did she leave the hotel?' Hall asked from the corner.

'She must have gone to her room to change. George.'

The carousel operator slid another slide into the frame. 'As you see from this angle of the body, she's wearing a sweater and jeans. The head waiter says she definitely had a burgundy-coloured dress on in the restaurant.'

Dave Watkiss was on his feet. 'We found nearly eight quid in loose change in her pockets. And a wallet containing forty more in notes, plus the normal credit cards in a bum bag. No handbag as such.'

'Can we rule out robbery then, guv?' somebody in the smoke-filled room had to ask the obvious.

'Rule out nothing,' Hall interrupted Watkiss's answer, 'until we have a little bit more. How did she leave the hotel, Paul?'

'Er . . . we assume taxi. We've got blokes out checking the ranks now. Her own car was left in the hotel car park.'

'Why's that, guv?' Jerry Manton wanted to know, trying to find an ashtray in the Incident Room's gloom.

'We don't know,' Hall said. 'Unless she thought her own car was too conspicuous. If she was going to meet someone, as seems likely, she perhaps didn't want the car to be recognized.'

'Dark green Megane, by the way,' Garrity chipped in. 'R reg, all the extras.'

'So, no one actually saw her leave the Grand,' Hall checked.

'No, sir,' Garrity said. 'Taxi information pending.'

'All right. SOCO – Bert?'

Bert Cameron shuffled into Watkiss's position. His feet hadn't touched the ground since seven that morning and he was no longer a young man. 'Body was found by a middle-aged couple out for a bracing walk. A Mr and Mrs . . . Doncaster, here on holiday.'

'Time?' Hall asked him.

'Six thirtyish,' Cameron confirmed.

'Middle-aged couple out at six thirty?' Manton knew a rat when he smelled one.

'Seems kosher,' Watkiss told him, sprawling back in his chair. 'We checked with their hotel. They've been here for nearly two weeks. Due to go home tomorrow. Arranged for a packed breakfast at six every morning. Twitchers.'

'What's that, guv?' Paul Garrity had led a very urban life.

'Bird watchers to you, Detective Sergeant,' Watkiss scowled.

'And to you, Detective Inspector,' Garrity bowed in his chair.

Hall quickly killed the chuckle that rippled round the room. 'The Doncasters found her as you saw in the first slide. Bert?'

'The body was face down,' Cameron went on. 'Clothing not rearranged. Apparently no money or personal effects taken. The problem is that, as most of you will know, the Shingle is a well-known shag-site . . . oh, sorry, Jacquie.'

Detective Constable Carpenter happened to be the only woman in the room at the time. She ignored the guffaws and grimaced at Cameron. Wait till he asked her to change shifts next.

'So that means the place is awash with tyre tracks, footprints, used condoms, the lot. There's more tissue paper up there than I've had hot dinners. Oh, and a rather unusual copy of "Sado" for those of you so inclined. See me afterwards.'

'Thank you, Bert,' Watkiss silenced the hoots and cat calls. 'I cancelled my subscription only last week. So how long will it be before you can isolate anything?'

'Well, Wednesday at the earliest,' Cameron offered.

'Monday night,' Hall corrected him. 'I'll square the overtime upstairs. You'll get all the men you need, but I want answers, Bert. Jacquie, Barbara Needham, the kind of woman she was, who knew her, liked her, hated her.'

'Yes, guv,' the girl said. It was a pattern she'd already established for Hannah Morpeth.

'Right. Eyes open, everybody. Dave, there'll be a press conference tomorrow at ten. I want you there, Paul, you and Jacquie. The rest of you, crack on. I want the link between these three deaths. And I want it fast. We are becoming a laughing stock, lady and gentlemen. The papers will have a field day unless we give them some answers. Jacquie.' He motioned her into his office as the Incident Room started to hum with phone calls and VDUs. The lights came on and the beam of the carousel died in the smoke.

'How did it go with Peter Maxwell?' he asked, when she'd closed the door, standing across the desk from her.

'You know Maxwell,' she hedged.

'Yes,' Hall nodded. 'Unfortunately, I do. And even more unfortunately, so do you.'

'Sir?'

'All right, Jacquie,' he motioned her to sit down. 'Drop the "sir" stuff. Did he get the message?'

'To stay out of the way? I think so.'

'You think so?'

'Perhaps you shouldn't have sent a woman to do a man's job,' she blurted and sat there shaking, instantly regretting it.

For a moment she thought she saw a flicker of a smile play around Hall's lips, but it must have been a trick of the light. Hall didn't do smiles. 'I didn't think I'd hear that sort of comment at this end of the 'nineties, Jacquie, and from you of all people. From equal opportunities to ball-buster. Isn't that it?'

'Perhaps . . .' She was in for a penny, she might as well go for the whole pound. 'Perhaps I'm not who you think I am, sir,' she said.

Hall leaned forward, clasping his hands on the desk. 'What's important, Jacquie, is who *you* think you are. Are you a copper or are you a woman?'

It was a question she'd asked herself countless times, especially when it had to do with Peter Maxwell. But it wasn't a question she'd ever expected to hear from the guv'nor; not from the DCI. 'Can't I be both?' she asked.

'Jacquie, Jacquie,' he leaned back, sighing. It had been another long, bad Friday. 'That's a question only you can answer.'

Patronizing bastard, Jacquie snarled inside, mentally promising herself that if he called her 'my dear' she'd push his lap-top up his arse. Seven years on the force had taught her directness like that.

'What does he know?' Hall asked, changing tack. His team's welfare was his concern too, but at the moment, he had three murders to solve.

'"Tiddly" and I quote, "squat".'

'And you believe him?'

She looked at the blank lenses, with no eyes behind them. And she hated Henry Hall at that moment for his facelessness. 'No, sir, I don't. He was outside Martin Bairstow's house because of something Wood and Stapleton had told him.'

'Who?'

'The first two re-enactors to leave. They went home to Brighton after Miles Needham was killed.'

'Ah, yes. They were in the clear, weren't they?'

'Nothing to hold them for, sir,' she said.

'But Maxwell thought otherwise.'

'Apparently.'

'How did he find them, Jacquie?' Hall had to ask.

He saw the girl's jaw flexing as she summoned up an answer. 'Not from me, Chief Inspector.'

Hall nodded, searching the girl's face, weighing her loyalty. 'Good,' he said. 'I'm glad to hear it. Maxwell's been bothering Dr Astley,' he went on. 'Shall we pick him up?'

'I don't know when he "bothered" Dr Astley, sir. Was it since I warned him off?'

'No,' said Hall, sensing a shift in the girl's stance. 'No, I don't believe so.'

'Then we should leave him well alone, sir. At least, that would be my advice.'

'Would it now?' Hall had placed his fingers together and patted his thumbs slowly as he spoke. 'Well, that may be sound enough advice, Jacquie, for now. That will be all, thank you.'

Interview over. Hook off. She scraped back her chair. At the door he stopped her.

'Jacquie,' he said with an edge in his voice he didn't usually let people hear. 'Just what *is* your relationship with Peter Maxwell?'

He watched her tense, her knuckles whiten, her neck mottle under the white blouse. 'I don't have a relationship with Peter Maxwell, sir,' she said, her eye clear, her head high.

'Barbara Needham,' the DCI said. 'That's the only relationship I want you to have at the moment, Jacquie. Clear?'

'As a bell, sir,' and she left him to the ringing phones and the pestering world.

All that was left of Barbara Jayne Needham lay on the slab

in Jim Astley's mortuary. The good doctor had let Henry Hall down a bit, it had to be admitted. His promised time had come and gone – Astley had grabbed what was billed as an apple Danish in the Cafeteria-from-Hell upstairs – and was back to the matter in hand thereafter. He spoke into the microphone suspended from the ceiling, the dead woman reflected like terrible twins in his glasses.

'No evidence of assault from the front,' he was saying as assistants came and went in green gowns and varying levels of professionalism. 'Crushed right cheekbone caused, almost certainly, by being hit from behind when the cheek was in contact with the ground.' The dead woman's face was a mask of bruises, her right eye bulging grotesquely out of its socket with the impact of the trauma around it. Astley travelled to her feet. 'One broken toe nail, big toe, left foot, caused I would think again, by the fall.' He looked along the curve of her thighs. 'Lividity very apparent,' he said in his post-mortem monotone, 'in consequence of the corpse having lain on its front for some hours. No apparent bruising to thighs, abdomen or genitals. No sign of sexual assault. No presence of semen,' he probed with no apology to the dead woman, 'internally. Turn her over, Joe, will you?'

Astley sneezed violently to one side of the table while Joe was doing the honours. 'Christ, I've been longing to do that.'

They'd already shaved off Barbara Needham's thick black hair and from the back, were it not for the damage to the skull, she looked like a mannequin with its sightless eyes and deathly pallor, that some shop assistant had laid aside ready to dress for the window. Barbara Needham, who would never buy a dress or have a window in her day again.

'Cause of death,' Astley was back at the microphone again, 'one severe blow to the parietal region of the skull. A hole,' he fumbled with his folding ruler, 'three point eight centimetres across the mid line. We've got cracks radiating out under the skin here,' he felt deftly with his gloved fingers, 'I'll confirm that later when we start cutting. Murder weapon is an object approximately fifteen or sixteen centimetres long, perhaps seven centimetres wide. Microscopy may give us something on that later. Will somebody answer that bloody phone?'

Someone did. 'It's Mr Hall, doctor,' a voice called through from Astley's office.

'Later!' Astley bellowed. 'Tell him I'll call him with news, not speculation.'

Henry Hall had caught Jim Astley at bad moments before. That would have to be good enough for now.

'I think he's still here, sir,' the girl on the Leighford police station switchboard said.

'Good,' Astley grunted, 'because I am.' It was half past eleven by his lab clock and the eleven fourteen to Hove was rattling past outside, its lights flaring, its seats empty. Jim Astley watched it go, through the slatted blinds. He couldn't remember when he'd caught a bus last.

'Hall,' a voice crackled over the line.

'Henry, it's Jim Astley.'

'Jim, good of you to ring.'

'I'm sorry for the hour. Do you want the rudiments?'

'I got savaged today, Jim,' the DCI confessed. 'First the Chief Constable, then the Press. I could do with a bloody miracle, to be frank.'

'Your lady died as near as I can ascertain at shortly after ten last night. Cause of death was a single blow to the back of the head. A heavy brass instrument.'

'Brass?' Hall frowned. 'What? A candlestick?' It was beginning to sound as though Colonel Mustard was in the frame after all, but on the Shingle, not in the library.

'Not my province, I'm afraid.' Astley knew a buck when he passed one. 'No sexual assault. It's my guess – and for all it's educated, it *is* a guess – that she was running away from her attacker – probably broke a toe nail as she tumbled – and wallop! Goodbye, Dolly Gray. Massive trauma to the brain of course. Neck muscles shot to hell. I'm not sure she'd have known very much about it.'

'Well, thanks, Jim. I appreciate that. Maybe it'll be some sort of comfort to whatever family she's got.'

'There's one more thing, Henry,' the DCI heard the doctor say. 'How old was Barbara Needham?'

'Forty-four according to our records. Why?'

'That's what I'd have put her at by the state of the body. We found something else. She was four and a half months pregnant.'

Silence.

'Henry?'

'Was she?'

'I don't suppose it would have shown. Small for a foetus of that age – and what with expensive designer clothes . . .'

'So it's a double murder,' Hall said grimly.

'Yes,' Astley had to agree. 'Technically, I suppose it is.'

'Can you do tests?'

'What, on the foetus?'

'Yes. Is that possible?'

'Yes. Poor little bugger had his own blood supply. What are we looking for? Paternity?'

'That's about the size of it, Jim,' Hall said. 'You see, I have reason to believe that Mr and Mrs Needham hadn't shared a marital bed for some time. Certainly not for the last four and a half months. It could give me a motive.'

'Yes, I see. Look, Henry, can this wait till morning? It's been a bugger of a day. Much longer in this bloody lab and I'll turn into a pumpkin.'

'Yes, of course, Jim. Tomorrow will be fine.' And the doctor hung up.

Tomorrow would be Sunday. Eighteen days since the murder of Miles Needham, fifteen since that of Hannah Morpeth. Henry Hall leaned back in his chair and tilted his glasses onto his forehead, just to prove to the contemptuous world that he had eyes after all behind those blank lenses. He picked up the little book of numbers and addresses, the one that Paul Garrity had found next to Barbara Needham's bedside at the Grand. He flicked it open to the letter 'I' and read the only name in it he recognized – 'John Irving, Caius College, Cambridge' and the number underneath. On a whim, he flicked to the 'M's. Damn, he found himself smiling, alone where no one could see in the dim light of the silent Incident Room. No Peter Maxwell. Well, never mind. Perhaps there'd be better luck next time.

# Chapter Twelve

Not for the first time in her seven years on the Force, Jacquie Carpenter found herself trying to put together the pieces of a person's life. Barbara Jayne Needham had come into the world on 4 August 1954. If she'd been the type to buy one of those copies of newspapers of the day she was born, she'd have known that Britain's first supersonic fighter, the 'Lightning' was screaming through the skies as she was screaming through the maternity unit at Harpenden Hospital. More relevantly to her future husband's calling, the Independent Television Authority was set up that afternoon under the chairmanship of Sir Kenneth Clarke.

Barbara Robinson as she was then wasn't exactly to the manor born, but the family had a bob or two. An only child, she went to an expensive London girls' school before becoming somebody's PA in advertising. She acquired a taste for fast men and fast promotion and seemed to get both with equal ease. She'd known Miles Needham for years before they married. In fact, they had a relationship of sorts, Barbara's mother told Jacquie, when Barbara was still at school. The Robinsons had a house near Bournemouth and Miles was a local boy.

'Bit of a ruffian, dear, in those days,' the old girl confided.

Jacquie had gone with the usual trepidation, to tell a mother that her daughter was dead. But Alice Robinson was of the old school. She'd never cried in front of servants as a child because she'd been told not to; she never cried in front of policemen; she didn't intend to start now. Time enough for that later.

Jacquie sat in the vast drawing-room of the Harpenden house where the Hertfordshire CID had directed her, aware of her heels clicking on the polished parquet whenever she moved. A ghastly ormolu clock struck the hour as the dead woman's mother came to terms with Jacquie's news.

'To be honest, I never really liked Miles. When Babs rang me to tell me he was dead, it was as though he was just a celebrity rather than my son-in-law. I felt the loss of dear old Frank Sinatra more keenly. Drinky, dear? Or don't you on duty?'

Jacquie smiled and declined, and the old girl tottered across to the tantalus. 'Oh dear,' she said, glancing up at the portrait over the Adam fireplace. 'I don't know what Ernest would have made of all this. You don't expect your children to go first, do you? Do you have children, my dear?'

'Er . . . no,' Jacquie told her, suddenly feeling very awkward in that huge chair in that vast room, staring out of the French windows and the endless grounds that stretched away into the summer sunshine. For all it was June it was strangely cold in that drawing-room with the old woman and her memories.

'Babs couldn't bear him, of course, latterly, I mean.'

'Who?' Jacquie had lost the thread of this conversation.

'Miles, dear.' Alice Robinson thought perhaps she'd better go more slowly. She'd never had much faith in the police ever since they lost that rotter, Lord Lucan. 'Her husband. The fire had gone, I think.'

'Mrs Robinson,' Jacquie had to broach it sooner or later, 'did you know that Barbara was pregnant?'

The old girl spun from the fireplace and sat down quickly, staring at Jacquie as if she were an alien entity.

'Obviously not,' Jacquie answered her own question. 'Is it possible . . . could the baby have been Miles's?'

The old girl sat upright like the dowager she was. 'My former son-in-law deposited his seed quite liberally, WPC, but never, since their honeymoon, where it was supposed to go. Are you absolutely sure of this?'

'Yes, Mrs Robinson,' Jacquie said. 'About four and a half months.'

Mrs Robinson frowned. 'Now I wonder whose child it was,' she muttered.

'We are carrying out tests,' Jacquie offered, 'but it's a long shot. There's no one you know . . . no one Barbara spoke of in her life at the minute?'

'Barbara and I were never all that close, my dear,' the old lady said through her rouge and lipstick. 'We talked on the telephone each week, but neither of us had anything to say. It sometimes happens that way with children. I hope you never find out.'

'Mrs Robinson,' Jacquie found herself fidgeting in the high-backed chair, 'as a couple, can you think of anyone who would want to see them both dead?'

'He was a noxious individual,' Alice remembered. 'From day one I warned Babs not to get involved. There was some trouble when she was in her early twenties. She rented the Bournemouth house from us then and we were staying there too. Miles would have been a little older. I remember the police calling. I don't remember the details now, something to do with the disappearance of a derelict, I believe. But I do remember a kindly old uniformed sergeant advising Babs to stay away from Miles. And of course for several years, she did. What she saw in him, I can't imagine. But as for her . . . Well, what mother doesn't imagine her goose is a swan, my dear? Babs had her faults. She was selfish, vain, rather headstrong and wilful – all that from her father of course, and I suppose that might have made enemies. But enough to kill her? No, I can't believe that. Tell me, my dear, when will I be able to have her back, her body, I mean? I would like to pay my last respects.'

Peter Maxwell leaned on the doorbell at the Larches. He seemed to have been leaning that way for ever when a small, solid-looking woman answered the door.

'You must be Helen's gran,' Maxwell raised his hat.

'That's right. Who are you?'

'Peter Maxwell, Head of the Sixth Form at Leighford High.'

She tried to slam the door in his face, but Maxwell was faster and jammed his foot in the way. 'Mrs Hetherington, we haven't seen Helen at school for nearly three weeks now. I'd like to talk to her.'

'She ain't here,' the woman snapped, infinitely more decisive face to face than she had been on the phone. Where was the tapioca woman now? 'Now, let go of this door or I'll call the police.'

'Gran!' a female voice called from upstairs. 'Who is it, Gran?'

'It's that Maxwell,' the old woman shrieked back into the hall. 'From up at the school.'

There was a slam from the bedroom door.

'There!' Mrs Hetherington said firmly. 'Now look what you've done. You've upset her now.'

'I'm sorry, Mrs Hetherington,' Maxwell said. 'That was not my intention. I just need to know why Helen isn't coming to school any more. If it's Giles Sparrow, I understand that she'd be upset . . .'

'Giles Sparrow?' the old woman trilled. 'What's he got to do with it? Bloody Sparrows everywhere! He's a bloody murderer. His uncle was a queer and killed hisself – which is the best thing to do if you're queer. My Helen's just going through a rough time that's all. She's under the doctor.'

'She's missing a lot of work, Mrs Hetherington,' Maxwell told her. 'I had some sent round, but it's not the same.'

'She's not well enough for that. I've told you, she's under the doctor,' and she kicked Maxwell's foot out of the way before slamming the door. 'Now, you go away before I call the police,' he heard her muffled voice from inside the hall.

Peter Maxwell knew when he faced his Waterloo. He'd fought wild women before – and men; shrieking parents who knew their rights and defended their demon offspring to the death. In his halcyon days, when W.E. Forster had passed the first ever Education Act and men walked in front of steam cars with scarlet flags, he'd have gone head to toe with Mrs Hetherington *and* the police officers she'd summon and come out on top. But Peter Maxwell was in the Autumn of his days. Oh, he was still 'battling Maxie' and mad as a March hare, but in life's battles now, he chose his own ground and kept his powder dry. This was a day for discretion. Time enough for valour later. He looked up to the bedroom window as he swung White Surrey away from the Hetherington fence. Helen McGregor looked down on him from behind the twitching nets. Four hundred years ago she'd have been sticking pins into a wax puppet of Peter Maxwell. But they were different days. She let two fingers in the air suffice.

'I've got two words to say to you, Chief Inspector Hall,' Jim Astley was on the phone in his lab, looking for somewhere to tap out the contents of his pipe. The recent Home Office directive on good laboratory practice would do.

'And they are?' Henry Hall was all ears.

'Haemoglobin S.'

'Sorry?'

Jim Astley liked to be smug. It was one reason why he'd chosen medicine as a career in the first place – you could use the long words and blind your fellow man with science.

'I won't bore you with the small print,' he chortled. 'The years of dedication, sleight of hand and enormity of brain power required for the tests I carried out this morning. Suffice it to say that I checked Barbara Needham's baby as per your request . . .'

'And?'

'It turns out the father is black or at the very least half caste.

'What?'

'Now, I realize this is not a crime,' Astley went on, 'at least not in West Sussex, but if you *are* looking for a motive, well, even in these politically correct days . . .'

'Can you be more specific?' Hall wanted to know.

He was lucky it was only Astley's eyes that rolled towards the ceiling and not the top of his head. 'Do you mean can I tell you the man's brand of aftershave and where he buys his Y-fronts, no, pardon me all to Hell, I can't. Contrary to what you may have been taught in the police academy, all that Sherlock Holmes stuff is bollocks. But I can tell you he is African. First or second generation, I'd say. Well, there it is; take it or leave it.'

'Oh, I'll take it, doctor,' Hall said. 'And thanks – I owe you one.'

The Chief Inspector flicked his intercom, ferreting in his desk drawer for his sandwiches and flask. 'Janet,' he said, 'get me Cambridge CID will you? And have a squad car standing by. I'm not sure the Chief Constable will wear me commandeering a plane in these stringent times.'

Lieutenant Henry Fitzhardinge Berkeley Maxse was coming on a treat. Maxwell sat in his lamp-lit garret that night crossing his eyes as he applied the very tip of his paint brush to the man's blue and gold pill box cap.

'Whaddya think, Count?' he asked the cat, 'Moustache, of course. De rigeur. Nobody would be seen dead in the Crimea without a moustache – and that included Mrs Duberley. Full dundrearies? Or is that over the top?'

He was still deciding what sort of facial hair to give his 54-millimetre soldier, sitting nonchalantly astride his roan when the phone rang.

'Bugger and shit!' Maxwell jerked the paintbrush away just in time before Maxse's entire head turned gold. He rammed the brush horizontally in his teeth and picked up the phone.

Metternich looked at him with utter contempt. What *was* this love affair with plastic? At least picking it up stopped that bloody noise.

'War Office,' Maxwell slurred over the wood between his molars.

'Max?'

'Who's that?'

'It's me, Bwana.'

'John!' Maxwell whipped out the brush and left a golden line across his cheek. 'How are you? Where are you?'

'Leighford Police Station.'

'What? Ah, so you talked to them after all.'

'Not exactly, Max. They talked to me. Listen, I need your help.'

'Go on.'

'Well, you know I'm allowed one phone call.'

'Yes,' Maxwell drew the word out. He somehow knew what was coming next.

'Well, you're it. You're my phone call.'

'Right. Give me your solicitor's number.'

'No.'

'What?'

'I don't want my solicitor, Max, Bwana. I want you.'

'Well, you're a funny age, John, me ol' Uncle Tom, but seriously . . .'

'Max,' the Head of Sixth Form could hardly miss the change of tone. 'This is me being serious. I've never been so serious in my life. I'm in a hole, Bwana. I need your help.'

'Mr Maxwell?' a different voice hummed along the wires.

'Who's this?'

'Inspector Watkiss. I'm on the other line.'

'Should you be eavesdropping on a private call?' Maxwell asked.

'There's nothing private that comes out of a police station, Mr Maxwell,' Watkiss told him. 'Especially in a murder inquiry. I have to caution you that Dr Irving's request is highly unusual. I assume you have no legal training?'

'I watch *Kavanagh QC*,' Maxwell said, straight-faced.

There was a brief silence. 'If you think this is some sort of game, Mr Maxwell . . .'

'Never played games if I could avoid it,' Maxwell said, hauling off the Crimean forage cap he always wore when painting to give him that sense of camaraderie with his plastic men. 'It was always more fun thinking up scams to get out of it.'

'Would you like a squad car, sir?' Watkiss sounded tired, unprepared to waste any more of his time.

'Thank you, no. I can do Leighford nick in fourteen minutes flat with a tail wind. And don't worry, Inspector – my vehicle does have lights and an anti-theft device; so do sleep well – don't have nightmares.' And he hung up, leaving Dave Watkiss wondering just how many books he could throw at the man when he arrived.

'Well, Count.' Maxwell switched off the lights and put lids on paint tins, not always in that order. 'I fear our swarthy friend has put his great size tens into it this time.' He paused while stuffing his trouser-bottoms into his socks, 'Did I or did I not urge him to give himself up only the other day?'

Metternich said nothing, but then he was like that.

'You know perfectly well I did,' Maxwell was looking for his keys, 'But not him as would. Oh, dear, no.' He found them under a copy of *Everyman His Own Jehovah's Witness* a strange caller had pushed through his letterbox the day before. He looked at the cat. 'I don't suppose *you'd* care to accompany me to the station, would you?'

Metternich's head sunk sullenly into his shoulders, his ears flat, his eyes closed.

'No, I thought not,' Maxwell murmured.

Detective Inspector Dave Watkiss was probably late thirties. He had a long, unfashionable face topped by an unfashionable fringe and because someone once told him he looked not unlike Jeremy Paxman, he'd grown a moustache to reduce the possibility. Well, it was that or plastic surgery. The other man, Maxwell didn't know, but he was glad in a way that it wasn't Jacquie Carpenter. He didn't need distractions tonight, of all nights.

'Interview commencing at . . . eleven thirteen. DI Watkiss, DC Firth in the presence of Dr John Irving and . . . Mr Peter Maxwell. Mr Maxwell, for the record, is not a solicitor and is here merely at the request of Dr Irving, said Dr Irving having been advised against this. Is that correct, Dr Irving?'

The coloured man nodded. They sat in Interview Room Number Two at Leighford Police Station, as bleak and forbidding a place as a guilty man could wish for.

'You have to speak, sir,' Watkiss said with what little patience he had left. 'Even equipment this sophisticated doesn't pick up a nod, I'm afraid.'

'Er . . . sorry.' Irving cleared his throat. 'Yes, that is correct.'

'You are John William Irving of 124, St Neot's Rd, Cambridge?'

'Yes,' Irving answered.

'And you are a lecturer in history at Caius College, Cambridge?'

'That's pronounced "Keys", Inspector,' Maxwell interrupted. 'For the record.' And he winked at his man.

'For the record, Mr Maxwell,' Watkiss leaned forward with as much menace as the whirring spools would allow him, 'This interview is to be conducted along strict procedural lines. You may not interrupt unless on a point of legality. And since you don't know any points of legality, I suggest you shut up. Okay?'

Maxwell beamed at him in silence, pleading the Fifth.

'What was your relationship with the late Mrs Barbara Needham?' Watkiss asked Irving. Firth was lolling back in shirt and tie. A young man with a bland face and blond hair, he could have been one of those children from the Village of the Damned. Maxwell knew the type – he'd been teaching them for years.

'I don't have a relationship with Mrs Needham,' Irving said.

'Really?' Watkiss's eyes narrowed and his nose became even more hawklike. 'Then how do you explain your phone number being in her phone book?'

'I can't,' Irving shrugged, staring ahead at Watkiss, not daring to turn to Maxwell, who watched his old mucker with a growing sense of unease.

'And how do you account for the fact that Mrs Needham made . . . four calls to . . . Keys . . . college in the last week of her life?'

'Once again,' Irving blustered, 'I am at a loss . . .'

'When we picked you up this lunch time, Dr Irving, your college secretary, Mrs Maguire? . . .'

'Yes,' Irving cleared his throat, dry and tight as it was.

'Yes,' Watkiss smiled, 'she was very helpful. She'd taken two of the calls. Apparently, you wouldn't speak to Mrs Needham at first.'

'That's almost certainly because I didn't know who she was.'

'But then you relented,' Watkiss said. 'Calls three and four you accepted. Though to be fair, Mrs Maguire was only able to tell us about call three. Call four came through direct after hours when she'd gone home. Give us those figures again, Roger, will you?'

DC Firth slid his note pad into the pool of light over the blank table top. 'Call three lasted four minutes, seven seconds,' he said. 'Call four two minutes eighteen seconds.'

'Wonderful service, British Telecom, isn't it?' Watkiss beamed. Then the smile vanished and his face darkened. 'Would you like to revise your previous statement, sir, in the light of all this? What *was* your relationship with Mrs Barbara Needham?'

Irving felt all eyes on him, boring into his soul. 'There was no relationship,' he insisted. 'She rang me a few times, that was all.'

'I see,' Watkiss leaned back, hands clasped across his shirt. 'Do you mind telling me why?'

'She wanted to enrol on a Cambridge summer course that I run.'

'Really?' This came as a surprise to DI Watkiss and still more of a surprise to Peter Maxwell. 'Is this at Keys?' Watkiss stressed the word each time for Maxwell's benefit.

'Yes, that's right. It's on the slave trade. Or at least she thought it was. Actually she got her dates wrong. It was at Easter.'

'Didn't you tell her that in her first call?' Watkiss asked, 'That she'd missed the boat, as it were?'

'Of course.'

'Persistent, was she?' Firth asked. He'd picked up the wheedling I'm-going-to-get-right-up-your-nose tone from his DI.

'Clearly,' Irving responded.

'Tell me, Dr Irving.' Watkiss cut in. 'What sort of car do you drive?'

'An Audi. Why?'

'Colour?'

'Silver.'

'Ah,' Watkiss took his time checking the notes in front of him. 'There was a silver Audi parked outside the Longshoreman pub on the night Mrs Needham was killed.'

Something in Dave Watkiss's tone didn't sit right with Peter Maxwell. He'd been lied to by a lot of people at the Chalk Face in his quarter of a century in the business, most of them his teaching colleagues and many of them far more consummate than DI Watkiss. 'That's not quite true, Inspector, is it?' he asked disingenuously.

The look on Watkiss's face said it all, and he dropped that particular line of inquiry. 'How well did you know Miles Needham?' he rattled the question at Irving.

'Hardly at all,' the Cambridge man told him. 'We met a few months ago in London. I suppose we had three or four meetings to discuss the script of *The Captain's Fancy*. I wouldn't say I knew him well at all, really.'

'And Barbara Needham wasn't present at any of these meetings?'

'No, of course not. They were purely business. I wouldn't expect the man to bring his wife.'

'Who was there?'

'I'm sorry?' Irving had not exactly slept for a while. The whole nightmare was exploding again and again whenever he shut his eyes. So he preferred not to shut his eyes.

'Those production meetings or whatever you call them. Who was there?'

'Well, Miles of course. Angela Badham, his PA. There was a bigwig or two at the first one – I'm sorry, I don't remember their names. Oh, at the last two was Erika Marriner.'

'Who's she?' Watkiss asked.

'The writer.'

'Got on with her, did you?' the Inspector probed, every avenue worth a wander.

'She's mad as a snake, Inspector,' Maxwell couldn't help himself.

'Dr Irving?' Watkiss continued to focus on his man.

'She's a little . . . eccentric, yes. She didn't like what Miles and I had done to her baby.'

'Baby, Dr Irving?' Watkiss had a strange look in his eyes.

'Her creation. *The Captain's Fancy*. I was brought in to add some gravitas, I suppose. Mr Maxwell here was brought in because I realized I needed help on the battle scenes.'

Watkiss and Firth shot sideways glances to the man of war to their right.

'Tell me,' Watkiss changed tack. 'How well did you know Hannah Morpeth?'

'I didn't,' Irving shrugged. 'I met her on the set, of course. She seemed charming.'

'Make a pass at her, did you?' Watkiss's barbs were all the sharper for being unexpected.

'Certainly not,' Irving insisted.

'No, I suppose she was a little young for you.' Watkiss was fishing. 'And a little unattached. You like 'em married, don't you, Doctor? Somebody else's wife? That's what they call race memory, isn't it?'

Maxwell slammed the desk with the flat of his hand.

'That was an interjection by Mr Maxwell,' Watkiss said calmly, 'timed at . . . eleven twenty-one. I withdraw the slur, if that's what it was. Do you know the Shingle, Dr Irving?'

'No. The constables who brought me from Cambridge told me it's where Mrs Needham's body was found. And I do read the papers. But know it? No, I don't.' Irving was looking resolutely at Watkiss again, anything rather than meet the gaze of his old oppo sitting beside him.

'Do you have any idea what Mrs Needham would be doing up on the Shingle late at night?'

Irving shrugged. 'Taking a walk? As I say, Inspector, I don't know the woman. I can hardly account for her movements.'

'And where did you say you were, sir,' Firth threw in his six pen'orth, 'the night before last?'

'At home, in Cambridge.'

'You live alone?'

'Yes. I have a housekeeper, but Thursday is her night off.'

'Now, how did I guess it would be?' Watkiss asked, wide-eyed.

For a moment all four men sat in silence, then Maxwell broke it. 'Will that be all, gentlemen?' he asked. 'We could make up a four at bridge if you like.'

Watkiss snapped off the tape-recorder. 'I'll rearrange your fucking face for you one of these days, Maxwell,' he growled.

Maxwell forced his fingers up so that the microphone was activated again. 'The blip you just heard, timed at . . . eleven thirty-two . . . was Detective Inspector Watkiss offering to rearrange my face. I won't embarrass the Bench with the Saxon adjective that punctuated his kind offer.'

Watkiss was on his feet, the colour drained from his face completely. 'Inspector Watkiss is standing up,' Maxwell said calmly, 'in a most threatening manner at . . . eleven thirty-three.'

The tug from Firth on Watkiss's sleeve broke the flood of red mist that was threatening to engulf the Detective

Inspector. Somehow he controlled himself and sat down, clearing his throat, loosening his collar. It had been a long, hot day and nobody's temper was over-long.

'Did you know,' Watkiss had found his composure again, 'that Barbara Needham was pregnant?'

Irving and Maxwell looked at him. Watkiss leaned forward, his nose inches from the coloured man's. 'And did you know,' his teeth were clenched, 'that the foetus we found in her battered body was that of a black man?'

There was no doubt about it. The long arm of the law didn't want to let John Irving go. But Maxwell gave sureties. Irving didn't have his car; he'd been brought south by the courtesy and petrol of the West Sussex CID. He wasn't carrying his passport either and he promised to stay at Peter Maxwell's that night and the Grand from then on, because DI Watkiss felt pretty sure they'd want to talk to him again. A spotty police driver took them to Columbine at an hour of the morning when even the all-seeing, all-sneering Miss Troubridge had hung up her trusty secateurs and gone to bed.

In the lamplight of his lounge, Maxwell checked through the slats of the blinds. Yes, there was an unmarked car down the road, a way back from the houses. There'd probably be another one, funds permitting, though he couldn't see it from the house, at the back, where his garden abutted the allotments and the corner of the park.

'What's this, for God's sake?' Irving's eyes widened at the size of the Southern Comfort Maxwell had poured for him.

'It's a tongue loosener,' Maxwell was gazing fiercely into his friend's eyes. 'Now it's that or the thumb screws or I knock seven kinds of shit out of you, John, but before dawn through yonder window breaks, I want the bloody truth out of you. All of it.' He was shouting now, throwing himself down on the settee. 'I sat in that stinking police interview room with Attila the Hun and Genghis Khan and listened to you lie through every orifice you've got. Now *this* time, *this* time,' and he skewered the air with his index finger, 'I kept shtumm. But you're a whisker, Johnnie my boy, from me picking up the phone and telling Inspector Watkiss you didn't really mean it. Now,' he subsided, his point made, 'do I get some answers?'

John Irving had never been on the receiving end of a full barrage from Mad Max before. The walls were still reverberating and beyond them, Miss Troubridge had not only woken up, but was rummaging about in the kitchen, looking for a suitable tumbler to place between her ear and Maxwell's adjoining wall.

'All right, Bwana.' Irving's sophisticated tones were all the more dulcet in comparison with the maelstrom that had gone before. 'I owe you that, at least.'

Maxwell was sitting comfortably. And John Irving began.

# Chapter Thirteen

'Babs Needham and I met three years ago,' John Irving said, 'at the Open University summer school I told you about. I said I didn't remember her – well, that was a lie. We went out a few times. She was bright, vivacious. We fell in love that summer. Stayed in love, I suppose until . . .'

'Until?' Maxwell didn't want to miss any of this. Like the Light Brigade assembling in his loft, Peter Maxwell had policemen to right of him, policemen to left of him. And a third had been practically up his nose all night.

'She changed, Bwana. People do, don't they? I didn't know why it was. She had her own life, separate from Miles, I mean. Oh, they appeared the loving couple on BAFTA and charity nights, but they hardly saw each other apart from that.'

'She rang you?'

'Yes. That was another thing. She'd stopped being discreet. It was easy for her to come to Cambridge. There's a little motel I know nearby. Like you, Max, I've been a bachelor too long. You've got a cleaner, neighbours – how much do they miss, huh? Believe me, there's nothing snoopier than a Cambridge college – but I don't have to tell you.'

'No, you don't,' Maxwell remembered.

'Sometimes I'd go to her place in Berkshire. Whenever Miles was away filming and I had a few days . . . er . . . research.'

'And the baby, John?' Maxwell was grimly serious.

'As God is my witness, Max, Bwana, I didn't know anything about that.'

'It *is* yours?'

Irving shrugged. 'I think we must assume it has to be,' the historian in him was weighing his words. 'That bastard Watkiss tried to plant the silver Audi sighting – thanks for bailing me out there, by the way – but I don't think even he'd go so far as to invent the baby.'

'No, I agree,' Maxwell nodded. 'Is that what Barbara wanted to see you about? On the Shingle? The reason for those phone calls?'

'I don't know, Max,' Irving shook his head. 'If only I'd got there just a few minutes earlier.'

It was Maxwell's turn to shake his head. 'It wasn't to be, John,' he said. 'If you'd been on time, if she'd been late, if she wasn't pregnant . . .' And his mind wandered away to other 'ifs' all those years ago – if he hadn't stayed in to watch that match, if his little girl hadn't gone to a party, if the roads hadn't been wet . . .

'It's funny,' Irving's voice brought him back to the here and now. 'It was about the time I told her I'd be working with Miles that she changed.'

'How did she change, John?' Maxwell asked.

'Colder. More distant. I'm not exactly the super stud type, Bwana. I hadn't had a relationship like that for years, perhaps never quite like that. It was . . . exhilarating. I'd find myself walking along the Backs grinning, going for beers with my students. Christ, I even gave one lad an A+.'

'Desperate!' whistled Maxwell. 'You'd got it bad, John.'

'I had. And so had she. Or so I thought. Did you ever have a woman like that, Bwana?'

'Hmm? Oh, yes.' Maxwell was far, far away, wreathed in the smiles of a girl who died, taking his daughter to a party. 'Yes, I did.'

'And then it was over,' he toyed with his drink, 'I behaved badly, I suppose. Rang her. Pestered her . . .'

'Wait a minute!' Maxwell's fingers clicked. 'I've just remembered it. The day you left the Grand. We were still filming and you said you had to get back to Cambridge. You almost knocked Barbara Needham over in the revolving door. I caught her on the ricochet, so to speak.'

'I know,' Irving grimaced. 'That was pathetic, wasn't it? Puerile. I saw her walking across the car park and I suddenly couldn't handle it – the introductions, the politeness, the strain. Worse – what if she blanked me, cut me dead? I just couldn't face her. I ran. Bloody silly.'

'Well, we've all done it.' Maxwell understood.

'Not you, Max Bwana,' Irving doubted. 'I don't believe you've run away from anything in your life.'

Maxwell chose to ignore the terminally dull Dr Nicholson. His old oppo didn't need to know anything about that. 'Well, there's always a first time.'

'Thanks, Bwana.' Irving held out his hand.

'What for?' Maxwell took it.

'Covering for me at the police station. I've never been in one of those places before. I didn't like it, Max. And thanks for, well, just being there.'

'Terrible film,' Maxwell smiled, 'the late, usually great, Peter Sellers being self-indulgent. Bed!' he suddenly ordered. 'You look peaky, John,' he winked. 'Quite pale, in fact. What do you want? Sofa or floor?'

'Floor, please. You know me, Bwana,' Irving smiled. 'Pegged out on the deck of a ship for months on end. Nothing my people like better.'

And they chorused together, 'Oh, Lordy, Lordy!' in the half light.

Boo Radley came out again that summer. No one had really believed Helen McGregor with her tale of a prowler on the cliffs. The rookie constable who'd investigated filed a report and then got sidetracked into the murder of Miles Needham. A Peeping Tom didn't fit that MO at all. The only other person who might have seen him was Giles Sparrow and Giles Sparrow had disappeared from the world like the Princes in the Tower, kept there by the wicked uncle they call Her Majesty's Government.

When they asked her, Helen McGregor couldn't say why she'd gone out at twilight on her own, wandering the place where it all happened. She couldn't say because she wouldn't say. It would have sounded so silly – she was walking where *he* had walked, reliving the sight of him in his scarlet and lace. She'd written to Marc Lamont at his Fan Club address, telling him all about herself, how she'd watched him on the beach and seen what a bastard that Maxwell had been to him. Never mind, she'd written; there'd be a time for revenge. She stood on the path that led to the Shingle and looked down on the beach and the rolling surf of Willow Bay. The gulls were far out to sea and the little kiddies had put their buckets and spades away and gone home.

In her imagination, she saw the thin blue and white line of Maxwell's Marauders fluttering like a police cordon in the breeze, then standing to attention with the glaring sun dazzling on their bayonet points and buttons. She saw that bastard Maxwell standing facing her beloved Marc, shouting something at him, pushing him over. She felt the hatred rise again as she trudged the ridge of the dunes. Bob Pickering's tent, the last one in the line, had gone now and a glossy new camper was parked in its place. She was still seething at the insult to her true love as she disappeared from view into a hollow of the dunes. Funny he hadn't written back, thanking her, saying 'Hi!'

Then she saw him, towering above her on the ridge. An unkempt mess of a man in tattered anorak, tied around his waist with string. His dark hair clung to his face where the wind blew it and his smile was a sneer of lust to the seventeen-year-old who saw it. She screamed. She ran, tumbling backwards with the depth and pull of the sand, rolling over in the sticky black debris an unusually high tide had thrown up. Hysterical, she looked over her shoulder as she scrambled to her knees. He was coming for her, his hair flying wild as he hurtled down the slope, spraying sand as he came, his voice harsh and guttural.

In the quiet confines of Leighford Police Station Incident Room later that night, she remembered it all a little differently. Her attacker's features had changed quite a bit. He had a shapeless tweed hat and a bow tie. And she knew his name – Peter Maxwell.

They came for him at lunch-time the next day, just as he was introducing order into the chaos that was the dinner queue at Leighford High. Police uniforms were not an unusual sight in comprehensive schools the length and breadth of the country. Shop-lifting was endemic with Year 10 girls in the Boots make-up department and white and brown substances changed hands with frightening rapidity in the amusement arcade along the Front.

Even so, no one expected the two burly policemen to march up to Mad Max and ask him to come quietly.

'Is there any other way?' he asked them once they had shown him some ID.

'What's he done?' was the question that ran in Chinese whispers down the ragged dinner line.

'To the back, Jason!' Bernard Ryan was desperately trying to stem the flow.

'Oh, I only wanted to see what happened to Mr Maxwell, sir,' Jason complained.

'What do you reckon?' Jez Harrap was in for the second part of his Physics exam that afternoon as the great man swept past him, past the lockers, 'Porn on the Internet would be my guess.'

'Nah,' his oppo said. 'He wouldn't know how to switch it on.'

'Max?' James Diamond was coming back on site after an excruciating budget meeting at County Hall. If he'd been anything other than a boring bastard, he'd have shot himself during it.

'Could you ask Roger or Bernard to cover me this afternoon, Headmaster?' Maxwell beamed at him. 'I'm afraid I'm helping these gentlemen with their inquiries.'

'Right!' Helen McGregor's allegations were the answer to a maiden's prayer. Except that this particular maiden was Detective Inspector Dave Watkiss and he was loving every minute of it. They were back in the Interview Room again. Same room. Different shit. 'We've established for the benefit of the tape that you are Peter Maxwell. Now tell us where you were last night.'

'What time?' Maxwell asked. 'Assuming you are going to be as reticent about the reasons for my being here as were the two gorillas you sent to collect me.'

'Dusk. Let's say nine thirty.'

'At home. No – I tell a lie . . .'

Watkiss didn't doubt it. He looked meaningfully at DC Firth.

'I was parched and popped out for a pint.'

'Where?'

'The Longshoreman.'

Watkiss leaned back, taking his time. 'Out on the Shingle,' he said.

'That's right,' Maxwell smiled broadly.

'That's over a mile from your home as the crow flies.'

'Nearly two the way I go,' Maxwell corrected him.

'How's that?' Firth asked.

'Bike. You're too young to remember the old road safety ad "Think Bike", Constable. But that's what I always do.'

'So what made you choose the Longshoreman, Mr Maxwell?' Watkiss wanted to know.

'Morbid curiosity,' Maxwell disarmed the man. 'I'm afraid I visited Barbara Needham's murder site.'

'I understood,' Watkiss relished, 'that we had made it clear you were not to get involved in this.'

'This? Oh, I'm sorry, Inspector. I understood that when Policewoman Carpenter spoke to me, it was to warn me off the cases of Miles Needham and Hannah Morpeth. I had no idea she was referring to a murder that hadn't even happened. Anyway, I'm not sure there is a law forbidding me from wandering on the Shingle, is there? Unless there's an obscure statute of Edward I I may have missed.'

'How did you get to the Shingle?' Watkiss ignored the man. 'The exact route, I mean.'

'Pratchett Street out of Columbine. West to the Flyover, then cut down Derwent Avenue and along the Front. It's the quickest way I know.'

'And from the Front,' Watkiss was trying to trace the route in his mind, 'you'd have skirted the dunes and the caravan park.'

'That's right.'

'Did you see anyone there?'

Maxwell had to think for a minute. 'A couple of kids from school,' he said. 'A few holidaymakers. You wouldn't expect that many people there. It was getting dark.'

'Go there often, do you, as it's getting dark?' Firth asked.

A happily married man himself, he was deeply, truly, madly suspicious of middle-aged bachelors.

'No, I told you. I wanted to see the spot where Barbara Needham died.'

'And what's that to you?' Watkiss put it to him.

'I told you, I'm morbidly curious.'

There was a long silence while the Inspector changed tack. 'Tell me, Mr Maxwell, do you own an anorak?'

'No,' Maxwell said.

'A Barbour, then? How about that?'

'I have a Barbour, yes. Is this relevant?'

'You asked me earlier why you'd been brought here, Mr Maxwell.' The Inspector had chosen his moment carefully. 'An allegation has been made against you.'

'Really?' Maxwell looked the man in the face. 'Of what? By whom?'

'The allegation is that you exposed yourself on the dunes at approximately nine thirty last night.' Watkiss opened a slim file on the desk in front of him. 'This is from the statement made by the young lady in question. "He stood on the top of the dune and undid his trousers. As I tried to get up he grabbed me but I pulled away. He was still masturbating as I got out of the hollow and he did not pursue me any further." Note the use of the word "grabbed", Mr Maxwell; that doesn't just make it indecent exposure, that makes it assault.'

'That makes it nonsense,' Maxwell looked levelly at his man, 'a sublime piece of nonsense.'

'Why? Because you're some sort of pillar of the local community? I've thrown away more keys than you've had hot dinners on men who were pillars of communities. They were also perverts and weirdoes. Scout leaders, vicars, children's home carers, teachers. Don't think you're anything special, Maxwell. You're just one of a happy little band of brothers, you are. Perverts 'R' Us.'

'It's Helen McGregor, isn't it?' Maxwell asked.

'You what?'

'The girl who made the allegations – Helen McGregor.'

'It might be,' Firth hedged.

'You know bloody well who it is.' Watkiss wanted to hurry things up now, get a confession, go home. He could barely remember where that was. 'Too crafty to shit on your own doorstep, of course. Couldn't touch her up at school. That would be asking for trouble. But wearing a derelict's get-up, using darkness as a cover. Did you seriously think she wouldn't recognize you?'

'My God!' Maxwell sat back, blinking at Watkiss. Here it comes, the Inspector thought. He's going to cough. *Could* it be that easy? 'If this were crime fiction, I'd say something like "Say that again, Inspector". And you would – the wrong phrase, of course – and I'd say "No, not that bit" . . .'

'What the bloody Hell are you talking about?' Watkiss shouted, his tether-end in full view.

'Your man was a derelict, yes? That was the word you used?'

'What of it?' Watkiss asked.

'Are you going to charge me, Inspector?' Maxwell wanted to know.

The Inspector looked at the detective next to him. He'd been shat on by Peter Maxwell twice in forty-eight hours, but there wasn't a damn thing he could hold him on. He knew it. Maxwell knew it. It was just the girl's word against his. The word of a girl, a school refuser as the educational establishment called them, who had already reported a Peeping Tom whom nobody else had seen. Dr Astley had examined her thoroughly. There wasn't a mark on her. She was no virgin, but that had nothing to do with what may or may not have happened last night.

'Or,' Maxwell was waiting for Watkiss's answer, 'are you going to let me go?'

The Inspector switched off the tape. 'If you go within half a mile of that girl,' he growled, 'I'll fucking lock you up for ever. Got it?'

Maxwell nodded and stood up. 'Thank you, gentlemen. It's been . . . an education. I expect the County Council will be sending you a bill for my supply cover this afternoon. And by the way,' he paused at the Interview Room door, 'I don't expect to be followed when I leave here. That would constitute police harassment, wouldn't it?' Maxwell smiled. 'And you wouldn't want to set the lad here a bad example, would you, Inspector? Please don't get up – I'll see myself out.'

He found himself going back to it again, like an itch he couldn't scratch. Maxwell sat in the offices of the *Advertiser* during his lunch hour the next day. At school, Jason had seen that Mr Maxwell was back, so he reckoned he must have paid the Bill wads of money. James Diamond had seen he was back too, but when he asked Maxwell about the visit of the two officers, Maxwell had muttered something about an overdue library book. You didn't push a man like Mad Max. Not even if you were a Headmaster; and James Diamond, BSc, MEd was very far from that.

The microfiche article flickered on the screen. 'Thomas Sparrow . . . well known in the gay community . . .' There was Astley, the tight-lipped bastard who wouldn't talk; some coroner who was probably dead; the journalist, Bill Donlan, who'd already told Maxwell all he could remember. And that left . . . the police – Maxwell's favourite people.

He flicked forward onto new reels. Going back to March of this year, he combed the columns for news of a vagrant, a down and out; things going missing from washing lines; anybody being moved on along the beach. Nothing. Whoever Helen McGregor's attacker was, he hadn't made the local headlines. There were those who might dismiss the whole McGregor statement as the meanderings of a warped, obsessive juvenile mind – that there'd been no exposure, no assault. But Maxwell wasn't one of them. He'd been around hormonal girls, pre and post the thing called puberty for years – it was what they paid him for. And he knew a lie when he heard one. *Somebody* had flashed at Helen McGregor; *somebody* had watched her coupling with Giles Sparrow. And something, some sixth sense perhaps, told him that that somebody had to do with all this – the blood that seeped through Leighford's sands that summer.

'Jacquie, can we talk?'

The girl jumped at her desk. Around her the Incident Room hummed with activity. Her pizza slice lay discarded on the pile of papers by her coffee and her VDU.

'Max,' she cupped the receiver with her hand, aware that all calls to the Incident Room were logged. 'Where are you calling me from?'

'Call box,' he told her, 'corner of . . .'

'Don't tell me,' she hissed. 'I don't want to know.'

'No more pratting about, Jacquie.' She heard an edge to his voice she hadn't heard before. 'A straight trade. I've got information you want. You've got information I need. Swap yer!'

She glanced left and right. Paul Garrity was deep in a phone conversation himself; Jerry Manton was typing up reports and his return key was giving him grief. Everybody else seemed busy.

'What? she whispered. 'What have you got?'

'Hannah Morpeth had a stalker.'

'What?' the girl's eyes widened and she tried to control her volume. 'Why didn't you . . .'

'Ask Buster Rothwell. I'll see you tonight. Your place. Twelve. I want you to pull a file, Jacquie, can you do that?'

'What?' Her voice was even louder this time and Jerry Manton glanced up. 'No, that's not possible.' She swung her chair so that its high back was between her and her colleagues.

'It'll be on record somewhere,' Maxwell was saying. 'June 1977. Here in Leighford. The death of one Thomas Sparrow. Thanks, Jacquie. See you tonight.'

She promised herself she wouldn't. Not again. The last time she'd helped Mad Max, she'd almost lost her job, her sanity. And Hall, Watkiss, probably Garrity and Manton – they all knew. But that was then. Now Mad Max was different. She was different. *They* were different. He was old enough to be her father, for Christ's sake. And she kept telling herself that as she went to records and found the file on Tom Sparrow. And all the way home through the leafy suburbs of a sleepy seaside town. So why was it then she saw his face in the steam of her bath that night? Heard his voice in the purr of her hairdryer? Why was she putting on *that* dress, of all dresses? In fact, she was just about to take it off again when she heard the rattle of her back door. She checked her watch – ten twenty-four. Couldn't be Maxwell. He'd said twelve. Who was that at this time of night?

'The postman always rattles twice,' Maxwell's beam lit her kitchen. She grabbed his sleeve and pulled him in, clawing down the blind behind him.

'For fuck's sake, Max. I don't believe you're here. I don't believe you called me today. You know, don't you, that Hall knows? He knows everything.'

'Does he?' Maxwell took the girl's hand and held it, then he kissed her softly, on the cheek. She closed her eyes. She wanted to sink her face into the rough tweed of his jacket, soak up the warm male scent of his neck and hair. Instead she pulled away.

'Max,' she wasn't looking at him, 'I'm falling in love with you.' As she said it, she felt fifteen again.

'Jacquie . . .' And for once the master of wit and repartee was lost for words.

She held up both her hands and turned away. 'The file you want is there – on the table. I haven't opened it. I don't know why you want it. It's a photocopy of course. The original is still back at Leighford nick.' She looked at him for the first time. 'Max, if *any* of this gets out. If you've been seen on your way here tonight, I'm finished . . . I think I am, anyway.'

'Buster Rothwell,' Maxwell said. 'Did you talk to him?'

'I managed to persuade Jerry Manton it was his idea that he should.'

'And?'

'You were right. Hannah had a stalker who was sending her threatening letters. We're having them analysed at the lab now. And Rothwell's likely to face charges of withholding. Which is exactly what I could charge you with, Max.'

The Head of Sixth Form nodded. 'You'd be within your rights,' he said. And he took up the file on Tom Sparrow.

'I hope it helps,' he said, 'the stalker information. Thanks for this.' He reached the kitchen door and turned to face her. 'Don't fall in love with me, Jacquie,' he said. 'I'm too old, too clapped out, too set in my ways. I'm going now. And when I do, you won't see me again. Unless it's to pass me on my zimmer frame one day and you'll say "There's that boring old fart Mad Max. We used to like each other, you know."'

'No, Max,' tears were trickling down her cheeks, splashing onto the black velvet of her dress. 'No, I couldn't bear not to see you again.'

'Well, then,' his throat felt iron-hard. 'If you need me,' he covered the moment with his best Bacall, 'just whistle. You know how to whistle, don't you? You just put your lips together and blow.' And her whole body shook as she heard his footsteps padding away across the grass.

Peter Maxwell sprawled in his lounge that night, his bow tie discarded, his slippers on, his third or fourth Southern Comfort firmly in his grasp. He'd read and re-read the police report on the death of Tom Sparrow. His body had been found along the shoreline at Willow Bay – the names of the two fishermen who'd found him were recorded. Dr James Astley, the newly appointed police surgeon back in 1977, diagnosed death by drowning. Excessive froth at the mouth, sea water in the lungs, blue finger nails – all the classic symptoms. The body was fully clothed except for the shoes and the weight of his saturated anorak had probably contributed to the death. There was no alcohol in the body, so it was unlikely he'd fallen in drunk. He could have slipped, the investigating officer speculated, but where and how was a mystery.

A number of witnesses were interviewed, as people who knew the deceased. One was George Sparrow, the dead man's nephew, who lived out at Glove Farm and had reluctantly identified the body. He had nothing to do with his uncle, whom he found an embarrassment because of his proclivities. And none of his family did either. Another was Miles Needham, a young man from near Bournemouth working in television in some unspecified capacity. The police had visited him at his girlfriend's parents' home. He said he'd known the deceased as a child, but hadn't clapped eyes on him for years. His drinking buddy Alan Rossiter said much the same.

But it wasn't so much these names that intrigued Peter Maxwell. And it wasn't these names that led him to pour his fourth or fifth Southern Comfort so smartly on the heels of the last one. It was another name altogether. Metternich the cat sensed the black mood at 38 Columbine and elected for a night on the tiles – it was safer.

*   *   *

He tried finishing Lieutenant Henry Berkeley Fitzhardinge Maxse, but horses' reins are tricky blighters when you're stone cold sober and Maxwell was far from that. He slammed the whole thing down in his attic workshop so that the ADC to Lord Cardigan lost his head completely along with his left arm.

He stumped downstairs to his bedroom and took up where he'd left off on *The Jew of Linz*; but he wasn't up to Hitler, never mind Wittgenstein at that hour of the morning. He was pacing his lounge on the floor below that, contemplating suicide or renewing his membership of the Conservative Party, when his eye lighted on something he'd forgotten about completely in the last murderous fortnight – the script of *The Captain's Fancy* lay abandoned on his magazine rack. He realized he'd never finished it and had no idea how it ended. He threw himself down heavily on the settee and flicked through its tatty pages. He could imagine the unimaginable Erika Marriner weeping buckets because her creation had been so hacked about by those dreadful television people. He couldn't wait to read her next opus on the '45.

He reached the part where Captain Fitzgerald aka that shit Marc Lamont got his in a hail of musket balls in the battle on the beach. Jemima Vawr, his light o' love, found his body after the marauding French had been repulsed and wandered the deserted camp, more or less wringing her hands. There, in one of the tents she found . . . Jesus Christ! Maxwell was sitting up sharply, his head spinning, his heart racing. He checked his watch. Quarter past three.

'Saddle White Surrey for the field tomorrow!' He gave himself – since he was on his own – his best Larry Olivier as Richard III and fumbled under the settee for his shoes. 'Look that my cycle clips be sound and not so tight. Come, come, caparison my bike. The foe . . .' And he looked down at the vital pieces of evidence he needed, *The Captain's Fancy* and the file on Tom Sparrow lying side by side on the settee. 'The foe vaunts in the field.'

He caught sight of his reflection in the darkling mirror and whispered to it, 'Conscience avaunt. Maxwell's himself again.'

# Chapter Fourteen

'Guv?' Paul Garrity was mumbling into his walkie-talkie.

'This had better be essential, Paul,' he heard a tired Henry Hall mutter.

'Peter Maxwell's just gone into the Grand.'

'Great!' he heard his guv'nor mutter before he put the receiver down with a click that hurt his eardrums.

'At least you're at home in bloody bed!' Garrity spoke to the dead mobile.

The hotel's video security picked up Peter Maxwell where Garrity's vigilance left off. There was a florid-faced kid at reception, amazingly not one Maxwell remembered teaching.

'Can I help you, sir?' the lad asked.

'Dr John Irving, please.'

'Is the gentleman expecting you, sir?'

'I don't suppose so for a moment,' Maxwell told him. 'It's half past three in the morning. Just ring his room, will you? Which one is it, by the way?'

'Er . . . I'm afraid we don't give out . . . sir? Sir?' But Peter Maxwell had that knack, vital to an amateur detective, of reading upside down. John Irving was staying in Room 105 according to the open register. He'd find it himself.

It was a bleary-eyed Fellow of Gonville and Caius who opened the door to Peter Maxwell. 'Christ, Bwana, the lad on the reception desk was all for having you arrested. Luckily for you I calmed him down.'

'Ah, it's not true what they say about you black chappies, then?'

'Hmm?'

Maxwell glanced knowingly down at Irving's bath robe and Irving instinctively closed it. 'Just joking,' he winked. 'Tell me,' he swept past his old oppo, 'does your room have one of those dear little . . . ah, it does. Do you mind?'

'Feel free.'

Maxwell helped himself to a Southern Comfort miniature from the drinks cabinet. 'Hair of the dog,' he said and threw himself down on Irving's twin bed. 'Tell me about *The Captain's Fancy*,' he said.

'What about it?' Irving sat in the bedside chair. 'Max, has it actually registered with you what time it is?'

'How does it end, John? Ms Marriner's load of tosh. What happens to the girl, Jemima Nicholas aka Vawr?'

'Er . . . well, she dies. Commits suicide, I think. Why?'

'How? How does she do it?'

'Er . . . Oh, Christ. She stabs herself.'

'With what?'

'With . . . a surgeon's knife.'

'A surgeon's knife,' Maxwell nodded.

'Is that what killed Hannah Morpeth? The papers just said a knife.'

'The police aren't giving all they've got to the papers, John, they never do.'

'So where did you get it from?' Irving wanted to know.

'Someone on the inside,' Maxwell tapped the side of his nose. 'And as always, my sources are impeccable.'

'But, Bwana, I don't see . . .'

'Had you filmed that bit? The suicide? You said you'd

done most of the indoor shots. It was the battle you still had to do.'

'Yes. No, we hadn't. Jemima is heart-broken at the Captain's death and she sees the surgeon's knife lying in a tent. I think the television people count that as an outside shot. Anyway, I'm pretty sure we hadn't done it.'

'Good. There's a bloke on the front door, John – a detective.'

'I know. Not the subtlest of surveillance, one way or another.'

'Between us, you and I have a total IQ measurement off the scale. Do you think we can put all that colossal brainpower to some use for a change and lose him come the morning?'

'I expect so. Why?'

'Because you and I have to take a little drive to Basingstoke.'

'Basingstoke?'

'I've heard better Roderic Murgatroyds,' Maxwell commented. 'That's where they keep Eight Counties Television.'

The sun was scarcely over the sound boom when Peter Maxwell bustled out to talk to Paul Garrity.

'Morning, detective,' he smiled breezily, tapping on the car window. Garrity's mouth felt like the bottom of a budgie's cage and he had a crick in his neck the size of the national debt. He'd spent nights in more interesting places than a hotel car park, it had to be said. 'Dr Irving and I are just about to have breakfast. I've ordered the full cholesterol and English. He's having the rather more debonair but probably no healthier croissant. Well, he always was rather cosmopolitan for obvious reasons. Would you like to join us or shall I send you out a doggy bag?'

Maxwell didn't wait for Garrity's reply, but he could read lips fairly well through the closed car window. He'd already seen, and Garrity hadn't, John Irving nip out of the side door and take his car round the back to the kitchen entrance. From the foyer, it was a simple matter to wander into the dining room, waving gaily to the disgruntled detective and reach nonchalantly for the orange juice. He then chose a table as far from the front car park as he could. And ducked past it into the kitchens.

'Can I help you?' a flustered waitress asked.

Maxwell looked at her closely. 'I shouldn't think so,' he said and walked on. At the back door, a waiter almost collided with him. 'Just offering my compliments to the chef,' Maxwell beamed and then he was in John Irving's Audi purring north to Basingstoke.

Eight Counties Television had its main studios to the south-west of the town where the old house of Basing had been besieged during the Civil War. It was a great, glass monolith, eloquent testimony to the advertisers' money that had built it.

An intercom crackled alongside an automatic barrier as Irving's car pulled up.

'Dr John Irving to see Daniel Weston,' he said through the Audi's open window.

'Who?'

'John Irving to see Daniel Weston – props department,' the good doctor repeated.

'Come to the main car park, turn left. You'll see a blue door facing you. Go straight ahead to reception.' And the electronic arm whirred upwards to allow them access.

Reception was vast, with lifts jockeying for space with palm trees in gravel beds. An enormous fountain played silver in the centre, its tinkling reverberations a nightmare for the incontinent.

'Dr John Irving and Mr Peter Maxwell to see Daniel Weston,' Irving said at the counter.

'Hello, I'm Sharon,' the blonde bubbled at them through several strata of make-up. 'Is Dan expecting you?'

'Yes,' Maxwell butted in. 'We're the historical advisers on *The Captain's Fancy*. One or two loose ends to tie up.'

'I'll just see if he's free.' Sharon pressed lots of buttons under her side of the desk. Behind her, vying with the piped muzak that filled the atrium, four screens, all showing Gloria Hunniford from different angles, flashed and bobbed as the cameras went to work on her.

'He's on his way down,' Sharon grinned. 'Can I get you a coffee while you're waiting?'

'No . . .' Irving began.

'That would be delicious,' said Maxwell, smiling at the girl.

She simpered and turned away to push buttons various. 'Black?' she called to Irving.

It had to be said that Dan Weston looked a little better than the last time Maxwell had seen him. Even under the unrelenting sun that filtered through Eight Counties' glass roof, it was obvious his colour had returned, he was upright and he was sober. Even so, the guilt of the Brown Bess had never left Dan Weston and he didn't need the faces of Maxwell and Irving to remind him.

'Dan,' Maxwell shook the man's hand, 'can we have a word?'

Dan Weston lived in a perpetual Aladdin's cave of goodies. He led them through labyrinths of uniforms and dresses, lace and froth without end as they took the short cut through Costumes and into Props proper.

'Here we are,' he said. 'This is the historical section. Most of the stuff we used on *The Captain's Fancy* is here. If this is about guns again . . .'

'No, no,' Maxwell assured him, 'I seem to remember,

Dan, that the script called for Jemima to kill herself with a surgeon's knife. What did you use?'

'Well, we didn't,' Weston told him. 'We still had odds and sods to film when Hannah was murdered. What with that and now both the Needhams, Upstairs have decided we ought to shelve the programme, at least for a while. Bad taste and all. As far as Hannah's role goes, we could probably get away with a few back shots, arty lighting, maybe a double if we've got one. It'll work.'

'Well, what had you *planned* to use, then?' Maxwell persisted. 'Let me put it that way.'

'Oh, let's see,' Weston consulted a clipboard with endless typed and annotated lists. 'Here. D18.' He slid out a vast, shallow drawer from a rack in the corner. 'This,' he said.

In the middle of a welter of gloves, fans and lorgnettes enough to furnish the Duchess of Richmond's ball on the eve of Waterloo, lay a canvas bag tied with cords.

'May I?' Maxwell asked. He untied the cords and rolled out the contents. 'Three pairs of forceps,' he listed them mechanically, 'tourniquet. Good, good. Chisel – Jesus. Needles, various. Ah, that's authentic – anti-gonorrhea gadget. And . . . three knives.'

'What's the matter, Max?' Irving asked, 'What did you expect to find?' He read the disappointment in his friend's face.'

'I hoped to find one missing,' Maxwell confessed. 'You see these loops here, John? Three of them. There were only ever three knives with this kit. Nothing's not here, if you see what I mean. Dan, was there a spare set? Another one like this?'

Weston checked his lists again. 'No,' he said, shaking his head. 'Only this one.'

'Right. Well, thanks, Dan. We appreciate your help. Look, I'd say we'd see ourselves out, but I'm not sure we'd make it.'

Weston got them back to the sunlit atrium again, where the four faces of Gloria Hunniford had been replaced by a quartet of identical gardening programmes and they said their goodbyes.

'Max? Mr Maxwell!' Both men turned.

'Angela!' Maxwell smiled. 'Good to see you.'

'You too,' Angela Badham shook their hands. 'What brings you to Eight Counties?'

'A wild-goose chase, Angela, as it turns out.'

She looked as harassed and agitated as ever – a walking billboard for Valium if ever there was one. 'Can I buy you both a coffee?'

'I thought you'd never ask.'

The staff canteen at Eight Counties beat the staffroom at Leighford High into a Napoleonic cocked hat. For a start, there were no piles of old *TES* in the corner and nobody's games kit abandoned across the photocopier. Maxwell wasn't privileged to peek inside the fridge, but he was prepared to bet it didn't contain last week's yoghurt or last term's milk suppurating at the bottom. John Irving, of course, was less impressed. Eight Counties, for all its state of the art and wall-to-wall extravagance, didn't have the Gothic grandeur of Gonville and Caius; not an oak panel in sight.

'Dan Weston tells us you've shelved *The Captain's Fancy*,' Maxwell munched through his Danish.

'We had to, really.' Angela fumbled with her ciggies from the huge portmanteau on her lap. 'I mean, I know Barbara Needham wasn't actually part of the show, but the powers-that-be decided hers was a death too far. What were you asking Dan about?'

'A surgeon's knife,' Maxwell said. 'The one that killed Hannah Morpeth.'

'You thought Dan might have it?' Angela blew smoke to the ceiling.

'To my shame,' Maxwell mopped his chin with his paper

napkin. 'I hadn't actually finished reading the script. I'll wager the law hadn't read any of it. Why should they? I thought it rather poetic that Hannah should die by the very weapon that she was to have killed herself with on screen.'

'How can Dan help you?' Angela was confused.

'The actual murder weapon was found by the police at Leighford. They've still got it, no doubt bound up in plastic as Exhibit A, m'lud. If the kit Dan Weston showed me had had just such a knife missing, I could have pointed Chief Inspector Hall in the direction of Eight Counties Television.'

'You still think someone from here is involved?' she asked.

Maxwell sucked his teeth. 'There's something about Hannah Morpeth's death I can't figure,' he said. 'It doesn't fit.'

'What doesn't?' Irving asked.

He looked at them both, did Peter Maxwell and leaned back in his chair. 'I'm pretty sure I know who killed Miles and Barbara Needham and I'm pretty sure I know why.'

'Who?' asked Irving after a moment's stunned silence.

'All in good time,' Maxwell waved a hand at him. 'I could be wrong.'

'Why is Hannah different?' Angela asked.

'Motive,' Maxwell said. 'I know why – correction, I *think* I know why the Needhams died. I haven't a clue why Hannah was killed.'

Another silence.

'For God's sake, Max, you've got to tell us,' Irving insisted. 'You can't leave us dangling like this, not after all I've been through.'

Angela looked at him. 'You poor man,' she said. 'Dr Irving, I haven't had a chance to see you since that dreadful day on the beach when dear Miles was killed. That dreadful

Marc Lamont calling you . . . what he did. And Barbara. I was so very sorry to hear about Barbara.'

Irving nodded. 'These things happen,' he said. It was limp enough, but he didn't know what else to say. 'Max, Bwana, are you going to the police with what you know?'

'Hah!' Maxwell guffawed. 'With what *I* know? Johnnie, Johnnie, you could barely fill a thimble with what I know. Come on, we'd better get back. Leighford High will be wondering where their star teacher is and that nice detective's replacement at the Grand will be looking out for us. Angela.' Maxwell stood up and stooped briskly to kiss her hand. 'Thanks for the coffee. It's good to see you again.'

'And you, Max,' she smiled, 'Dr Irving.' And they made their farewells.

It had been a long time since Peter Maxwell had been back to Cambridge. He was a Jesus man himself, attracted by that prettiest of colleges along Jesus Lane. Coleridge the poet had gone there before him (they'd never met) and its port and claret were legendary.

The town had changed a little, but the colleges were the same, the tourists just as annoying, if slightly more Japanese, and there seemed to be fewer bikes around than he remembered. But what with the summer term having ended and most students having gone down, not to mention the fact that many of them had cars these days, that was hardly surprising.

But it wasn't Jesus Maxwell had come to visit. It was Gonville and Caius.

That Wednesday was a Heaven-sent day for Peter Maxwell. It was Open Day in which hordes of palpitating sixth formers from all over the country chattered together in groups with their proud, overweening parents, many of whom had bought hats fit for Ascot. It was swelteringly hot in the old court as a bowler-hatted official in civil-service black was giving the conducted tour.

'The college was founded in 1348 by the priest Edmund Gonville and well endowed later by Dr John Caius, physician in ordinary to King Edward VI and his sisters Bloody Mary and Elizabeth. The court in which you are standing has an eighteenth-century façade built over the original medieval and Tudor buildings . . . er . . . can I help you, sir?'

Maxwell was making rather a spectacle of himself, edging towards a stairway off the grassy area to his right.

'Er . . .'

'Are you a parent, sir?' the bowler hatted man was patience itself.

'Er, no, no,' Maxwell beamed as the crowd of parents and their appallingly precocious offspring looked on. 'Student. Intending.'

'*Mature* student, sir?' the bowler-hatted gent *was* having some difficulty with the intensity of the sun in his eyes.

''Fraid so,' Maxwell gushed, giving the man his Forrest Gump.

'For that you need Wolfson College, sir. Turn right out of College and look for Barton Road.'

'No, no, History here at Caius. I was told to look up a Doctor Irving.'

'Well, that wouldn't be today, sir,' the bowler-hatted man's crowd were growing a little restless. 'You'll need to come back another time.'

'Could we see a student's room?' a loud woman, probably from Leeds, wanted to know.

'Of course,' said the bowler-hatted gent, 'Now, if you'd all care to step this way . . .'

That wasn't the way Maxwell cared to step at all. He hung back for as long as he could, carefully inspecting the wisteria, then nipped up the staircase and along a shadowed corridor. A blonde girl cradling a pile of books met him halfway, which is more than most people were prepared to do.

'Excuse me,' Maxwell tipped his hat, 'I'm looking for Dr Irving's rooms.'

'Just along there,' the girl jerked her head behind her, 'but I'm not sure he's here at the moment.'

'Many thanks.'

John Irving's study door contrasted quite favourably with Maxwell's at Leighford High. For a start, it was made of wood. The Gothic panelling was streets ahead of the County hall woodstain that Maxwell met every morning. The Head of Sixth Form fished in his pockets. No jemmy. No switchblade. And the credit-card thing in the lock-jamb would hardly work on Gothic – not that Peter Maxwell knew how to do the credit-card thing. All he had was his house key. It seemed sacrilege, but needs must when the devil drives and he slotted the key into the door jamb, twisting this way and that. Through the little oriel window behind him, he could see the visiting group crossing the inner court, perhaps coming his way. He'd have to move quickly.

'Shit!' the door opened as Maxwell leaned on it in desperation, and he was inside.

Around the walls of Irving's study were wall-to-wall academe. Maxwell found himself wandering them, shaking his head every so often at titles he'd long forgotten, titles he'd never read.

'I bought you that one, you ungrateful shit,' he whispered into the silence. But he hadn't come to ogle and he hadn't come to reminisce. He'd come to snoop. And he set to work on Irving's drawers with the key . . .

'Peter Maxwell's just gone into the Grand,' Paul Garrity was talking to the mobile again, his second night of surveillance of John Irving.

'When did you last see Irving, Paul?' It was DI Watkiss at the other end of the line.

'Not since . . . last evening. He strolled in the grounds.'

'You sure he's there now?'

'Oh, yeah,' Garrity nodded. 'No probs.'

There had been probs earlier in the day. After that idiot Maxwell had come out to offer him breakfast, Garrity noticed that Irving's silver Audi had gone. But it wasn't in Paul Garrity's nature to panic and it wasn't in Paul Garrity's nature to tell his bosses anything they didn't need to know. He told his replacement that Irving's car was round the back, valet parked and didn't have a hope in hell of getting out. Well, what was a little fibbette between friends?

All the more confusing then, when Irving's silver Audi had purred back into the car park a little after lunch-time and the coloured gentleman had strolled in for a late bite to eat.

'Say nothing,' was Garrity's advice to his shift partner. The partner shrugged. He'd heard it all before.

John Irving wasn't prepared for the sight that met him as he opened his hotel room door to Peter Maxwell. He found himself staring at a bundle of letters covered in messages stuck on from crude cuttings from newspapers, clutched in the hand of a Head of Sixth Form whose tether-end had been reached.

'Where did you get those?' he asked.

'Would you like me to tell the whole fifth floor?' Maxwell asked him.

Irving let him in.

'I got these,' Maxwell threw them down on Irving's bed, 'as you very well know, from your rooms at college.'

'Max . . . Bwana, how could you?'

Maxwell's jabbing finger was threatening the other man's nose, 'Don't come that Bwana, holier-than-thou stuff with me, John. You lied to me. You've been lying to me from the start.'

'Now, Max, I . . .'

'Something didn't ring quite true – about Barbara Needham, I mean. I've been around people a long time, John. I know when they're lying. Why didn't you tell the police about the meeting? About finding her body?'

'What would it look like?' Irving shouted. 'It all points to me.'

'It does indeed, John,' Maxwell threw himself down in Irving's chair. 'You know, I'm tired. Dog tired. After you dropped me at home this lunch-time, I toyed with going in to my place of work. Then I thought . . . stuff it. And I *like* teaching, John. For all people whinge about education today and the youth thereof, there are still some of us who get a kick out of what we do. So I actually resented not going in. And I resented having to catch the train to Cambridge and lying my teeth off in the college grounds. And I resented most of all breaking into your study desk – send me the bill for the damage, by the way.'

'Nobody asked you to . . .'

'*You* asked me to, John!' Maxwell thumped both arms of the chair with his hands. 'You asked me to help you on the Eight Counties location and since then three people have died. Now, either you tell me what this is all about – *all* of it now, without the bullshit – or I'm going to tell that nice and equally hoodwinked detective in the car park out there everything I know about who found Barbara Needham's body.'

For a moment, the silence deafened. Then John Irving sat down on his bed, sifting the four letters Maxwell had stolen to make a point.

'All right,' he said, 'I owe you this, Max, Bwana. Most of it you know. I've no idea where they came from, but Babs was receiving them too. They accused us of betraying Miles, carrying on behind his back. Hers were more specific than mine. More vile and polluted. What kind of sick mind . . . ? Anyway, we couldn't trace them ourselves. And I couldn't go to the police, although she suggested we should. My college position. I had to think of that.'

'Oh, yes,' Maxwell nodded. 'You had to think of that.'

'And anyway, as I told you, Babs was changing.'

'Yes, you said.'

'Yes,' Irving looked at him, 'but I didn't tell you why. She knew Miles was unfaithful and she claimed not to care. Perhaps when they were younger, she didn't. But she was getting older – and the bits on the side were getting younger; Hannah Morpeth was the last straw.'

'I don't see . . .'

'She wanted me to kill him,' Irving said.

'What?'

'Babs wanted me to kill Miles. I know, it's preposterous. I'm hardly the hit man type. But that was a side to Babs I'd never seen before. She was a bitter, twisted woman, Bwana. I got cold feet.'

'You wanted to end it?'

'Yes. I told her so. When I saw her here at the Grand that day I left in such a hurry, I knew she'd come to sort things out. At first I assumed she'd think I'd done it – killed Miles just as she wanted me to. But she did it, Max. It was Babs. God knows how – I don't want to know how. It had to be her.'

'Except you weren't the only ones getting letters like that,' Maxwell told him.

'What?'

'Hannah Morpeth got them as well, from someone her minder calls her stalker.'

'Jesus!'

'If you were getting cold feet, why did you come to meet Barbara on the Shingle?' Maxwell asked.

'I'd got another letter – that one,' Irving waved to it. 'I knew I couldn't leave things as they were. Nothing resolved. As far as Babs was concerned, we were in the clear. Miles was dead. So, for that matter, was Hannah Morpeth. It could be me and her, love's middle-aged dream.'

'Except the dream had become a nightmare,' Maxwell said softly.

'I had to see her one last time. Tell her I had nothing to do with Miles's death; find out if she had. Oh, God, Max, she must have killed Hannah as well.'

'No,' Maxwell shook his head. 'No, she didn't kill Miles and she didn't kill Hannah. The question is, John, who killed her? Now, are you going to go to the police – or am I?'

# Chapter Fifteen

Mad Max looked at himself in his shaving mirror next morning and shook his head, 'Whatever happened to you, Max? Victor Ludorum at fifteen; Victor Meldrew at fifty-three. Jesus!'

It had been a rough night in Jericho aka Room 105, the Grand Hotel. And a rougher day lay ahead. It started with a phone call that caused Metternich to despair. He rolled over with his back firmly to the world, his face to the wall.

'Mr Maxwell?'

'Yes,' Maxwell couldn't place the voice.

'Mr Maxwell who is the historical adviser to Eight Counties Television?'

'In a way,' Maxwell sat down slowly on the bed, trying to find his other sock. 'Who is this?'

'Oh, forgive me, Mr Maxwell, my name is Edward Stubbington, I keep Things Ancient and Modern in the High Street – the antique shop.'

'Ah, yes, of course, Mr Stubbington,' Maxwell could picture the man now, centre parting, glasses on a chain, seemed to be having perpetual conflict with his sexuality.

'I'm most dreadfully sorry to bother you at home, particularly so early in the morning, but I was anxious to catch you before you went to work.'

'Very wise,' Maxwell said. Once lost in the bowels of Leighford High, there was no telling when – or if – he'd come out again.

'I wonder if it would be at all possible for you to call into the shop today? I have something here which . . . well, I don't really know what to do with it now.'

'Er . . . what is it, Mr Stubbington?' Maxwell was confused.

'It's a British Army surgeon's knife, probably 1840s. It's not Napoleonic, I'm afraid . . .'

But he was talking to himself. Maxwell grabbed the half-drunk coffee on the mantelpiece and screamed at the cat, 'You've had my bloody sock, Count, I know you have.' He rattled out another series of numbers on that white thing again and fumbled at its cord's full length with his bow tie, wound inextricably around a coat hanger in the wardrobe.

'Thingee!' he shouted across the wires to the girl on the Leighford High switchboard, 'You're there already. Wonderful! Remind me to see Mr Diamond about your promotion.'

'Morning, Mr Maxwell,' the switchboard girl trilled, 'Are you coming in today? Only Mr Ryan's ever so short-staffed.'

'And ever so short-IQed as well, isn't he?' Maxwell told her free and gratis. 'I don't suppose Paul Moss is in yet?'

'I haven't seen him, Mr Maxwell.'

'Right, Thingee. When he comes in, tell him I'll be in by ten. If he can bung on a video for 7A1 . . . er . . . *Dances With Wolves* will keep them busy.'

'Right-o, Mr Maxwell,' Thingee always sounded as if she had a perpetual cold, 'I'll tell him.' And he hung up on her too.

'Only in teaching, Count,' Maxwell opted for an odd sock and what the Hell? 'does one have to arrange one's day when one isn't even bloody well there. Take my advice, Count.'

Maxwell threw something fishy onto a plate for the animal, 'Don't go into teaching.'

Metternich sniffed the breakfast goodies. Mackerel, huh? A likely story. What was the silly old sod talking about now?

Things Ancient and Modern hadn't actually opened as Maxwell hammered on the glass of the door. Banks and antique shops, he'd noticed in all his years in the world, didn't play by everybody else's rules. They didn't open until at least 9.30 and until recently, probably because Joe Public had sussed them, they were closed by three. What a doddle!

'Ah, Mr Maxwell?' the door was opened by the fussy cardigan-wearer Maxwell remembered from his earlier sojourns in Victoriana-land.

'Mr Stubbington,' Maxwell was still in his cycle clips, but the antique dealer said nothing at all about his odd socks. 'I came as quickly as I could.'

'Well, there was no great hurry,' Stubbington said. 'It's just that I didn't quite know what to do with the item.'

'May I see it? I'm sorry to call so early, but I won't be able to make it later in the day.'

'Of course. Come in.'

He led Maxwell past the faded memories of an earlier era, another time, through his beaded curtain to an inner office. He held up a silver-hilted scalpel, handsomely mounted. 'This is the best I could do. I know it's not the correct period. And I'm afraid it's a hundred and fifty pounds.'

'Is it?' Maxwell blanched. 'You'll have to forgive me, Mr Stubbington, but I've no idea why you contacted me about this.'

'Oh, I'm sorry,' Stubbington lifted the chained glasses onto the bridge of his nose and looked at the man, 'It's just that the young lady said . . .'

'Young lady?'

'Yes, the one who called in for the knife the other week. Yours was the one name I knew. Local teacher and so on.'

'A young lady called in for it?'

'Yes, but I didn't have one in stock. She said she needed it as a surprise for her husband. He was here with the film crew working at Willow Bay. I said I'd do my best, but it might take a few days. Well, she never called back and here it is. I suppose I should have contacted Eight Counties Television. But, as I say, yours was a name I knew and the *Advertiser* said you were their historical adviser.'

'This young lady,' Maxwell said, 'Did she give a name?'

'No, that was just it. She was staying in the town for a while and would call back.'

'Do you remember, Mr Stubbington, what she looked like?'

'Oh, yes, I do,' the antique dealer said, 'Very well. She was very attractive. Jet-black hair. I remember thinking it was the colour of mourning. I have several items of jewellery in the shop . . . Mr Maxwell?'

'Sorry,' Maxwell had crashed through the curtains and was halfway to the door. 'I must be away. I'm afraid I can't help with the knife, Mr Stubbington. You see, the lady who asked for it won't be coming back, ever.'

7A1 were still entranced by Kevin Costner turning the Indians into the good guys when Maxwell breezed onto the second floor. He waved at Paul Moss and winced at the row emanating from the room where Anthea Edwards was attempting to maintain order with 9C4, Morons 'R' Us.

'Thingee,' he grabbed the History Department's internal phone, 'get me the Grand Hotel, will you, there's a good Communicator?'

'Grand,' a sable voice purred.

'Wally, is that you? It's Peter Maxwell.'

'Mr Maxwell,' the sable voice had vanished, 'How are you, all right?' Maxwell's old pupil sounded more like Barrymore than ever.

'In the pink, thanks, Wally. Room 105 please; Dr Irving.'

He put his hand over the receiver as a child drifted in to the History Inner Sanctum. 'You don't *have* to knock on the door to be allowed to live, Colin,' Maxwell growled at him, 'but it helps. The scissors are there look. No, left. *Left*. Steel things. Blunted for your own protection. That's it. Good lad. Hurry back to Mr Moss's lesson now and try not to fall over. Ah, John.'

'Max,' Irving's voice crackled over the ether. 'What's up?'

'To cut a long story short, I got a call from a local antique dealer this morning. He tried to sell me a surgeon's knife.'

'Christ.'

'He'd put it on hold for a lady who'd ordered one as – and I quote – "a surprise for her husband". John, the woman had black hair.'

'Babs,' Irving whispered.

'You're thinking what I'm thinking, aren't you?' Maxwell checked.

'Babs wants Hannah Morpeth dead,' Irving talked him through it, concentrating, working it out. 'But how's she going to do it? She thinks I've killed Miles, but that isn't enough. She wants her revenge on the girl, too.'

'She's read the script of *The Captain's Fancy*. Would you say she had a poetic nature, John? Would the knife have had a delicious irony?'

'It's possible,' Irving nodded at his end of the line.

'But she couldn't use the props from Eight Counties because there'd be tight security after Miles Needham. Dan Weston would have died at his post rather than let anybody else have access to anything.'

'Which meant getting a knife from elsewhere,' Irving realized.

'But that was easier said than done,' Maxwell went on at full tilt. 'Then dear old Mr Stubbington had the answer. He didn't have one himself, but he knew a man who had. Unfortunately, time was running out. She couldn't wait for him . . .'

'She must have got another knife from somewhere else. After all, double bladed, x number of inches long, so many millimetres wide, they must be reasonably standard . . .'

'And of course,' Maxwell said, 'Barbara didn't expect not to be able to collect Stubbington's knife herself, did she? He'd have had no reason to contact me then.'

'So I was right,' Irving growled. 'Not that it gives me any pleasure, Max, Bwana.'

'I'm going to the police with this, John,' Maxwell said. 'Tomorrow. There's one little errand I've got to run first. Will I see you there? John?'

'Yes,' the voice came back, resigned, beaten. 'Yes, tomorrow.'

'Half four?' Maxwell asked, his life, as ever, revolving around his school.

'Half four will be fine.'

She rang the doorbell at the Larches a little before lunch-time. There was no reply. She stepped back into the road, brandishing her warrant card in the air, shouting at the window.

'Helen!' she yelled, 'Helen McGregor! I know you're in there. Now, either you open up or I get a warrant and break down the door. What's it going to be?'

The nets twitched in the bedroom window, upstairs right. There was a thunder of feet on the stairs like a distant storm over the mountains and the girl-most-likely-to put her plump, sullen head around the door.

'I'm Detective Constable Carpenter,' Jacquie showed her card again. 'I'd like a chat.'

She held the door open, letting the policewoman in the neat-pleated skirt into the hall and then the kitchen.

'Have you got him?' Helen asked. 'That Maxwell?'

Jacquie was half a head taller than the sixth former, slimmer, older, everything Helen was not. 'I'm not looking for Mr Maxwell,' she said, sliding back an upright chair and sitting by the Formica-topped table. 'I'm looking for the man who attacked you.'

'It was him,' Helen insisted defiantly. 'It was Maxwell. I told them other policemen. They believed me.'

'Well, I don't, Helen,' Jacquie told her. 'I happen to know that Peter Maxwell is one of the gentlest men around. He wouldn't hurt a fly.'

'Oh yeah?' Helen too slid back a chair and sat opposite the policewoman, 'Sleeping with him, are you?'

Jacquie hadn't snapped in a long time, especially with a witness, but she couldn't help herself that morning. She grabbed the girl's plump arm and forced it down onto the kitchen table, leaning forward and putting her nose inches from the girl's. 'Look, you foul-mouthed little cow. You claimed someone attacked you on the dunes. Now you know and I know it wasn't Peter Maxwell. So who was it? If you're telling anything approximating to the truth, you've got a duty to any other girls out there. Whoever it is, is still out there, watching, waiting.'

She let go of the girl's arm, 'Who's going to be next, Helen, because of you?'

'All right!' The girl's face wore a mask of pain and the tears were starting as she rubbed her arm. 'It wasn't Maxwell. And he didn't do anything, the bloke. All right? He just scared me, that's all. It was the same bloke I'd seen before, when I was with Giles. He just scared me.'

Jacquie sat back in the chair. She'd just broken every

rule in the book and she knew it. Now it was time to build bridges, set the record straight.

'Right, Helen,' the voice was softer, more gentle, 'now you put the kettle on, yeah? We'll have a nice cup of tea, you and me, and you can tell me what this bloke *really* looked like.'

'What's this?' Henry Hall looked up from the detective's warrant card on his desk to the detective herself.

'My resignation, sir,' Jacquie Carpenter was staring straight ahead.

Hall leaned back in his chair, weighing the moment. 'Do you want to tell me why?' he asked, his face as expressionless as ever.

'I lost my temper this morning, sir,' Jacquie confessed, 'while interviewing a witness.'

'Who?' Hall asked.

'Helen McGregor.'

'What did you do?'

'Grabbed her wrist. Told her her fortune.'

'With what result?'

'She now admits that it was not Peter Maxwell who attacked her. More than that, there was no attack at all.'

'This obtained under duress?' Hall checked.

'You could say that, sir.' She was still staring straight ahead. 'That's why I'm resigning. I went too far.'

Hall paused, his fingers clasped, his lips pursed. 'In the calmer light of day,' he said, 'does the girl hold to her new story?'

'Yes, sir,' Jacquie said. 'And the description she's now given is pretty good. PC Bannerman even thinks he knows who it is.'

Hall leaned forward again in his chair. 'Close the door on your way out,' he got back to his paperwork, 'and take that with you.'

Fluster crossed Jacquie Carpenter's face, and she looked at the bland bastard forever doomed to sit in the hot seat. 'Sir?'

'Call it a cooling off period, Jacquie,' he said softly. 'Give it some time before you come to me with that again. If you do, we'll talk then.'

She picked it up. 'Thank you, sir,' she said and choked back the tears.

'Anyway,' Hall's voice stopped her at the door, 'I never accept resignations in the course of a murder inquiry,' he told her. 'It's bad for morale.'

Mums don't wait outside High Schools. For a start they don't need to, their offspring being too big to need collection; and for follow on because said offspring would die of embarrassment if they did.

So it was odd to find an attractive young woman sitting in a plain, dark car in the space reserved for parents and other school visitors. She'd almost collided with the Head of Media Studies roaring away at the end of another long day. And when she saw the Head of Sixth Form pedalling like a thing possessed through the staff cars, she hung her head out of the window.

'Have you got a licence for that?'

Maxwell screeched to a halt, his rear wheel spraying dust in all directions. 'The doctor told me I shouldn't do wheelies at my age,' he smiled at her. 'I might lose the wheel to live.'

'I don't usually pick up middle-aged men,' she said as he swung out of the saddle, 'but there's someone I'd like you to meet.'

The All Angels Crypt Centre was the place to be if you were nobody in Leighford. It was run by the Reverend Michael Chapman, one of the few genuinely nice people in the Church of England, but everyone just called him Father Mike and he saved his dog collar for Sundays. He was used to visits from the police at all hours of the day and night because the Centre was a temporary home for the flotsam and jetsam of that part of the south coast – the people that time forgot. They felt safe here. There was a bed and an endless supply of tea and coffee, fresh rolls and warming soup. And Father Mike didn't push it. He preached no gospel, delivered no sermon, took no side.

'Can we have a word with him, Mike?' Jacquie asked, taking the vicar's proffered coffee cup. 'The two of us? This is Peter Maxwell, by the way. Leighford High.'

'You're Mad Max!' Chapman shook his hand.

'Only when I stand in a certain light,' Maxwell said. 'I'm secretly delighted you've heard of me, of course . . . if suspicious.'

Chapman laughed. 'I run a youth group on Friday nights,' he said, 'You are a legend among that lot.'

Maxwell bowed. 'They're lying, of course.'

'Of course,' Father Mike winked. 'He's on the patio, Jacquie,' and the vicar vanished.

In the car, Jacquie Carpenter had said nothing to Peter Maxwell about where they were going or why. She was just happy to be there with him, in the sun of that afternoon. For her, it was one day at a time for the moment. Perhaps it would always be like that.

The patio was a paved area under the shelter of the churchyard wall on one side and the church on the other. There was a scattering of garden furniture the local B&Q had donated to Mike Chapman's good cause and a solitary figure sat with his back to Maxwell as he approached. He had dark, wild hair and a scruffy anorak, for all it was flaming June, tied at the waist with string. It was Boo Radley.

'Max,' Jacquie sat down next to the man, 'I'd like you to meet Alan Rossiter. Alan, this is Max.'

Maxwell sat opposite him, staring first at Jacquie, then at Rossiter.

'Hello,' he said, his voice high and wavering.

'Hello, Alan,' Maxwell stuck out his hand.

For a moment it looked as if Rossiter didn't know what to do with it, then he took Maxwell's hand in his own, limp and clammy.

'Alan's been in hospital for a long time,' Jacquie said, 'but he used to come to Leighford a lot when he was younger. Didn't you, Alan?'

'Yes,' Rossiter said, looking wistfully at the girl. A broken Eccles cake lay on the plate in front of him and a half drunk cup of tea. 'That was a long time ago.'

'Remember what you told me earlier today, Alan?' Jacquie was sitting hunched over, her hands clasped, filling Rossiter's vision, holding his concentration. 'About Miles? About Miles Needham? He was your friend, wasn't he?'

For a moment, Rossiter smiled. 'Miles,' he said, 'yes, he was my friend. I haven't seen him in a long time. But I saw him the other day.'

'Where was that, Alan?' Jacquie coaxed. 'Was that on the beach? Was that at Willow Bay?'

Rossiter's face had darkened. He wasn't there any more, on the Crypt Centre patio with the sun burning onto his bald head. He was back, back in the mists of time he'd never really left.

'He wasn't a bad man,' he told Jacquie, suddenly holding her hand.

'No,' Jacquie smiled. 'We know that.'

'Miles shouldn't have done it,' Rossiter shook his head sadly. 'He shouldn't have pushed him, because he wasn't a bad man. He couldn't swim, you know.'

'We know,' Jacquie said. 'What was his name, Alan? The man Miles pushed? Do you remember his name?'

Rossiter frowned. God alone knew what jumble of thoughts

cascaded in that man's mind. Then he smiled, 'Tom,' he said. 'The man's name was Tom.'

The A27 snaked before them in the evening sun, Jacquie rattling up through the gears as she drove east, east, ever turning as the road took her.

'Is it me?' Maxwell broke the silence, 'or have you achieved a minor miracle today, Woman Policeman Carpenter?'

'I got lucky, Max,' she said. 'That's all. I had a peek at that bloody file you got me to lift for you. That's where I found the name Alan Rossiter. He was a witness called in when Tom Sparrow's body was found. A friend of Miles Needham's. Both of them were interviewed, held for a while on suspicion. But there was nothing to go on. Nothing that would stick.'

'How did you find him?' Maxwell asked.

'That's where luck comes in,' Jacquie said, slowing a little as a sleek white patrol car purred past. 'First I talked to your friend Helen McGregor. I didn't know she'd made an allegation against you until I saw the reports yesterday. What a little madam!'

'Oh, she means well!' Maxwell gave Jacquie his best Mrs Hetherington.

'The fuck she does!'

Maxwell was horrified. 'All right, so she's a deeply disturbed psychotic nymphomaniac. What's new?'

'What's new is that with a little . . . shall we say help . . . from me, she admitted she'd made the whole thing up. I expect DI Watkiss is at your door as we speak, with a grovelling apology and a year's supply of Southern Comfort.'

'No doubt,' Maxwell chuckled.

'Not only had *you* not attacked her, but no one had.'

'Surprise, surprise,' he gave her his best Cilla.

'One useful thing did emerge, however, from my chat with Helen – one approximation of the truth. She gave me what I hoped was an accurate description of the man she'd reported seeing, twice, on the dunes. He was a derelict.'

'There's that word again,' Maxwell murmured.

'And I thought "Where's the place to look for someone like that?" Answer? All Angels Crypt Centre! And I was right. Father Mike has had him here for the past few weeks. He just turned up out of the blue. No one seemed to know who he was or anything about him. And, needless to say, Rossiter himself wasn't very forthcoming. Now Father Mike doesn't pry, but this one seemed so . . . well, forlorn, I think was the word he used . . . he made an exception.'

'Not snooped, surely?' Maxwell was aghast.

Jacquie gave him the most old-fashioned of looks. 'Mental hospitals will tell vicars things they won't tell the likes of you and me, Max. Whatever Alan witnessed back in '77 affected him so badly, he had a nervous breakdown. He was a local Middleton boy with an Oxford degree and a glittering career in television ahead of him, but all that crashed in the late summer of '77.'

'So he saw Needham kill Tom Sparrow?'

'You heard him,' Jacquie shrugged.

'Would he make a good witness, do you think, when this comes to court?'

Jacquie shook her head. 'Shambolic,' she said. 'You'd have so-called expert witnesses outsmarting each other as to his competence to testify. And assuming they let him, he'd be crucified by some bastard of a silk. Have you ever been in court, Max?'

'No,' Maxwell told her. 'One of my keenest regrets. I've always fancied doing the *Twelve Angry Men* bit.'

'Don't,' she warned him. 'A clever lawyer will drive you into a corner and there's no way out. I know. I've been there and done that.'

Maxwell looked at the girl beside him, the wind whipping through her chestnut hair. 'Children dear,' he said softly, 'was it yesterday, that I said you wouldn't see me again.'

She glanced at him, as much as the traffic flow would allow. 'I can't see you, now, Max,' she smiled. 'As far as my bosses go – Hall, Watkiss, all of them – you're the invisible man.'

Maxwell smiled too. Sitting next to him was a different girl from the stop-go dilemma he'd known for the last two years. There was a kind of maverick restlessness he recognized; recognized because it was like looking into a mirror.

'Jacquie,' he said after a mile or so, 'it's very good of you to show me Alan Rossiter and to confirm what I thought I knew, but isn't this rather a long way round to get to Columbine Avenue?'

She looked straight ahead. 'We're not going to Columbine Avenue, Max,' she said. 'We're going where you would have gone, I guess, by train, if I hadn't turned up at Leighford High. We're going to Brighton.'

But he wasn't where Jacquie Carpenter thought he'd be, the man they'd come to see.

'Down the pier, love,' the aproned neighbour called, leaning out of her upstairs window and twisting a curler into her thick ringlets. 'Can't miss it.'

They couldn't. Brighton pier stretched like a beached whale in the dying sun, its ribs black with the dangling weed that had enfolded for a while the passing body of Tom Sparrow all those years before. The surf roared along the shingle ridges, the incessant plaintive backing to the music of tonight, blaring from the PA systems and a thousand throbbing speakers.

Lights and laughter. The sun was a ball of fire sinking silently into the sea as Maxwell and his policewoman reached the pier's entrance. Here, Joe Melia had switched on the coloured light bulbs that welcomed a generation to World War One in *Oh, What A Lovely War!* Here, proud Brighton citizens had called it 'the finest pier in the world' when they opened it in 1899, one thousand seven hundred and sixty feet of promenade deck with ornate wrought-iron ridged domes and sun verandahs with magical coloured glass. The paint was peeling now, behind the flying ice-cream signs that offered 99s without number, and the glass was cracked and dusty in that already tired summer. The waft of hot dogs and doner kebabs, the smells of Old England, filled Maxwell's nostrils as he crossed the glass threshold. The management, the posters told him, reserved the right to refuse admittance and he looked down to make sure he was wearing shoes.

He felt Jacquie grab his arm, 'Too many people here, Max,' she said, 'If he feels threatened, there could be trouble. A pier is a cul-de-sac. He'll feel cornered, trapped . . .'

'With your powers of arrest and my legendary public-school right hook, policewoman, we're invincible.'

'Max, listen to me,' Jacquie was facing him in the carpeted vestibule where determined grannies with blue rinses and specs on chains were milking the fruit machines. 'This is wrong. In his flat, okay, but not here. You shouldn't be here. *I* was wrong.'

'Jacquie,' he grabbed her shoulders, shaking her gently, 'you said it – I'd have come by train anyway. Now, let's do this.'

'No,' she shook her head. 'We need back-up. You wait here, Max. You don't go any further. Not until I've found a copper.'

Maxwell shook his head. 'There's never one around,' he said. But Jacquie had gone, running through the milling holidaymakers, jabbing the buttons on her walkie talkie.

'Wait there!' she shouted.

Maxwell half turned. A whiskered old timer on the fuzzy screen of the shoot-out game was beckoning to him. 'Howdy, stranger,' he croaked. 'We've got some trouble here. Mad Dog McGee's in town. D'you reckon you can take him?'

'There's one way to find out,' Maxwell drawled in his best Randolph Scott.

An intrigued eight-year-old who should have been home hours ago stood by him. 'That won't work, mister,' he said, 'You ain't supposed to talk to him. You gotta put a quid in the slot and shoot the baddie.'

Maxwell looked down on him, along with Gary Cooper and Clint Eastwood and John Wayne. 'I don't think it'll come to that,' he said. 'Here,' he tossed the kid a coin. 'Why don't you do it for me?'

The boy caught the pound expertly and drew a bead on the video madman who had taken over the video town. Maxwell was gone past the screaming skulls that came at him from the House of the Dead, beyond the hurtling road of the Mille Milia. A Street Fighter swung at him, grunting, growling. Kids. Everywhere he looked. Thirteen-year-old tarts with naked arms, legs and bellies, flaunting their nubile bodies in stolen makeup and navel jewellery, tottering on outsize fuck-me shoes. Young thugs who saw themselves as the street fighters, twelve if they were a day, swaggering and swearing, lighting up from each other's ciggies, spitting obscenities at the girls, who ignored them or cackled at them, depending on their level of sophistication.

Beyond the thump and flash of the amusement arcade, the night air hit Maxwell like a sledgehammer. From nowhere, the long June day had turned dark and bleak and cold. The sun was only a glimmer now, faint on the sea and the summer seemed to die there, on that Brighton night.

He passed the popcorn and the silly '30s postcard hoardings with the cut out faces. Behind him, the video games screamed their message of death and destruction and the naked bulbs fluttered on their wind-blown cables overhead like stars in some mad, meteoric night.

Then he heard it. Above the crescendo of the Spice Girls and the All Saints, the false girl power that was the rage of that insane summer, the quaint, out of time tune that Napoleon's Old Guard had made their own – that '*Ça Ira*' which would strike terror in the hearts of all the enemies of France.

'Step this way, Mr Maxwell,' a familiar voice called. 'See if you can shoot the hat off old Wellington.'

There he stood, upright behind the counter of his shooting gallery, resplendent in the blue, red and white of the Ninth Voltigeurs, the black-braided hair dangling on the white cross-belts and the shining brass buttons – Maxwell's Maréchal de Logis, Bob Pickering.

'What brings you here, Mr Maxwell? Haven't you got enough amusements in Leighford?'

'Ah, it's the quality, Bob,' Maxwell said. 'Where else, other than Brighton, could you find a gallery like this, eh?'

'Only a quid for five shots,' Pickering presented the musket across his chest. 'But to you,' he threw the gun at Maxwell, 'it's on the house.'

Maxwell looked at the musket. 'This is clever, Bob,' he smiled. 'Did you adapt this mechanism yourself?'

'It's not that difficult,' Pickering told him, 'what with the workshop. I've got all the gear.'

'I'm sure you have,' Maxwell dropped the first pellet into the breech. 'Tell me, Bob, does this one have any peculiarities I should know about? Does it kick to the right – or high, perhaps? I always had the impression the shot that killed Miles Needham was a bit high . . .'

'I wouldn't know about that, Mr Maxwell,' Pickering's smile had frozen. 'You just aim for the centre of old Hooky's nose. That'll do it. Roll up! Roll up!' he called in time-honoured tradition for the benefit of the milling crowds.

Maxwell slid the butt against his shoulder, taking the weight of the gun on his left elbow. He closed one eye.

'Tut, tut, Mr Maxwell. *That's* not how it's done, is it? You keep both eyes open in the shooting business.'

Maxwell jerked off a shot, but it pinged into the metal backdrop above Wellington's cocked hat.

'Ooh, so close,' Pickering smiled. 'Have another go.'

Maxwell straightened and dropped the second pellet into its niche.

'Of course,' he said, settling back into the firing position. 'Miles Needham had it coming, didn't he?'

'They say nobody liked him,' Pickering commented. 'That's it, shoulder up just a little, get that nose in the centre of your sights.'

'Ah, but it's not just that, is it?' Maxwell eased back the serpentine so that it clicked and stayed. 'It's got more to do with what he did to Tom Sparrow.' He squeezed the trigger and Pickering jumped as the pellet hit Wellington's nose dead centre and his plumed hat sprung off to land in the sand tray below. 'Bull's eye.'

'Very good, Mr Maxwell,' Pickering said as the man straightened. 'One more like that and you get the prize.'

'One more like that,' Maxwell loaded up for the third time. 'Well,' he said, smoothing down the barrel, 'the first one was for Miles Needham. Stop me if I go wrong, Bob. You knew Tom Sparrow when you were a kid. You liked him, hung around on street corners with him – that would be the year before I came to Leighford. You must have liked him, to ignore the stories. You must have heard them. Tom Sparrow was well known in the gay community. But not everybody liked him, did they? Miles Needham for one. Alan Rossiter for another. What happened, Bob? Did they take Tom for a car ride one dark night? Probably more to frighten him, that was all.' Maxwell eased back the serpentine, 'But it all went horribly wrong, didn't it?'

'I'm sorry, Mr Maxwell,' Pickering's laugh was brittle, 'you've lost me.'

'No, I haven't, Bob,' Maxwell looked at him. 'You see, your name is on a police report from the time. The fourteen-year-old Robert Leonard Pickering interviewed by such and such on such and such a date. Needham and Rossiter picked up Sparrow in Needham's car while you were chatting to him. They drove west, out of town. It's all in the report.'

'Yes,' Pickering said. 'I remember that. But it was all a long time ago.'

'Oh, it was,' Maxwell agreed, 'but you were a kid, Bob. And it hurt, didn't it? When they took that sweet old man away? And there was nothing you could do. So Needham had got away with it. The perfect murder, in fact. And you lived with that for . . . what? Twenty-one years.'

'A soldier's lifetime,' Pickering nodded.

He was right.

'Then you saw him, when you signed on with the Eight Counties production team, on the beach at Willow Bay, the very place they'd found Tom Sparrow's body. And it all came back, didn't it? The hurt. The pain. You had the gun all along, the real one you used for target practice. All you had to do was put it in somebody else's hands, somebody who could use it. Somebody you knew, because you found out no doubt in chatting to him, was a crack shot and wouldn't miss. Especially when you placed him where you did, front rank, left flank. And there'd be other chances. If Giles Sparrow missed the first time, if he aimed for something else, there'd be other opportunities. You must have been delighted when it worked first time.'

'Oh, I was,' Pickering's voice had changed. Maxwell was still in the firing position, crouching with the rifle in his hands. He felt something cold against his temple. And he knew he couldn't move. 'But I didn't want to pin it on Giles. He's a nice kid. I had no choice.'

'Ironic,' Maxwell said carefully, 'that it should be that family, of all families. Quite poetic, really.'

'Over here, policewoman!' Pickering shouted. 'Or your friend's head will be all over Brighton pier.'

There was a scream. Women and children scattered, men moved away. Out of the corner of his eye, Maxwell could see Jacquie Carpenter standing with a crowd behind her. One uniform. Two. He didn't know how many coppers she'd found, but she'd been right, of course. He should have waited. He saw her edge forward.

'Closer,' Pickering called. 'Mr Maxwell here was just telling me how I arranged Miles Needham's death.'

'I want you to put that gun down, Mr Pickering,' Jacquie was saying, her hands clenched by her side.

'I'm sure you do,' Pickering nodded, 'But if I did that, your boys in blue over there would kick the shit out of me, wouldn't they? By the way, Mr Maxwell, you can't see it from where you are, can you? But this is a replica New Land pistol, and as you know, like all my replicas, this one kills.'

'1802 pattern, I hope,' Maxwell's finger was still on his trigger, as was Pickering's. 'I'd like to see that some time.'

'I'm sure you would, Mr Maxwell,' Pickering said. 'But if you or your lady friend here move just one fraction, you'll certainly see what it can do.'

'Bob . . .' Jacquie began.

'That's Mr Pickering to you, cow,' he snarled, the pistol jamming into Maxwell's temple.

'It's all right, Jacquie,' Maxwell's spare hand flapped to his left, urging the girl back. 'Bob here was just going to tell us why he killed Barbara Needham, weren't you, Bob? I can't believe she was in on Tom Sparrow's murder.'

'Of course not,' Pickering said, 'but she knew about it.

The longer the law probed, the more chance there was of finding the Sparrow case in their files. If they talked to her about it – I remember them cruising the seafront together at Leighford, laughing at Tom, calling him names – it'd all come out. I had to keep her quiet.'

'So you followed her?'

Pickering nodded. 'She went out to the Shingle at night. Took a taxi from the hotel. Going to meet somebody, I suppose. I put a musket butt through her skull. Perhaps it was that one you're holding there, Mr Maxwell.'

'But you missed your chance with Alan Rossiter, didn't you?' Maxwell said, his right arm tingling with numbness, his eyes burning in his head as he stared straight at Bonaparte's nose, his next target.

'What are you talking about?'

'The weirdo on the dunes. The one that frightened Helen McGregor. It was him.'

'Never!' Maxwell felt the pistol muzzle waver a fraction. 'Stand still, I said!' Pickering was screaming at Jacquie. She froze. How much longer could the man keep that same pressure on the trigger?

'You saw him yourself, didn't you?' Maxwell asked. 'And after all these years, you didn't recognize him. Pity – you could have got them both.'

'Well, well,' Pickering seemed to relax, choosing his moment. 'Better luck next time, eh? You've certainly done your homework, Mr Maxwell. That's something us kids forget, isn't it? That teachers are better at homework than we are.'

'One thing I didn't find out in my homework, Bob,' Maxwell said softly, keeping the quiet tone going, not moving, not blinking, 'is why Hannah Morpeth? She was only a child when Tom Sparrow died.'

'That's got nothing to do with me, Mr Maxwell. I'll put my hand up to the other two. But not her.'

'He's got one shot in this pistol,' Maxwell suddenly shouted. 'When he's fired it, he's all yours.'

He squeezed the trigger, both eyes open, his shoulder bucking backwards instinctively. Bonaparte's nose exploded with the impact of the pellet and his hat shot skyward. In the same instant, there was the deafening roar of Pickering's horse pistol and the smoke of it stung Maxwell's eyes and filled Maxwell's throat.

Everyone was screaming, running, ducking for cover. Only Maxwell stood there, the empty musket across his chest, presenting arms. Jacquie rushed to him, cradling him, kissing him, the tears splashing on his shirt. The two policemen were there, jumping over the counter, seeing what could be done for Bob Pickering.

In that split second as Maxwell fired, the re-enactor had swung the pistol up to his own head and blown away his cranium. Blood glistened on the red, white and blue of the draped flags and '*Ça Ira*' sounded cracked and broken on the worn-out, blood-spattered tape.

Peter Maxwell pressed his face into Jacquie's hair and Jacquie's shoulder. Then he looked over the counter at all that was left of Bob Pickering – and wished he hadn't. The policemen began clearing the horrified crowd, going through the routine mechanics of sudden death.

The blood-soaked black wig with its leaded braids and centre parting had blown off in the impact of the shot. It lay like a rag on Pickering's counter, his hand still wrapped in its curls.

# Chapter Sixteen

They held a memorial service for Miles Needham in the church of Michael and All Saints. He who hadn't set foot in a church since his own christening, he who had broken the sixth commandment. It was Eight Counties Television who chose the church, appropriately enough little more than a musket shot from where he died. Father Mike did the honours one bright Saturday as Maxwell's summer term came to an end. The flowers were astonishing. And the music. Half of showbiz was there and Sir Anthony Hopkins read the lesson.

Waiting in the crowds outside, along with the tourists and the sun-seekers and the groupies, Mad Max leaned against the church wall. There were security men everywhere, and television crews angling their shots at the door through which the famous would emerge into a harsh, unflattering world.

'Max,' he turned at the softness of the voice. 'How have you been?'

'Jacquie,' Maxwell nodded, smiling at the girl. She was dressed in her finery, starched blouse and dark suit. 'For Needham?' he frowned.

'For me,' she said. 'I'm resigning today.'

He stood up. 'What?'

'It's been hanging over me for some time,' she said. 'I've got no choice now.'

'Jacquie . . .'

'I endangered the life of a civilian, Max,' she said, 'I can't just walk away from that.'

'If you're talking about me,' he smiled, 'think nothing of it. I hijacked you, remember, forced you to take me to Cuba, or failing that, Brighton . . .'

'Max,' she shook her head, smiling back at him, 'you know Henry Hall. Does he have *any* sense of humour at all?'

'No,' Maxwell said. 'I suppose not.'

'I didn't have much respect for Miles Needham,' she looked at the church where the organ was playing and the doors swung back, 'and even less now. But he *was* a human being. I thought I owed him that.'

'Jacquie,' Maxwell said suddenly, turning the girl round and taking her to the far side of the flying buttress, 'do you *really* want to resign? I mean, is Hall going to ask for your shield?' Maxwell couldn't help himself – he'd lapsed into Clint Eastwood again.

'I think that's very likely,' she said. 'And I *do* want to resign – no. No, I don't. I want to be a little ray of light in a naughty world – is that arrogant of me, Max?'

He chuckled, took her face in his hands and kissed her quickly on the nose. 'No,' he said, 'it isn't. How would Hall feel, do you think, if you handed him a murderer's head on a plate?'

Jacquie blinked. 'Pickering's dead, Max.'

'Indeed he is, Jacquie,' Maxwell nodded. 'So who killed Hannah Morpeth?' He patted the side of his nose. 'Stick with me, kid,' he drawled, although the Thin Man was well and truly lost on her. He spun round to watch the dark-suited, feather-hatted famous glide from church, careful to present their best sides to the cameras that flashed and whirred as the paparazzi closed in.

'Angela!' Maxwell extricated the woman from the throng, whisking her away to the deserted patio of the All Saints crypt. And Jacquie came too.

'Was it a moving service?' Maxwell held out one of Father Mike's plastic chairs for her like the public schoolboy he was.

'It was,' Angela nodded, sitting down. 'Hello,' she'd just caught sight of Jacquie some paces to the rear. 'It was good of you both to come.'

'Our pleasure, really,' Maxwell said. 'I can't speak for DC Carpenter, but I wanted to make sure the shit was well and truly dead.'

'Max . . .' Angela Badham blinked. 'That's not a very nice thing . . .'

'Ah, sorry, Angela,' Max frowned. 'Not really Benenden language, is it? At least, not officially. Tell me, where *did* you get the replica surgeon's knife in the end?'

'I don't know what you're talking about, Max,' Angela was suddenly on her feet. 'Now I really must be going.'

'Well, it wasn't from the props caravan,' Maxwell hadn't moved, 'because Dan Weston had that well and truly under lock and key. And it wasn't from that dear old fusspot Mr Stubbington because he couldn't get you one in time, could he? By the bye,' and he stood up behind her, 'he's got one now. Nip along there, to his antique shop in the High Street and he'll be so glad you called back for it.'

She spun round, her face hard behind the dark glasses, her eyes invisible to the prying world. 'Max,' she almost snarled, 'I repeat – I don't know what you're . . .'

'Save us the clichés, Angela,' Maxwell rested his hands on his hips. 'You loved Miles Needham. That was the bottom line, wasn't it? The only sad thing was that he didn't love you back. But that didn't matter somehow, did it? The important thing was that anybody who crossed him must pay. John Irving was having an affair with his wife, so he got the offensive, threatening letters. Marc Lamont hated him, but you'd barely started on him when I stepped in and did a little of your job for you – I knocked him down, toppled him off his perch. *And* in full view of his adoring fans. But it was Hannah you really reserved the best for, wasn't it? That's why, DC Carpenter tells me, there was no sign of a struggle in her hotel room. She never suspected you. Dear, fussy, clipboard-carrying Angela, everybody's favourite exec? "Beware the smiler with the knife."'

'What?'

'It's a quotation, my dear,' Maxwell humoured her, 'From dear old Geoffrey Chaucer, the most unlikely pilgrim of them all.'

'You've been too long in the sun, Max,' Angela had the calmness of ice. She looked at Jacquie Carpenter writing silently at Max's elbow on her grim little notebook. Then she turned and walked away.

At the corner, where the buttress jutted from shadow to sunshine, a figure in a cardigan emerged, his glasses dangling on a chain.

'Hello,' he beamed, 'I've got your knife, you know,' and he looked past her to Maxwell, a little pained, 'although I'm not sure you want it now.'

Angela Badham stood there, quivering, her nerve gone, her life over. She didn't feel Jacquie's hand, firm on her elbow. She didn't hear Jacquie's time-honoured words in her ear.

'How did you know, Max?' Jacquie asked, quietly slipping the steel cuffs on Angela's wrists.

'One little thing,' Maxwell said, still looking at Angela's grim, impassive face behind the shades, 'when John Irving and I went to see Dan Weston at Eight Counties, we bumped into Angela – although I'm not sure it was that much of a coincidence on her part. Angela told John how sorry she felt for him – for Marc Lamont being offensive to him on the set at Willow Bay and how sorry she was to hear about Barbara. Now, as far as Angela was supposed to know, what was Barbara Needham to John Irving? She couldn't even be sure they'd met. It was she who told me that Barbara had nothing to do with Eight Counties. No, somehow, Angela here had found out all about Babs and John – hence the threatening letters to them both. That was silly of you, wasn't it, Angela?'

The Johanna Factotum held up her head. She was staring straight in front of her saying nothing. Suddenly she turned to Maxwell. 'I didn't mean to,' it was another cliché. 'I merely went there at her request. She wanted to try out the knife – to practise with it. We started talking about Miles. And yes, you're right, Mr Maxwell, I did love him. She laughed at me. That cold, self-centred bitch. Laughed at him, too. She said she was sorry he was dead, but she didn't mean it, not a word of it. I don't normally lose my temper, Mr Maxwell – you can't in this job. But I did that once, that night. And I stabbed her. It was surprisingly easy, really, using two hands.'

'Was it really worth it, Angela, to kill someone, just because they laughed at the man you loved?'

Angela Badham's face was a mask again. She turned away from him, in silence. And that was how it would stay, all through her remand, her trial and her years in Holloway.

'I'll be back, Max,' Jacquie turned to him, smiling, leading the woman away.

'Fine,' he said, 'and make sure you've got your shield with you, Woman Policeman Carpenter.'

'It was that wig, Mr Maxwell,' Stubbington dithered. 'She looks a little different without the black wig. By the way,' he was frowning, 'a moment ago – I didn't understand all that conversation you had with the young lady, but I wasn't too keen on the "dear old fusspot" bit.'

'Bit of artistic licence, Mr Stubbington,' Maxwell winked at him. 'You aren't old at all.'

Peter Maxwell wandered down in his jacket and bow tie and shapeless hat to the water's edge, where the surf roared along the line of Willow Bay and the last surfer was curling in to the blood-red shallows in another dying sun. For a moment he thought he saw Tom Sparrow's body rising and rolling with the tide, but it was driftwood, nothing more. For a moment, he fancied he heard the muskets rattle and the bayonets level and the haunting catch of *'Ça Ira'*.

'I don't know,' he said to himself, 'I came here to re-enact a war and I ended up fighting one.' This time next week, it would be the Summer Fête Worse than Death. He must get his larynx into tannoy mode.

DC Jacquie Carpenter picked up the phone in the closing Incident Room at Tottingleigh. She'd become a celebrity in the nick that day, bringing in Angela Badham on a charge of murder. There'd been cheers all round and hugs and kisses and pats on the back. A smacker from Jerry Manton, a squeeze from Paul Garrity, a nod from Dave Watkiss. The DCI thought he might overlook the Peter Maxwell business, the whole Brighton incident. After all, they'd got their man, messy as it turned out to be. And Jacquie? Well, promotion was not out of the question. As long, and Hall had underlined the words by taking off his rimless glasses, as long as in the future, Jacquie Carpenter behaved with full propriety and did not involve members of the public. Especially members of the public who were plainly mad and called Maxwell.

Peter Maxwell was placing Lieutenant Henry Fitzhardinge Berkeley Maxse, glued and painted to perfection, in his place to the left rear of Lord Cardigan in his attic as the phone rang. Metternich the cat lifted one disapproving eyelid. He couldn't believe it. Maxwell was doing it again, picking up that white plastic thing – the one that always got him into trouble. He buried his ear under his paw and pretended not to hear his master's voice:

'War Office.'